# The Lemonade war

## 3 BOOKS IN 1!

The Lemonade war
The Lemonade crime
The Bell Bandit

by
Jacqueline
Davies

Houghton Mifflin Harcourt

Boston   New York

## ACKNOWLEDGMENTS

*The Lemonade War*

I would like to thank the astute and devoted first readers of this book: Mary Atkinson, Tracey Fern, Jennifer Richards Jacobson, Sarah Lamstein, Carol Antoinette Peacock, and Dana Walrath. Thanks also to members of the $100K Club: Toni Buzzeo and Jennifer Ward. For her support in so many guises: my agent, Tracey Adams. And last, but never least in my heart: Ann Rider. *Thank you.*

*The Lemonade Crime*

Many thanks to the good people who helped shepherd this book: Tracey Adams, Mary Atkinson, Henry Davies, Mae Davies, Tracey Fern, Jennifer Jacobson, Sarah Lamstein, Carol Peacock, and Dana Walrath. A special thanks to Ann Rider, who knew when to push and when to step back—and then push again.

*The Bell Bandit*

Thanks go, as always, to the Gang of Four: Carol Peacock, Sarah Lamstein, Tracey Fern, and Mary Atkinson. A special thanks also to Kevin Sullivan of Paul Davis Restoration for providing information on home repair following a fire and to Lucia Gill Case for sharing the tradition of ringing a village bell on New Year's Eve. And thank you to Tracey Adams, the angel on my left shoulder, and Ann Rider, the angel on my right. To all the students in Ms. Amy Cicala's fourth grade class at Hillside Elementary, thank you for helping me with Evan's handwriting, especially Ryle Sammut, who wrote Evan's note for me.

—J.D.

*The Lemonade War* © 2007 by Jacqueline Davies
*The Lemonade Crime* © 2011 by Jacqueline Davies
*The Bell Bandit* © 2012 by Jacqueline Davies
Illustrations by Cara Llewellyn

Pronunciations in *The Lemonade War* and *The Lemonade Crime* are reproduced by permission from *The American Heritage Dictionary of the English Language, Fourth Edition* © 2006 by Houghton Mifflin Harcourt Publishing Company.

Bell illustration on page 31 of *The Bell Bandit* courtesy of the Eric Sloane Estate.

The text was set in Guardi and Child's Play.
The illustrations are pen and ink.

Library of Congress Cataloging-in-Publication Data for individual titles is on file.

ISBN: 978-1-328-53080-6 paper over board

Printed in the United States of America
DOC 10 9 8 7 6 5 4 3
4500800176

# The Lemonade War

by
Jacqueline
Davies

Houghton Mifflin Harcourt
Boston  New York

For Tom, Kim, and Leslie.
*All roads lead back.*

# Contents

# Chapter 1
# SLUMP

**slump** (slŭmp) n. A drop in the activity of a business or the economy.

Evan lay on his back in the dark, throwing the baseball up in a straight line and catching it in his bare hands. *Thwap. Thwap.* The ball made a satisfying sound as it slapped his palm. His legs flopped in a V. His arms stretched up to the ceiling. And the thought that if he missed he'd probably break his nose made the game *just* interesting enough to keep going.

On the floor above he heard footsteps—his mother's—and then a long, loud scraping-groaning sound. He stopped throwing the ball to listen. His mother was dragging something heavy across the kitchen floor. Probably the broken air conditioner.

A week ago, right at the beginning of the heat wave, the air conditioner in his mother's attic office had broken. The man from Sears had installed a brand-new one but left the old one sitting right in the middle of the kitchen floor. The Treskis had been walking around it all week.

*Scra-a-a-ape.* Evan stood up. His mom was strong, but this was a two-person job. Hopefully she wouldn't ask him why he was hiding in the dark basement. And hopefully Jessie wouldn't be in the kitchen at all. He'd been avoiding her for two days now, and it was getting harder by the minute. The house just wasn't that big.

Evan had his hand on the railing when the scraping noise stopped. He heard footsteps fading to silence. She'd given up. *Probably the heat,* he thought. It was that kind of weather: giving-up kind of weather.

He went back to lying on the floor.

*Thwap. Thwap.*

Then he heard the basement door open. *Psssshhh.* Evan caught the ball and froze.

"Evan?" Jessie's voice sounded echo-y in the darkness. "Evan? You down there?"

Evan held his breath. He lay completely still. The only thing that moved was the pins-and-needles prickling in his fingers.

He heard the door start to close—*long breath out*—but then it stopped and opened again. Footsteps on the carpeted stairs. A black outline of Jessie standing on the bottom step with daylight squirting all around her. Evan didn't move a muscle.

"Evan? Is that you?" Jessie took one short step into the basement. "Is that . . . ?" She inched her way toward him, then kicked him with her bare foot.

"Hey! Watch it, would ya?" said Evan, swatting her leg. He suddenly felt stupid lying there in the dark.

"I thought you were a sleeping bag," she said. "I couldn't see. What are you doing down here? How come the lights are off?"

"It's too hot with the lights on," he said. He talked in a flat voice, trying to sound like the most boring person on the whole planet. If he kept it up, Jessie might just leave him alone.

"Mom's back in her office," said Jessie, lying down on the couch. *"Working."* She groaned as she said the word.

Evan didn't say anything. He went back to throwing the ball. Straight up. Straight down. Maybe silence would get Jessie to leave. He was starting to feel words piling up inside him, crowding his lungs, forcing out all the air. It was like having a chestful of bats, beating their wings, fighting to get out.

"She tried to move the air conditioner, but it's too heavy," said Jessie.

Evan tightened up his lips. *Go away,* he thought. *Go away before I say something mean.*

"It's gonna be hot *a-a-a-all* week," Jessie continued. "In the nineties. All the way up 'til Labor Day."

*Thwap. Thwap.*

"So, whaddya wanna do?" Jessie asked.

*Scream,* thought Evan. Jessie never got it when you were giving her the Big Freeze. She just went right on acting as if everything were great. It made it really hard to tell her to bug off without telling her to *BUG OFF!* Whenever Evan did that, he felt bad.

"So, whaddya wanna do?" Jessie asked again, nudging him with her foot.

It was a direct question. Evan had to answer it or explain why he wouldn't. And he couldn't get into *that.* It was too . . . too complicated. Too hurtful.

"Huh? So, whaddya wanna do?" she asked for the third time.

"Doin' it," said Evan.

"Nah, come on. For real."

"For real," he said.

"We could ride our bikes to the 7-Eleven," she said.

"No money," he said.

"You just got ten dollars from Grandma for your birthday."

"Spent it," said Evan.

"On what?"

"Stuff," Evan said.

"Well, I've got . . . well . . . " Jessie's voice dribbled down to nothing.

Evan stopped throwing the ball and looked at her. "What?"

Jessie pulled her legs tight to her chest. "Nothin'," she said.

"Right," said Evan. He knew that Jessie had money. Jessie always had money squirreled away in her lock box. But that didn't mean she was going to share it. Evan went back to throwing the baseball. He felt a tiny flame of anger shoot up and lick his face.

*Thwap. Thwap.*

"We could build a fort in the woods," said Jessie.

"Too hot."

"We could play Stratego."

"Too boring."

"We could build a track and race marbles."

"Too stupid!"

A thin spider web of sweat draped itself over his forehead, spreading into his hair. With every throw, he told himself, *It's not her fault*. But he could feel his anger growing. He started popping his elbow to put a little more juice on the ball. It was flying a good four feet into the air every time. Straight up. Straight down.

*Pop. Thwap. Pop. Thwap.*

The bats in his chest were going nuts.

"What is the matter with you?" asked Jessie. "You've been so weird the last couple of days."

*Aw, man, here they come.*

"I just don't wanna play a dumb game like Stratego," he said.

"You *like* Stratego. I only picked that because it's *your* favorite game. I was being *nice*, in case you hadn't noticed."

"Look. There are only six days left of summer, and I'm not going to waste them playing a dumb game." Evan felt his heartbeat speed up. Part of him wanted to stuff a sock in his mouth, and part of him wanted to deck his sister. "It's a stupid game and it's for

7

babies and I don't want to play a stupid baby game."

*Pop. Thwap. Pop. Thwap.*

"Why are you being so mean?"

Evan knew he was being mean, and he hated being mean, especially to her. But he couldn't help it. He was so angry and so humiliated and so full of bats, there was nothing else he *could* be. Except alone. And she'd taken even that away from him. "You're the genius," he said. "You figure it out."

*Good.* That would shut her up. For once! Evan watched the ball fly in the air.

"Is this because of the letter?" Jessie asked.

*Crack.*

Evan had taken his eyes off the ball for one second, just for one second, and the ball came crashing down on his nose.

"Crud! Oh, CRUD!" He curled over onto his side, grabbing his nose with both hands. There was a blinding, blooming pain right behind his eyes that was quickly spreading to the outer edges of his skull.

"Do you want some ice?" he heard Jessie ask in a calm voice.

"Whaddya think?" he shouted.

"Yeah?" She stood up.

"No, I don't want any stupid ice." The pain was starting to go away, like a humungous wave that crashes with a lot of noise and spray but then slowly fizzles away into nothing. Evan rolled to a sitting position and took his hands away from his nose. With his thumb and index finger, he started to pinch the bridge. Was it still in a straight line?

Jessie peered at his face in the dim light. "You're not bleeding," she said.

"Yeah, well, it *hurts!*" he said. "A lot!"

"It's not broken," she said.

"You don't know that," he said. "You don't know *everything*, you know. You think you do, but you *don't*."

"It's not even swollen. You're making a big deal out of nothing."

Evan held his nose with one hand and hit his sister's knee with the other. Then he picked up the baseball and struggled to his feet. "Leave me alone.

9

I came down here to get away from you and you just had to follow. You ruin everything. You ruined my summer and now you're going to ruin school. I hate you." When he got to the bottom of the steps, he threw the baseball down in disgust.

*Thud.*

# Chapter 2
# Breakup

**breakup** (brāk′up′) n. Dissolution of a unit, an organization, or a group of organizations. The Justice Department sometimes forces the breakup of a large corporation into several smaller companies.

Jessie didn't get it. She just didn't get it.

What was Evan's problem?

He'd been acting like a weirdo for two days now. And it was two days ago that the letter had arrived. But why would he be so upset about that letter?

*This is a puzzle,* Jessie told herself. *And I'm good at puzzles.* But it was a puzzle about feelings, and Jessie knew that feelings were her weakest subject.

Jessie sat in the cool darkness of the basement and thought back to Monday, the day the letter had come. Everything had been normal. She and Evan were putting together a lemonade stand in the driveway when the mailman walked up and handed Jessie a bundle of letters. Evan never bothered to look at the mail, but Jessie was always entering contests and expecting to win, so she flipped through the letters right away.

"Boring. Boring. Boring," said Jessie as each letter flashed by. "Hey, something from school. Addressed to Mom." She held up a plain white envelope. "What do you think it is?"

"Dunno," said Evan. He was in the garage, uncovering the small wooden table they usually used for a stand. It was buried under two sno-tubes, two boogie boards, and the garden hose. Jessie watched while Evan gave a mighty pull and lifted the table up over his head. *Wow, he's gotten so big,* thought Jessie, remembering what Mom had said about Evan's growth spurt. Sometimes Jessie felt like Evan was growing twice as fast as she was.

Growing up. Growing away.

"It looks important," said Jessie. *It looks like bad news* is what she thought in her head. Was there a problem? A complaint? A mix-up? All the nervousness she'd been feeling about skipping to fourth grade suddenly burbled up inside her.

"This table's really dirty," said Evan. "Do you think we can just cover it with a lot of cups and the pitcher and no one will notice?"

Jessie looked. The table was streaked with black. "No."

Evan groaned.

"I'll clean it," said Jessie. Evan had only agreed to have a lemonade stand because it was one of *her* favorite things to do. The least she could do for him was clean the gunk off the table. "Maybe," she said, holding up the envelope again, "they're postponing school? Maybe the first day isn't going to be next Tuesday? Ya think?"

That got Evan's attention. "Let's ask Mom to open it," he said.

Up in the humming cool of her office, Mrs.

Treski read the letter through once. "Well," she said. "This is a curve ball." She looked right at Evan. Jessie thought her face looked worried. "Evan, you and Jessie are going to be in the same class this year. You'll both have Mrs. Overton."

Jessie felt relief flood her entire body. The same class! If she could have wished for one thing in the whole world, that's what she would have wished for. She would be with Evan, and Evan would make everything easier. He would introduce her to all those fourth-graders. He would show them all that she was okay. Not some puny second-grader who didn't really belong.

But Evan didn't look happy. He looked angry. "Why?" he asked in an almost-shouting voice.

Mrs. Treski scanned the letter. "Well, the classes were small to start with. And now some of the fourth-graders they thought would be attending aren't because they're moving or switching to private schools. So they need to combine the two small classes into one bigger class."

"That is so unfair," said Evan. "I wanted Mrs.

Scobie. And I don't want—" He looked at Jessie. "That is *so* unfair!"

Jessie was surprised. This was great news. Why didn't Evan see that? They always had fun together at home. Now they could have fun in school, too. "It'll be fun," she said to Evan.

"It will not be fun," said Evan. "School. Isn't. Fun." And then he stomped downstairs and locked himself in his room for the rest of the afternoon. They never finished the lemonade stand.

And here it was, two days later, and Evan was still all locked up, even though he wasn't in his room. He wouldn't talk to her, and he wouldn't play with her.

So Jessie went up to her room and did what she always did when she was upset or angry or sad or confused. She started reading *Charlotte's Web*. She had read the book about a hundred times.

She was at the good part, the happy part. Wilbur had just been named "some pig," and he was getting all kinds of attention from the Zuckermans and the whole town. But Jessie couldn't settle into that happy feeling, the one that usually came when Charlotte said:

I dare say my trick will work and Wilbur's life can be saved.

Instead, she kept noticing an unhappy feeling tap-tap-tapping on her shoulder. And it wasn't the unhappy feeling that came from knowing that Charlotte was going to die on page 171.

It was Evan. She couldn't stop thinking about what he had said.

Jessie could only remember one other time that Evan had said "I hate you" to her. Grandma had been over and Evan needed help with his math homework. He had that frustrated, screwed-up-mouth look that he sometimes got with math or spelling or writing reports. Mom called it his "he's-a-gonna-blow!" look. But Grandma couldn't help him because it was "all Greek" to her. So Jessie had shown him how to do each problem. Well, she'd just sort of jumped in and done the problems for him. That was helping, wasn't it? Grandma had called her a girl genius, but Evan had ripped his paper in half and run upstairs, shouting "I hate you!" just before slamming his door. That was last year.

Jessie rested the book on her stomach and stared at the ceiling. People were confusing. She'd rather do a hundred math problems than try to figure out someone else's mixed-up feelings, any day of the week. That's why she and Evan got along so well. He'd just tell her, straight out, "I'm mad at you because you ate the last Rice Krispie's Treat." And then she could say, "Sorry. Hey, I've got some Starburst in my room. You want them?" And that would be that.

Evan was a straight shooter.

Not like the girls at school, the ones who had started that club. She rolled over onto her side to get away from *those* thoughts.

Across the room, against the opposite wall, she noticed the three pieces of foam core her mom had bought for Jessie's Labor Day project. Every year, the Rotary Club sponsored a competition for kids to see who could come up with the best display related to the holiday. This was the first year Jessie was old enough to participate, and she had begged her mom to buy foam core and gel pens and fluorescent paper and special stickers for her display. She was determined to win the prize money: a hundred dollars! But she hadn't been able to come up with a single idea that seemed good enough. So here it was, just five days before the competition, and the foam core was still completely blank.

Jessie reached for her book. She didn't want to think about the girls at school and she didn't want to think about the competition. She started reading again.

Wilbur and Charlotte were at the fair, and Charlotte was beginning to show her age. Jessie read the words that Wilbur said to his best friend.

I'm awfully sorry to hear that you're feeling poorly, Charlotte. Perhaps if you spin a web and catch a couple of flies you'll feel better.

Well, the second part didn't apply at all, but Jessie imagined herself saying the first line: *I'm awfully sorry to hear that you're feeling poorly, Evan.* It sounded about right. At least it would show him that she cared, and Jessie knew that this was important when someone was feeling upset. She decided to go downstairs and give it a try. She would do just about anything to get Evan back to the way he was before the letter.

Jessie looked in the kitchen and the backyard—no Evan. She was halfway down the steps to the basement when she heard a noise coming from the garage. She opened the door and felt the full heat of the day on her skin. It was like some giant had blown his hot, stinky breath on her.

In the garage, she found Evan and Scott Spencer. *Weird,* she thought. *Evan doesn't even like Scott Spencer.* They'd been on-again, off-again friends from kindergarten. But ever since Scott had purposely put Evan's bike helmet under the wheel of the Treskis' minivan so that Mrs. Treski ran over it when she backed out, the friendship had definitely been *off.*

Jessie looked from Evan to Scott and back again. Now she had no idea what to say. *I'm awfully sorry to hear that you're feeling poorly, Evan,* didn't seem to make much sense when Evan was obviously having fun with his friend. She tried to think of something else to say. All she could come up with was "What're you doing?"

The boys were bent over a piece of cardboard. Evan was writing letters with a skinny red felt-tipped pen. The purple cooler was in the middle of the garage and two plastic chairs were stacked on top of it. On the top chair was a brown paper bag.

"Nothing," said Evan, not looking up.

Jessie walked over to the boys and peered over Evan's shoulder.

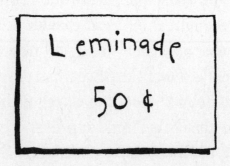

She said, "You spelled *lemonade* wrong. It's an *o*, not an *i*." But she thought, *Oh, good! A lemonade stand. My favorite thing to do!*

The boys didn't say anything. Jessie saw Evan's mouth tighten up.

"You want me to make the lemonade?" she asked.

"Already made," said Evan.

"I could decorate the sign," she said. "I'm good at drawing butterflies and flowers and things."

Scott snorted. "*Huh!* We don't want *girl* stuff like that on our sign!"

"Do you want to use my lock box to keep the money in? It's got a tray with separate compartments for all the different coins."

"Nope," said Evan, still working on the sign.

"Well," she said, looking around. "I can clean the table for you." The small wooden table, still covered in black streaks, was pushed up against the bikes.

"We're not using it," said Evan.

"But we always use the table for a stand," said Jessie.

Evan pushed his face in her direction. "We don't want it."

21

Jessie took a couple of steps back. Her insides felt runny, like a fried egg that hasn't cooked enough. She knew she should just go back into the house. But for some reason her legs wouldn't move. She stood still, her bare feet rooted to the cool cement.

Scott whispered something to Evan and the two boys laughed, low and mean. Jessie swayed toward the door, but her feet stayed planted. She couldn't stand it that Evan wanted to be with Scott—who was a real jerk—more than her.

"Hey," she said. "I bet you need change. I've got a ton. You could have all my change. You know, as long as you pay it back at the end of the day."

"Don't need it," said Evan.

"Yeah, you do," insisted Jessie. "You always need change, especially in the beginning. You'll lose sales if you can't make change."

Evan capped the pen with a loud *snap!* and stuck it in his pocket. "Scott's bankrolling us. His mom keeps a change jar, so we've got plenty."

The boys stood up. Evan held the sign for Scott to read, turning his back on Jessie. "Awesome," said Scott.

Jessie knew that the sign was not awesome. The letters were too small and thin to read from a distance. (Evan should have used a fat marker instead of a skinny felt-tipped pen. Everybody knew that!) There weren't any pretty decorations to attract customers. And the word *lemonade* was spelled wrong. Why wouldn't Evan take a *little* help from her? She just wanted to help.

Scott turned to her and said, "Are you really going to be in fourth grade this year?"

Jessie's back stiffened. "Yep," she said.

"Wow. That is so freaky."

"Is not," she said, sticking her chin out.

"Is too," said Scott. "I mean, you're a *second*-grader and now you're gonna be a *fourth*-grader. That's just messed up."

Jessie looked at Evan, but he was busy taping the sign to the cooler.

"Lots of people skip grades," said Jessie. "It's not that big a deal."

"It's completely weird!" said Scott. "I mean, you miss everything from a whole year. You miss the whole unit on Antarctica, and that was the best.

23

And the field trip to the aquarium. And the thing where we sent letters all over the country. Remember that, Evan? You got that letter from Alaska. That was so cool!"

Evan nodded, but he didn't look up.

"It's not that big a deal," said Jessie again, her voice stretched tight like a rubber band.

"It's like you miss a year of your life," Scott said. "It's like you're gonna *die* a whole year earlier than the rest of us because you never had third grade."

Jessie felt cold and hot at the same time. Part of her wanted to yell, "That doesn't make any sense!" But the other part of her felt so *freakish*—like Scott had just noticed she had three legs.

Evan stood up and tossed the paper bag to Scott. Then he grabbed the plastic chairs with one hand. "Come on. Let's go." He reached down to grab one handle of the cooler. Scott grabbed the other, and together they lifted it and began to walk out of the garage.

"Hey, Evan," said Jessie, calling to their backs. "Can I come, too?"

"No," he said, without turning around.

"Come on. Please? I'll be a big help. I can do lots of things—"

"You're too young," he said sharply. "You're just a baby."

The boys walked out.

*You're just a baby.*

Jessie couldn't believe Evan had said that. After all the stuff they'd done together. And he was only *fourteen months* older than she was. Hardly even a full year. She was about to yell back something really harsh, something stinging and full of bite, like *Oh, yeah?*, when she heard Scott say to Evan, "Man, I can't believe you have to be in the same class as your little sister. If that happened to me, I'd move to South America."

"Yeah, tell me about it," replied Evan, crossing the street.

The words died on Jessie's lips. She watched Evan walking away, getting smaller and smaller.

He was deserting her.

He *wasn't* going to stand by her at school. He

wasn't going to smooth the way for her. He was going to be on the *other* side, with all of *them,* looking down on her. Telling everyone that she was too young to be part of the crowd. Telling everyone that she didn't belong.

"Fine for you, Evan Treski," she said as she marched into the house, her fists balled up at her sides. "I don't need *you.* I don't need *you* to have fun. I don't need *you* to run a lemonade stand. And I don't need *you* to make friends in the fourth grade."

Halfway up the stairs, she stopped and shouted, "And I am *not* a baby!"

# Chapter 3
# Joint Venture

**joint venture** (joint vĕn′chər) n. Two or more people joining forces to sell a certain amount of goods or to work on a single project. When the goods are sold or the project is finished, the joint venture ends.

"Your sister is really—"

"Shut up," said Evan.

"Huh?"

"Just shut up. She's okay. She just . . . she doesn't . . . look, she's okay. So just shut up."

"Y'okay," said Scott, holding up his free hand to show he meant peace.

Evan was getting abused on both sides. The

heavy cooler was banging against his inside leg with every step. And the plastic chairs were scraping against his outside leg. *Bruised and bloodied,* he thought to himself. *All for the fun of hanging out with Scott Spencer.*

Why couldn't Jack have been home? Or Ryan? And why did Adam have to be on the Cape this week? It stunk.

"How far are we walking?" grunted Scott.

"Just to the corner." Evan watched as drops of sweat fell off his face and landed on the hot sidewalk.

"We shoulda stayed in the driveway. It was shaded."

"The corner's better. Trust me," said Evan.

He remembered when Jessie had said the same words to him last summer. They were setting up a lemonade stand together, and Evan had been grumbling about dragging the cooler across the street and down two houses, just like Scott. But Jessie had insisted. "There's sidewalk on this side," she'd said. "So we'll get the foot traffic coming in both directions. And people in cars coming around the curve will have time to see us and slow down. Besides, there are a bunch of little kids on the side street and their mothers won't want them crossing Damon Road. The corner's better. Trust me."

And she was right. They'd made a ton of money that afternoon.

It took ten seconds to set up the lemonade stand. Evan unfolded the chairs and set one on each side of the cooler. Scott tilted the sign toward the street for maximum effect. Then they both sat down.

"Man, is it hot," said Evan. He took off his baseball cap and wiped the sweat from his face with his shirt. Then he grabbed an ice cube from the cooler, balanced it on his head, and stuck his cap back on.

"Yeah," said Scott. "I'm thirsty." He reached into the paper bag and pulled out a cup. It was one of those large red plastic cups that vendors use at professional baseball games. Then Scott took one of the pitchers from the cooler and filled the cup to the brim with lemonade.

"Hey, not so much," said Evan, pouring himself a cup, too, but only partway. He glugged down half his drink. *Not bad*, he thought, though he noticed a dead fruit fly floating on the top. His mom had been battling a mad fruit-fly infestation ever since the weather had turned really warm. The kitchen sink area, where they kept their fruit bowl, was dotted with tiny, feathery fruit-fly corpses.

Scott drained his cup and tossed it on the ground. "Aahhh," he said, satisfied. "That was good. I'm gonna have another."

Evan reached for the trashed cup and stowed it under his seat. "Nah, c'mon, Scott. You're gonna drink all our profits if you do that." He stretched his legs out by putting his feet on top of the cooler. "Just chill."

"I'm gonna chill by having another cup," said Scott.

There it was. That mean bite in Scott's voice. Evan's shoulders tensed up.

"Move your feet," said Scott. "It's hot out here."

"Dude, you're—" Evan sat up expectantly and looked down the street. "Hey, here comes our first customer."

A mother pushing a double stroller came into view. At the same time, one of the kindergartners from down the street rode her bike up, noticed the sign, and quickly pedaled back to her house. Within five minutes, there was a small crowd of neighborhood kids and pedestrians buying lemonade from the stand.

Evan let Scott handle all the money while he took care of the pouring and the "sweet talk." That's what his mother called it when a salesperson chatted her up. "Trust me," she had once told Evan and Jessie. "Buying something is only *half* about getting something. The other half is all about human contact." Mrs. Treski knew about these things because she was a public relations consultant. She'd even written a booklet called *Ten Bright Ideas to Light Up Your Sales* for one of her clients. And Evan was like her: He was good at talking with people. Even grownups. It was easy for him. So he kept the conversation flowing, along with the lemonade. People hung around. Most of them bought a second cup before they left.

Evan was so busy, he almost didn't notice Jessie flying out of the garage on her bike and riding down the street toward town. *Good riddance,* he thought—but at the same time he wondered where she was going.

During a lull in business, Evan walked all around the stand, picking up discarded plastic cups. Scott sat in his chair, jingling the coins in his pocket.

"Man, we are gonna be so rich," said Scott. "I bet we made five bucks already. I bet we made ten! How much you think we made?"

Evan shrugged. He looked at the stack of used cups in his hand and counted the rims. Fourteen. They'd sold fourteen cups so far. And each cup of lemonade cost fifty cents. Evan heard Mrs. DeFazio's voice in his ear. Mrs. DeFazio had been his third-grade teacher, and she'd done everything she could to help Evan with his math.

*If one cup of lemonade sells for fifty cents and you sell fourteen cups of lemonade, how much money have you made?*

Word problems! Evan hated word problems.

And this one was impossible anyway. He was pretty sure the right equation was

$$14 \times 50 =$$

but how was he supposed to solve that? That was double-digit multiplication. There was no way he could do a problem like that. And besides—some of those fourteen people had bought refills but used the same cup. How many? Evan didn't know.

Still, he knew they'd made a pretty good amount of money. That estimate was close enough for him.

"How much do you think we could make if we sold it *all?*" asked Scott.

"I don't know," said Evan. "Maybe twenty bucks?" That sounded high, even to him, but Evan was an optimist.

"Do you really think?"

Both boys looked in the cooler. Three pitchers were empty. They only had half a pitcher left.

"You were pouring the cups too full," said Scott. "You shoulda poured less in each one."

"You're the one who brought the huge plastic cups. You could fit a gallon in one of those!" said Evan. "Besides, I wasn't gonna be chintzy. They're paying a whole half a buck for it. They deserve a full cup. And anyway, we can just go home and make more. My mom has cans of lemonade in the freezer."

"So go home and make more," said Scott.

"Oh, yes, Your Majesty. O High Commander. Your Infiniteness. Why don't *you* go make it?"

"Cuz I'm chillin'," said Scott, leaning back in his chair with a stupid grin on his face.

Evan knew he was just joking, but this was exactly why he didn't like Scott. He was always thinking of himself. Always looking for some way to come out on top. If they were playing knockout, Scott always came up with a new rule that helped him win. If they were doing an assignment together, Scott always figured out how to divide it so he had less work to do. The kid was a weasel. No two ways about it.

But everyone else was out of town. Evan didn't want to spend the day alone. And Jessie—Jessie was on his "poop list," as Mom called it when the dog did something he wasn't supposed to do. Evan might never play with Jessie again.

Evan crossed the street and went into the house. He was surprised to find that there were no more cans of lemonade in the freezer. Wow. There'd been so many this morning. Luckily there was a can of grape juice in the freezer and a bottle of ginger ale in the fridge. *It'll work,* he thought. *People just want a cold drink. They don't care if it's lemonade.*

He mixed up the grape juice at the sink. The fruit flies were more out of control than ever, thanks to the lemonade the boys had dribbled on the countertop. Evan swatted a couple, but most of them drifted out of his reach and settled on the fruit bowl. He wished his mother believed in chemical warfare. But for Mrs. Treski, it was all-natural or nothing. Usually nothing.

When he went back outside to the lemonade stand, Evan noticed that the last pitcher was turned upside down on the cooler.

"Aw, c'mon, Scott," he said.

"What? It was hot! And you said we could always make more."

"Yeah, well, we didn't have as much in the house as I thought. I've got grape juice and ginger ale."

"I hate ginger ale," Scott said. "I wouldn't give you a penny for it."

It turned out that a lot of people felt the same way. Business was definitely slower. The day got hotter. The sun beat down on them so ferociously that it was easy to imagine the sidewalk cracking open and swallowing them whole.

Fanning himself, Evan asked, "How much money do you really think we could make?"

"I dunno," said Scott, pushing his baseball cap down over his eyes.

"I mean, on a hot day like this," Evan said, silently adding the words *or tomorrow*. "If we sold eight pitchers of lemonade. Whaddya think we'd each make?"

"Eight pitchers? I don't know." Scott shook his head. His baseball-capped face wagged back and forth. "Too hot for math. And it's summer."

Evan pulled the red pen out of his pocket and started to write on the palm of his hand.

$$8 \times ?$$
$$8 \times 50 ? \quad \div 2 ?$$

That didn't seem right.

Jessie would know. She'd do that math in a second.

Evan capped the pen and jammed it into his pocket. "But I bet it's a lot," said Evan. "I bet on a hot day like this, we could actually make some real money in the lemonade business."

"Yeah," said Scott. "Then we'd be rich. And I'd get an Xbox. The new one. With the dual controls."

"I'd get an iPod," said Evan. He'd been saving for one for over a year. But every time he had some money put away, well, it just disappeared. Like the ten dollars from Grandma. She'd even written in her card, "Here's a little something to help you get that music thing you want." But the money was gone. He'd treated Paul and Ryan to slices of pizza at Town House. It had been fun.

"That would be so great, to listen to music

whenever I want," said Evan. *I could tune you out,* he added in his own head.

They sat in silence, feeling the heat suck away every bit of their energy. Evan was hatching a plan. The heat wave was supposed to last at least five days. If he and a friend (*not Scott*) set up a lemonade stand every day for five days, he'd definitely have enough to buy an iPod. He imagined himself wearing it as he walked to school. Wearing it on the playground. *Hey, Megan. Yeah, it's my iPod. Sweet, huh?* Wearing it in class when the teacher droned on about fractions and percents. *Nah.* But it would be so cool. At least there would be one thing, *one thing,* that didn't totally stink about going back to school.

After two hours they decided to call it quits. Sales had dropped off—fast—and then stopped altogether.

"Hey, did you notice something?" asked Evan, stacking the chairs.

"What?" said Scott.

"When we started the stand, most of our business came from that direction." He pointed down the street toward the curve in the road. "But after an hour, not one person who walked past us from that direction bought a cup. Not one. They all said, 'No, thanks,' and kept on walking. Why do you think?"

"Dunno," said Scott.

"Boy, you're a real go-getter," said Evan. "You know that?"

Scott socked him in the chest, but Evan defended and knocked Scott's cap off. While Scott was scrambling for his hat, Evan said, "Just hang here for a minute, okay?" and set off down the street. As soon as he rounded the curve, he knew why business had fallen off so badly.

There was Jessie. And *Megan Moriarty* from his class. They were standing inside a wooden booth, and their sign said it all.

LEMONADE
frosty! delicious!
thirst-quenching!
Wow! Only 50¢ per cup!

By the looks of it, their business was booming.

Evan watched as Jessie accepted a fistful of dollar bills from a mother surrounded by kids. At that moment, Jessie looked up and saw him. Evan had a weird feeling, like he'd been caught cheating on a test. He wanted to run and hide somewhere. Instead, he froze. What would Jessie do?

Evan couldn't believe it: She sneered at him. She cocked her head to the side and gave him this little I'm-so-much-better-than-you smile. And then— and *then*—she waved the money in her hand at him. She *waved* it! As if to say, "Look how much *we've* made selling lemonade! Bet you can't beat that!"

Evan turned on his heel and walked away. Behind him, he could hear Megan Moriarty laughing at him, clear as a bell.

# Chapter 4
# Partnership

**partnership** (pärt′nər-shĭp′) n. Two or more people pooling their money, skills, and resources to run a business, agreeing to share the profits and losses of that business.

Jessie had been waiting for this moment—the moment when Evan would see their lemonade stand, see the wonderful decorations they had made, see the crowds of people waiting in line, see *Megan Moriarty* standing by her side. He would see it all and be so impressed. He would think to himself, *Wow, Jessie is one cool kid. She sure knows how to run a lemonade stand right!* And then he'd jog over and say, "Hey, can I help out?" And Jessie would say, "Sure!

We were hoping you'd come over."

And it would be like old times.

Why hadn't it worked out like that?

With one part of her brain, Jessie continued to take money from customers and make change. That was the part of her brain that worked just fine. With the other part of her brain, Jessie went over what had happened with Evan. That was the part of her brain that tended to run in circles.

She and Megan were selling lemonade. Business had been good. Then Mrs. Pawley, a neighborhood mom, walked up. She had had a bunch of kids in her backyard running through the sprinkler, and now they wanted twelve cups of lemonade. Twelve! It was the biggest sale of the day. Megan got cracking pouring the lemonade and Jessie took the six singles that Mrs. Pawley handed her. All the kids from Mrs. Pawley's backyard were chanting, "Lemon-ADE! Lemon-ADE! Lemon-ADE!"

A fly buzzed by Jessie's ear—they'd been having a problem with flies because of the sticky lemonade spills on their stand—and she cocked her head to one side to shoo it since her hands were busy with the money. And that's when Jessie looked up and saw Evan standing there, staring.

So she smiled.

But he didn't smile back.

So she waved, even though she had all that money in both hands. She waved so he'd know that she was happy to see him.

And then he stalked off, all stiff-legged and bristly. And she never got to say, "Sure! We were hoping you'd come over," like she'd rehearsed in her head.

And just then, Tommy Pawley, who was two years old, pulled down his bathing suit and peed right on the lawn. And Megan laughed so loud, Jessie was sure you could hear it all over the neighborhood.

That's what had happened. That's exactly what had happened. But Jessie knew that something else entirely had happened. And she didn't get it. The way she didn't get a lot of things about people.

All she knew was that the sight of Evan walking

away—walking away from her for the second time that day—made her feel so sad and alone that she just wanted to run home to her room and curl up on her bed with *Charlotte's Web*.

"Hey, Madam Cash Register," said Megan, nudging her. "You're falling behind. Ring three for this lady and one for this kid here."

Jessie turned away from the retreating figure of Evan. "That's a dollar fifty," she said to the woman standing in front of her. She took the five-dollar bill the woman was holding out and made change from her lock box, focusing all her energy on the part of her brain that worked just fine.

It's true that when Evan had first walked out of the garage, Jessie had banged up to her room and tried to think of every way possible that she could make his life a living misery.

She'd thought of telling Mom that Evan was the one who broke the toaster (by playing hockey in the house, which is not allowed). She'd thought of taking back every one of her CDs from his room (even though she knew that would mean she'd have to give back all of *his* CDs). She'd even thought of putting peanut butter in his shoes. (This was something she'd read in a book, and she loved to imagine that moment of horror when he'd think he'd somehow gotten dog doo *inside* his shoes.)

But when these ideas had finished bouncing around her brain, and when her breathing had returned to normal and her fists weren't clenched at her sides anymore, she knew that what she really wanted was to get the old Evan back. The one who was so much fun to be around. The one who helped her out of every jam.

Like when she ate all the Lorna Doones that Mom had set aside for the Girl Scout meeting. And Evan had ridden his bike to the 7-Eleven and bought a new package before Mom even noticed. Or when she accidentally—well, not accidentally, but how was she supposed to know?—picked the red flowers in Grandma's garden that were a hybrid experiment. Evan had said they'd both done it so that Grandma's disappointment was spread around.

Or the time that Jessie had smashed the ceramic heart that Daddy had given her because she was so mad that he had left them. And then, when she had cried about her broken heart, Evan had glued every single last piece back together again.

She wanted back the Evan who was her best friend.

But Evan didn't want *her,* because he thought she was a baby and she was going to embarrass him in Mrs. Overton's class. So she had to prove to him that she was a big kid. That she could keep up with the crowd. That she could fit in—even with his fourth-grade class.

*I'll show him I can sell lemonade, too. Just as good as him and Scott. I won't embarrass him.* So Jessie got down to business.

She knew she needed a partner. From past experience, she'd learned that having a lemonade stand alone wasn't considered cool—it was considered pathetic. And her partner would have to be a fourth-grade girl, because that's what this was all about—showing she could fit in with the fourth-graders. So the question was *who?*

It had to be a girl who lived in the neighborhood, or at least close enough to bike to her house. And it had to be someone that Jessie had talked to at least once. No way could she call up a girl she'd never even talked to. And it had to be someone who seemed nice.

This last part was a problem, because Jessie knew that she often thought people were nice and then they turned out to be not nice. Case in point: those second-grade girls. So Jessie decided it had to be someone who *Evan* thought was nice. Evan knew about these things. He was the one who had explained, with his big arm around her shoulder, "Jessie, those girls are making fun of you. They are *not* nice."

When Jessie thought about all these different requirements, there was only one obvious answer: Megan Moriarty. She lived less than three blocks down the street. Jessie had said hi to her a few times while biking in the neighborhood. And Evan must have thought she was nice because Jessie had found

47

a piece of paper in his trash can with Megan's name written all over it. Why would he cover a page with her name if he didn't think she was a nice person?

Jessie went to the kitchen and climbed onto a stool so that she could reach the cabinet over the stove. She took down the school phone book and looked through the listings for both of last year's third-grade classes. No Megan Moriarty. *Duh,* Jessie remembered—she'd moved in halfway through the school year. With a sinking heart, Jessie checked the town phone book. No Moriarty family listed on Damon Road.

"Okay," said Jessie, slapping the phone book shut and putting it back in the cabinet over the stove. "Time for Plan B."

Jessie went to the hall closet and got out her backpack, which had been hanging there, empty, since the last day of school. Inside she put three cans of frozen lemonade from the freezer and her lock box full of change. (She put the ten-dollar bill, still paper-clipped to last year's birthday card from her grandmother, in her top desk drawer.) Then she went to the garage, strapped on her helmet, and rode off on her bike. As she left the driveway, she could see Evan and Scott's lemonade stand on the corner, but she was careful not to make eye contact. She didn't want to talk to Evan until she was ready to (*ta-da!*) impress him. Her heart leaped when she imagined him ditching Scott to be with her.

Megan's house was so close that Jessie got there in less than thirty seconds. And less than thirty seconds wasn't *nearly* long enough for her to plan what she was going to say. So she rode back and forth in front of the house about fifteen times, trying to pick the right words.

"What're you doing?" a voice shouted from the upstairs window.

Jessie slammed on her foot brakes and looked up. Megan was staring down at her. She looked huge. Her voice did not sound nice.

"Riding my bike," said Jessie.

"But why are you riding back and forth?" asked Megan impatiently. "In front of my house?"

"I dunno," said Jessie. "Ya wanna play?"

"Who are you?" asked Megan.

"Jessie," said Jessie, pointing down the street toward her house.

"Evan's little sister?" asked Megan.

Jessie felt like a deflating balloon. "Yeah."

"Oh," said Megan. "I couldn't tell 'cause of the helmet."

Jessie took her helmet off. "So ya wanna?" she asked.

There was a long pause.

"Where's Evan?" asked Megan.

"He's out, somewhere, with a friend," said Jessie.

"Oh," said Megan. Jessie looked down at the ground.

*People tell you things,* Evan had told her once, *with their hands and their faces and the way they stand. It's not just what they say. You gotta pay attention, Jess. You gotta watch for the things they're saying, not with their words.*

Jessie looked back up. It was hard to see Megan at all, she was so far up and behind the window screen. Jessie sucked in her breath. "Do you want to do something?"

Another long pause. Jessie started counting in

her head. *One one thousand, two one thousand, three one thousand, four one thousand, five one thousand, six one thousand . . .*

"Sure," said Megan. Then her head disappeared from the window.

A minute later Megan was at the front door. "Hey," she said, opening the screen.

Jessie raised her hand in something that was halfway between a wave and a salute as she walked in. Her sweaty bangs stuck to her forehead where the helmet had mashed them down. She was so nervous about saying something stupid, she didn't say anything at all. Megan leaned against the banister of the stairs and crossed her arms.

"So," said Jessie. She stared at Megan, who was fiddling with the seven or eight band bracelets on her arm. Jessie counted two LiveStrongs, one Red Sox World Champs, one March of Dimes, and one Race for the Cure. "What's that one?" she asked, pointing to a band bracelet with tiger stripes.

Megan stretched it off her wrist and gave it to Jessie. "It's for the Animal Rescue League. My mom gave them some money, so they gave us this and a

51

bumper sticker. I've got twenty-two band bracelets."

"Cool," said Jessie, handing the bracelet back. Megan flipped it back on. She continued to play with the bracelets on her arm, running them up and down, up and down.

"So, whaddya wanna do?" asked Megan.

"I don't know," said Jessie. "We could—I don't know. Let me think. We could—have a lemonade stand!"

*"Enhh,"* said Megan, sounding bored.

"Aw, it'll be fun. Come on!"

"We don't have any lemonade," said Megan.

"I've got three cans," said Jessie. She slipped the backpack off her back and dumped out the three cans of frozen lemonade. Her lock box came rattling out, too.

"What's that?" asked Megan.

"My lock box," said Jessie. "We can use it to make change." She felt her face getting red. Maybe fourth-graders weren't supposed to have lock boxes?

"How much money have you got?" asked Megan.

"You mean in change, or all together?"

Megan pointed at the lock box. "How much is in there?"

"Four dollars and forty-two cents. Fourteen quarters, five dimes, three nickels, and twenty-seven pennies." Jessie didn't say anything about the ten dollars she'd left at home.

Both of Megan's eyebrows shot up. "Exactly?" she asked.

*What do those eyebrows mean?* Jessie wondered in a panic. Why was Megan smiling at her? *Jessie, those girls are making fun of you. They are* not *nice.*

Jessie didn't say anything. She had a sick feeling in her stomach that this was going to turn out badly.

Megan straightened up. "Wow, you're rich," she said. "Wanna go to the 7-Eleven? We could get Slurpees."

"But—" Jessie pointed to the cans of lemonade on the carpeted hallway floor. The frost on them was already starting to sweat off.

"We could do the lemonade stand later," said Megan. "Maybe."

Jessie thought of Scott and Evan, racking up

sales two blocks down. How was she going to prove herself to Evan if she couldn't even get Megan to *have* a stand?

"How about the lemonade stand *first?*" Jessie said. "And then Slurpees with our earnings. I bet we'd even have enough for chips. And gum!"

"You think?" said Megan.

"I *know*," said Jessie. "Look." She held up a can of lemonade. "It says right on the can: 'Yields sixty-four ounces.' So we get eight cups from each can and sell each cup for half a buck, so that's four bucks, and then there're three cans, so that's twelve bucks altogether. Right?" The numbers flashed in Jessie's brain so fast, she didn't even need to think about what she was multiplying and dividing and adding. It just made sense to her.

"Hey, how old are you?" Megan asked, looking at her sideways.

"Eight," said Jessie. "But I'll be nine next month."

Megan shook her head. "That math doesn't sound right. No way we can make twelve dollars from just three little cans."

"Yuh-hunh," said Jessie. "I'll show you. Do you have a piece of paper?"

Jessie started to draw pictures. She knew that other kids couldn't see the numbers the way she did. They needed the pictures to make sense of math.

"Look," she said. "Here are three pitchers of lemonade, 'cause we've got three cans of lemonade. And each pitcher's got sixty-four ounces in it.

"Now, when we pour a cup of lemonade, we'll pour eight ounces, 'cause that's how much a cup holds. You don't want to pour less than that, or people will say you're being a cheapskate. So each pitcher is going to give us eight cups. 'Cause eight times eight equals sixty-four, right?

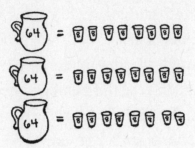

"Now, we'll sell each cup for fifty cents. That's a fair price. That means that every time we sell *two* cups, we make a buck. Right? Because fifty cents plus fifty cents equals a dollar. So look. I'll circle the cups by twos, and that's how many dollars we make. Count 'em."

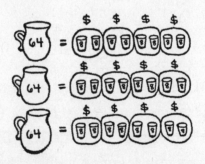

Megan counted the circled pairs of cups. "... ten, eleven, twelve."

"That's how much money we'll make," said

Jessie. "*If* we sell all the lemonade. And *if* we do the lemonade stand."

"Wow," said Megan. "You're really good at math." She puffed her cheeks out like a bullfrog and thought for a minute. Then she popped both cheeks with her hands and said, "Whatever. Let's do the lemonade thing."

Jessie felt soaked in relief. Maybe this was going to work after all.

An hour later, Jessie and Megan had transformed the little wooden puppet theater in Megan's basement into the hottest new lemonade stand on the block. The stand was decorated with tissue-paper flowers, cut-out butterflies, and glittery hearts. It was a showstopper.

And, boy, did people notice it. Kids in the neighborhood, strangers walking their dogs, moms strolling with carriages—even the two guys fixing the telephone wires. They all came to buy lemonade. And just when Jessie and Megan were on the verge of running out, Mrs. Moriarty went to the store and bought three more cans—free of charge!

So when Mrs. Pawley asked for twelve cups at exactly the moment that Evan rounded the curve and saw her lemonade stand, Jessie felt like she'd just scored a hundred on a test *and* gotten five points for extra credit.

So why did Evan stomp off?

And how come she didn't feel like she'd won anything at all?

# Chapter 5
# COMPETITION

**competition** (kŏm'pĭ-tĭsh'ən) n. Rivalry in the marketplace.

Dinner that night at the Treskis' was quiet. So the explosion that followed seemed *especially* loud.

It was Jessie's turn to clear and scrape the dishes, Evan's turn to wash and stack. Evan looked at the pile of dirty plates on his left. Jessie was ahead. She was always ahead when it was her turn to clear, but tonight it felt like she was taunting him. To Evan, every plate-scraping sounded like "Can't keep up. Can't keep up."

Evan was scrubbing the casserole pan when

Jessie stacked the last dirty dish by his elbow. Then she stuck her hands under the faucet to rinse without even saying excuse me and shook her hands *practically right in Evan's face* and said, "So how much money did you make?"

That was it! He couldn't hold it in any longer!

"Why'd you do it, huh? Why'd you have to ruin the one thing I had going?" For a second, Evan wasn't sure if he meant the lemonade stand or Megan Moriarty. In a mixed-up way, he meant both.

And there was *no way* he was going to tell Jessie that after paying back his mother for the four cans of lemonade, one can of grape juice, and one bottle of ginger ale (she'd been pretty irritated when she came down from the office and there wasn't a single cold drink in the house), he had walked away with two dollars and eleven cents. On top of that, he was pretty sure Scott had kept the five-dollar bill they'd earned. Well, what was Evan supposed to do? Ask Scott to turn his pockets inside out? Evan hadn't kept track of the sales, so he couldn't be sure.

"Why'd *I* do it? Why'd *you* do it? Why'd you invite that *jerk* over for a lemonade stand?" shouted Jessie. "And how come you wouldn't let me play? You're the one who was mean."

"You're such a showoff," said Evan. "You always have to let everyone know that you're the smart one."

"I wasn't showing off. I was just trying to have a little fun. Is that against the law? You won't do a lemonade stand with me. Then I won't do a lemonade stand with you. I'll do one with my friend Megan, instead."

"You can-*not* be her friend. You can-*not* be her friend!" shouted Evan.

"Why not?"

"Because you're a little kid. You don't even belong in the fourth grade. And because you're just an annoying showoff pest and no one likes you!"

The words felt like disgusting spiders running out of his mouth. They were horrible. But it felt so *good* to get rid of them.

Then Evan saw Jessie's lip tremble. Uh-oh. Jessie was a howler. She didn't cry often and she didn't cry long. But when she did, it was loud. Mom would come down from her office. Evan would catch the blame. *Unfair*.

But Jessie didn't let loose. Instead, she stood as tall as her runty height would allow and said, "Megan likes me. She invited me over to her house tomorrow. We're going to make another lemonade stand and earn *twice* what we did today."

Oh, that was *it!* She was going to ruin everything. Show him up right in front of Megan. Even before the school year started! Make Megan think he was just some stupid loser who couldn't even beat out his baby sister at a lemonade stand. Evan boiled over.

"I wouldn't count on it, *Juicy,*" he said. Jessie hated that nickname, and Evan only used it when he had to. "I'm going to have a lemonade stand every day until school starts. And I'm going to earn a hundred bucks by the end of the summer. Enough for an iPod."

"Oh, *please*. Like you *could* if you even wanted to," said Jessie. "Megan and I already made twelve bucks each today. We could have a hundred dollars like *that*." Jessie snapped her fingers.

"And then what?" said Evan. "You'd lock it up in your lock box and save it 'til you were fifty years old. You're the biggest miser on this planet."

Jessie stiffened up. Her mouth made a funny O. But then she put a hand on her hip and smirked at Evan. "For your information, I'm going to make a one-hundred-dollar donation to a *charity*."

Evan snorted. "Yeah, right. What charity?"

There was a long pause. And then Jessie said, as smooth as whipped cream, "The Animal Rescue League. Megan and I talked about it today."

"You don't even like animals," said Evan.

"Everybody likes animals!" shouted Jessie. "And I'm going to give them a hundred dollars. So you can't *ever* call me a miser again."

"I hope I never have to *talk* to you again," shouted Evan.

"Hey!" a sharp voice called from the stairs. Mrs. Treski had a pencil stuck in her hair and a worried look on her face. "I could hear you two all the way

63

in the attic. With the air conditioner on high. What's up?"

Evan looked at Jessie. Jessie looked at Evan.

They had taken a vow. A spit vow.

Ever since Dad had gone, they had vowed not to fight in front of Mom. It made her sad. Sadder, even, than when Dad left.

"Nothing," said Evan.

"Nothing," said Jessie.

Mrs. Treski looked at the two of them. "Come on. Out with it. What are you two yelling about?"

"It wasn't a fight, Mom," said Evan. "We were just joking around."

"Yeah," said Jessie. "We were goofing. Sorry we got you out of your office."

Mrs. Treski looked at both of them with her laser eyes. Jessie hung the dishtowel on the oven handle and fiddled with it until it was perfectly straight. Evan bent over the casserole pan and scrubbed as if his life depended on it. He scrubbed so hard, his elbow bumped the fruit bowl. A cloud of fruit flies rose into the air and then settled back down.

"Oh, God," said Mrs. Treski. "Would you look at those fruit flies!" Her shoulders slumped. "All right. Well, I'm going back up. Can you guys handle showers and reading, and then I'll be down to tuck and turn off lights?"

"Sure, Mom," said Jessie.

"No problem," said Evan.

Mrs. Treski disappeared upstairs. Jessie turned to Evan at the sink.

"Let's make a bet," she said. "Whoever earns a hundred dollars wins. And the *loser* has to give all their earnings to the winner."

Evan shook his head. "Not fair," he said. "You've already got money saved up."

"That money doesn't count," said Jessie. "We'll start with today's earnings. And it's *all* got to be from selling lemonade. No mowing lawns or sweeping out the garage or anything else."

"Aw, what if neither one of us makes a hundred?" said Evan, not liking the sound of this deal.

"Then whoever makes the closest to a hundred wins. And even if we *both* make over a hundred, whoever makes the most money wins the bet."

"When do we count up the money?" asked Evan.

Jessie thought about that. "Sunday night. Right before the fireworks." She looked straight at Evan. "Huh? Whaddya say?"

Evan didn't like bets. He really wasn't that into competition. He loved to play basketball and always gave it his all. But winning or losing—it didn't make much difference to him. He just liked to play.

But this. This was different. This mattered. If he didn't beat Jessie at this bet, if he couldn't win against his little sister in a lemonade war, then— Evan thought of the school year stretching in front of him—it was all over. He might as well just give up on everything right now.

"It's a bet. A hundred bucks by Sunday night. Winner takes all." He shook his wet hands over the sink, dried them on the dishtowel, and gave Jessie his most menacing look. "You better pray for mercy."

# Chapter 6
# underselling

**underselling** (un'dər-sĕl'ĭng) v. Pricing the same goods for less than the competition.

Jessie knew that Evan was up to something. First of all, there were all those phone calls last night. At least ten of them.

Then, he'd come knocking on her door this morning, asking if he could have the pieces of foam core she had leaning against her bedroom wall.

"No way," she'd answered. "That's for my Labor Day display."

"Oh, give it up. Today's Thursday. The contest is on Monday, and you don't even have an idea," Evan said.

"I do too have an idea. I'm just not telling *you*." Jessie still didn't have a clue about her Labor Day project, but she wasn't going to give Evan the satisfaction of knowing that.

"Then how come you haven't done anything?" Evan said, pointing at the blank foam core and the bags of untouched art supplies. "You're supposed to have pictures and typed-up information and a big title. It's supposed to be like a school report."

Jessie scrunched her eyes and pursed her lips in a you're-such-an-idiot look. "Don't worry. It's going to be great, and it's going to win first prize. And anyway, Mom bought all those supplies for *me*, and I'm not giving anything to *you*."

Jessie heard Evan mutter, "Miser," just as she slammed the door in his face.

And now three of Evan's friends were over— Paul, Jack, and Ryan. And all three had shown up with paper bags. And they were all in the garage making a lot of noise, with a big KEEP OUT sign taped to the door. Not that Jessie would have gone in there anyway. Who cares what a bunch of boys are doing? But she wished Megan had invited her to come over before lunch instead of after.

Jessie went into the kitchen to make a turkey sandwich. The boys had left a slimy mess of peanut butter, Doritos, and—yes—sticky puddles of lemonade mix. Jessie quickly looked in the trash can under the kitchen sink. There were twelve empty cans of frozen lemonade mix. Twelve! That was ninety-six cups' worth of lemonade. Ninety-six possible sales. Holy cow!

Where had Evan gotten the lemonade? He hadn't gone to the store, and he didn't have any money anyway. Then Jessie remembered the paper bags that Paul, Ryan, and Jack had carried in. She bet the boys had all raided their freezers and brought over a stash.

That didn't seem fair! She and Megan had to buy their lemonade today, using the money they'd made yesterday. How were they going to stay ahead of the game if the boys had free lemonade to sell?

"Think, Jessie, think," she whispered to herself. She couldn't let those boys win.

By the time she finished her lunch and cleaned up her mess (she wasn't going to lift a *finger* to clean up the boys' mess), she had the beginning of a plan in her head.

Which is why she found it doubly confusing when she knocked on Megan's screen and Carly Brownell came to the door. Jessie'd been all ready to say, "I've got a great idea." But then there was Carly, looking down at her like she was an earwig.

"Um, is Megan home?" asked Jessie.

Carly didn't open the screen door as she looked left and right behind Jessie. "Where's Evan?"

"Huh?" said Jessie.

Megan came running down the stairs carrying bottles of nail polish. "Oh, hi, Jessie," she said, opening the door. She poked her head out and looked around. "Where's Evan?"

"He's at home. Why?" asked Jessie. Carly made a noise like a snorting hippopotamus.

"I thought you said he was coming," said Megan.

"No, I didn't," said Jessie. "You said it would be fun to make a lemonade stand with all three of us, and I said, yeah, that would be fun."

"So, didn't he want to?" asked Megan.

"I never asked him," said Jessie.

"Oh. I thought you were going to," said Megan.

"Then you should have said, 'Hey, Jessie. Ask Evan if he wants to make a lemonade stand tomorrow.' And then I would have asked him." This was exactly what drove Jessie crazy about girls. They always said things halfway and then expected you to get the other half. And Jessie never got the other half.

Carly gave Megan a look. Jessie wasn't positive what the look meant, but she was pretty sure it wasn't a nice one.

That was the other thing that Jessie hated about girls. They were always giving looks. Looks that contained all kinds of strange and complicated messages.

Last year, in second grade, there had been four girls who were always exchanging looks with one another—Becky Baker, Lorelei Sun, Andrea Hennessey, and Eileen Garrett. Jessie watched them and knew that Evan was right: They talked without words. They used their eyes to pass secret messages. She also knew they didn't like her, but only because Evan had finally explained it to her over Christmas vacation. Jessie was surprised when he told her this. They laughed so much—how could they be mean?

They were the four who started the club: the Wild Hot Jellybeans Club. Or, as they called it, the WHJ Club. Becky was president, and she was always telling the others what to do. They made signs and paper buttons and membership cards. The teacher, Mrs. Soren, didn't usually allow clubs in the classroom, but she made an exception, telling the girls, "I'll let you wear your buttons in class, but only if you let all the other kids join—if they want to." By the end of the day, every kid in class was wearing a WHJ button—even Jessie, who'd never belonged to a club before.

It had seemed like Becky was being so nice to her. "That should have been your first clue," Evan told Jessie later. Becky made extra buttons for Jessie and even helped tape them all over her shirt. And she made a special membership card for her and even a

WHJ sign that she helped Jessie glue onto her Writers' Workshop folder.

Jessie remembered all the girls laughing and Jessie laughing, too. And all those strange looks that Becky and Lorelei and Andrea and Eileen kept flashing back and forth, like secret notes passed in class that Jessie could never read.

The very next day, Mrs. Soren collected all the buttons, gathered up all the membership cards, and even replaced Jessie's Writers' Workshop folder. "No clubs in the classroom," she said. "I made a bad choice by allowing it, even for one day."

On the playground, Jessie went up to Becky. "Why is she breaking up the club?" she asked.

Becky gave her a sour look. She'd been grumpy all morning. "Don't you get it, you dummy? WHJ doesn't stand for Wild Hot Jellybeans. We just said that to Mrs. Soren. It stands for We Hate Jessie. It's the We Hate Jessie Club, and everyone in the class is a member."

Jessie stared at Becky. Why did they hate her? What had she ever done to them? It didn't make sense. And then Lorelei, Andrea, and Eileen had laughed, and even Becky had managed a smirky grin.

"Jerks," Evan said later, when Jessie told him the whole story. "They've got rocks for brains. But Jess, you gotta be on the lookout for girls like that."

Standing in Megan's front hall, Jessie stared at Carly. Something inside told her Carly was a "girl like that."

"Look," said Jessie. "It doesn't matter. Evan can't come over. He's busy. And we've got to get going on our lemonade stand. I've got a great idea."

"We don't want to do a lemonade stand," said Carly.

Jessie looked at Megan.

"It's just that . . ." Megan fiddled with the bottles of nail polish in her hand the same way she'd fiddled with her band bracelets the day before. "It's kind of hot. And we did the lemonade thing already. And now Carly is over. So. Ya know?"

"You said you wanted to," said Jessie. *And I thought you liked me,* she added in her head. She felt her lower lip tremble. *Not now,* she shouted inside. *Don't you be a big baby!*

Megan stood there, saying nothing, fiddling with the bottles. Then she turned to Carly. "Aw, c'mon, Carly. It'll be fun. We made a *ton* of money yesterday. And it was really . . . fun."

Carly crossed her arms, tightened her lips, and raised one eyebrow. It was amazing how high she could raise that eyebrow. Jessie had never seen an eyebrow go that high.

"Aw, c'mon, Carly," Megan said again. Carly didn't move a muscle.

"Well, then I guess . . . " Megan's voice trailed off. She clicked one bottle of nail polish against another so that it made a tapping sound that filled the long silence. "I guess me and Jessie will do the lemonade stand alone then."

Carly dropped her eyebrow and her arms. "What-*ever*," she said as she walked out the door. "Spend the day baby-sitting if you want." The screen door slammed, followed by a huge bucketful of silence.

"What-*ever*," said Megan, imitating Carly's voice.

Jessie laughed, even though she was still sting-ing from the baby-sitting remark. "Thanks for doing the lemonade stand with me," she said.

"Are you kidding?" said Megan. "She's such a stuck-up jerk. I didn't even invite her over. She just rode by, and when I said that you and Evan might be coming over, she just walked into the house."

"Are all the girls in fourth grade like her?" asked Jessie. She tried to sound casual.

"Some are, some aren't," said Megan. She sat down on the stairs and opened a bottle of sky blue nail polish. With quick expert strokes, she started painting her toenails. "Hey, that's right. You're going to be in our class this year. That's so weird. Jumping a grade."

"A lot of people skip a grade," said Jessie.

"Really? I never met one before. Here. Do your toes green and then we'll be coordinated."

Jessie ended up getting more polish on her toes than on her toenails. But by the time they were done, Jessie had explained her plan for the day: Value-added.

"See," she said, pulling *Ten Bright Ideas to Light Up Your Sales* from the back pocket of her shorts. She turned to Bright Idea #2 and pointed with her finger.

> VALUE-ADDED: SOMETHING EXTRA (SUCH AS A SPECIAL FEATURE OR ATTRACTIVE PACKAGING) ADDED BY A COMPANY TO A PRODUCT THAT MAKES THE PRODUCT MORE DESIRABLE IN THE MARKETPLACE.

"That means we give customers something extra they didn't expect," explained Jessie. "I mean, anyone can go home and mix up their own batch of lemonade. Right? So if we want them to buy from us, we've got to give them something extra. We *add value*."

"Great," said Megan. "What are we going to add?"

"Well, how about chips? And maybe pretzels. Everyone likes chips and pretzels. We'll just have a bowl on the table, and anyone who buys lemonade can have some free snacks."

"So we're adding value—snacks."

"Yeah, except—" Jessie had stayed up late last night reading her mom's booklet. "You know what we're really adding? Fun. That's the one thing people can't get all by themselves. It *looks* like we're selling lemonade and snacks. But we're really selling fun. And everyone wants fun."

"Wow," said Megan. "That's really smart. It'll be like a party. Who doesn't like a party?"

Jessie nodded her head. She carefully tore out the definition of *value-added* from the booklet and put it in her lock box. Her mother always said: *Some ideas are like money in the bank.*

An hour later, they were all set up. The lemonade stand was newly decorated with streamers and balloons. Three bowls of snacks—Cheetos, potato chips, and pretzels—were set on top. Jessie had lugged Megan's boom box all the way downstairs, and Megan was doing the DJ thing with her CD collection. It looked like a party had somehow sprung up right in the middle of the hot concrete sidewalk. To anyone passing by, the lemonade stand shouted out, "Come over here! This is where the fun is!"

As soon as the music had come on, customers

had started drifting over. One of the moms across the street set up a sprinkler in her front yard, and soon all the kids in the neighborhood were running through the sprinkler and grabbing handfuls of Cheetos. Two women walking their dogs stopped for a nibble and ended up staying an hour. And three or four of the neighborhood mothers set up lawn chairs nearby and talked and ate pretzels while their kids ran through the water.

But Jessie noticed a funny thing. Even though there was an endless buzz of activity around the stand and the chips were flying out of the bowls faster than Megan could restock them, they weren't selling much lemonade.

"Hey, Jordan," said Jessie, as a four-year-old boy ran by in a bathing suit. "Don't you want a cup of lemonade?"

Jordan dive-bombed the pretzel bowl and came up with a fistful. "I had too much already. Four glasses!" and off he ran.

"Four glasses!" said Jessie to Megan. "He didn't buy any! Mrs. Doran, don't you want a cup of lemonade?"

"Sorry, Jessie, I have to pass," said Mrs. Doran. "I had two already, and I'm trying to cut down on sugary drinks."

*Where's everybody drinking so much lemonade?* wondered Jessie. She looked down the road. *Oh, wait a minute.* "Megan, hold down the fort," said Jessie. "I'll be right back."

"Sure thing," said Megan, dancing to the music. "This lemonade stand was the greatest idea. It's like a birthday for the whole neighborhood!"

Jessie headed down the road. As she rounded the bend, she prepared for the worst: Evan's lemonade stand crowded with customers. But there was nothing. Absolutely nothing. The corner was deserted.

She crossed the street and went into the garage. There was the cooler, dirty and empty. And there were the stacked plastic chairs, four of them this time. And there was—wait a minute. Those were *new* signs.

Jessie pulled out three large pieces of foam core. On the back of each one was part of the penguin project Evan had done last year in third grade. On the front were big letters:

Slow down!
Cheapest lemonade in
town!
Ahead!

Yesterday's prices!
Today's lemonade!

You won't believe
your eyes!
Icy cold lemonade!
Just 10¢ a cup!

Jessie *couldn't* believe her eyes. *Ten* cents a cup. That was crazy! Even if they sold all ninety-six cups, they'd only make $9.60. And split four ways— that was just $2.40 for each boy. Evan was never going to earn a hundred dollars with that kind of profit.

Jessie went down into the basement. Evan and Paul were playing air hockey. *Whashoo*. The puck flew into Evan's goal and Paul threw his arms into the air in a victory **V**.

"Oh, snap!" said Evan. "You're winning."

"Winning? Winning? Are you kidding me?" said Paul. Then he dropped his voice to a gravelly growl and said, "I don't play to win. I play to *pul-ver-ize*." Just like that muscle-guy actor in *Agent Down*, the movie that all the boys were talking about. Paul was even flexing his muscles like that actor— except that Paul didn't have any muscles. At least none that Jessie could see.

When Paul saw Jessie, he dropped his arms. "Hey," he said. Paul was Jessie's favorite of Evan's friends. He always joked around with her, but in a nice way. And he never minded when Evan invited her to come along with them.

"Hey," said Jessie. "What's up?"

Evan turned off the air hockey table. "Nothing," he said. "We were just going out."

Paul dropped his hockey paddle onto the table and followed Evan into the garage. Jessie trailed behind.

"Where are you going?" she asked.

"Down to the tracks," said Paul as he strapped on his bike helmet. "We put pennies there this morning, so we're gonna get 'em now. Squash! Ya wanna—"

"YO!" shouted Evan.

"My B," muttered Paul. "So, see ya," he said to Jessie.

Jessie hated this feeling of being shut out. Like she wasn't wanted. Evan had never made her feel that way before, even when sometimes he *did* want to be just with his friends. He'd always say things like, "Jess, we're going to go shoot hoops just the two of us, but when we get back we'll play spud with you." So that she knew he still liked her, even when she wasn't invited along.

But this. This was like he hated her. Like he never wanted to play with her again. And Paul was going right along with it.

Jessie scowled. "So you really cleaned up today at the lemonade stand, huh?" she said.

"Yep, we sold out," said Evan.

"So what did you make, like three dollars?" she asked.

"Actually, we made a ton. What was it, Paul?"

"Forty-five bucks," said Paul.

Jessie's mouth went slack. Forty-five dollars! "There's no way," she said. "Not at ten cents a cup."

"Oh, just the little kids paid that," said Evan. "The grownups all gave us way more. 'That's too cheap!' they said. 'It's such a hot day and you're working so hard. Here, take a dollar. Keep the change.' It was crazy!"

"Unreal," said Paul. "They kept pushing all this money at us 'cause they thought it was so sweet we were selling lemonade for a dime. We made a killing."

Bright Idea #5—Jessie remembered it immediately. "That's called *goodwill,*" she said slowly, picturing the exact page from her mother's booklet with the definition on it.

GOODWILL: AN INTANGIBLE BUT RECOGNIZED ASSET THAT RESULTS FROM MAKING/SELLING GOOD PRODUCTS, HAVING GOOD RELATIONSHIPS WITH YOUR CUSTOMERS AND SUPPLIERS, AND BEING WELL REGARDED IN THE COMMUNITY.

"It's when you do something nice in business and it ends up paying you back with money." She sighed. Why hadn't she thought of that? She would be sure to tear out that definition and put it in her lock box when she got back to the lemonade stand.

"Well, whatever. We cleaned up," said Evan.

"Even so," said Jessie, trying to find some way to prove that Evan had *not* had a good day selling lemonade. "You had four people working the stand. So if you split forty-five dollars four ways, that's only eleven twenty-five each." *Which is still way more than I'm going to make today,* she thought, *since the whole neighborhood has already filled up on cheap lemonade.*

"We're not splitting," said Evan. "The guys said I could keep it all."

"Right," said Paul. "All for a good cause!"

"That's not fair!" said Jessie.

"Sure it is," said Evan as he got on his bike and pushed off. "In case you didn't know, that's what it's like to have *friends*." Evan crossed the street.

"Ouch," said Paul. "TTFN, Jess." He followed Evan.

Jessie was left standing alone in the driveway.

## Chapter 7
# Location, Location, Location

**location** (lō-kā′shən) n. Real estate term that refers to the position of a piece of real estate as it relates to the value of that real estate.

Evan was in trouble. So far, he'd earned forty-seven dollars and eleven cents, which was more money than he'd ever had in his whole life. But today was Friday. There were only three days left. Three days to beat Jessie. He needed to earn almost fifty-three dollars to win the bet. And that meant each day he had to earn—

Evan tried to do the math in his head. Fifty-three divided by three. Fifty-three divided by three. His brain spun like a top. He didn't know where to begin.

He went to his desk, pulled out a piece of paper—his basketball schedule from last winter—and flipped it over to the back. He found the stub of a pencil in his bottom desk drawer, and on the paper he wrote

$$53 \div 3 =$$

He stared and stared at the equation on the page. The number fifty-three was just too big. He didn't know how to do it.

"Jessie would know how," he muttered, scribbling hard on the page. Jessie could do long division. Jessie had her multiplication facts memorized all the way up to fourteen times fourteen. Jessie would look at a problem like this and just do it in her head. *Snap*.

Evan felt his mouth getting tight, his fingers gripping the pencil too hard, as he scribbled a dark storm cloud on the page. His math papers from school were always covered in *X*'s. Nobody else got as many *X*'s as he did. Nobody.

*Draw a picture.* Mrs. DeFazio's voice floated in his head. She had always reminded him to draw a picture when he couldn't figure out how to start a math problem. *A picture of what?* he asked in his head. *Anything,* came the answer.

*Anything?* Yes, anything, as long as there are fifty-three of them.

Dollar signs. Evan decided to draw dollar signs. He started to draw three rows of dollar signs. "One, two, three," he counted, as he drew:

$

$

$

"Four, five, six." He drew:

$ $

$ $

$ $

By the time he reached fifty-three, his page
looked like this:

$ $ $ $ $ $ $ $ $ $ $ $ $$ $$ $$ $

$ $ $ $ $ $ $ $ $$ $ $ $$ $ $$ $ $

$$ $ $ $ $ $ $ $ $$ $$ $$ $ $$ $ $

There were seventeen dollar signs in each row.
And then those two extra dollar signs left over.
Evan drew a ring around those two extras.

$ $ $ $ $ $ $ $ $ $ $ $ $$ $ $$ ($)
$ $ $ $ $ $ $ $ $ $$ $ $ $$ $ $ $ ($)
$$ $ $ $ $ $ $ $ $$ $$ $ $ $$ $ $

Seventeen dollar signs. And two left over.
Evan stared at the picture for a long time. He
wrote "Friday" next to the first row, "Saturday"
next to the second row, and "Sunday" next to the
third row.

Friday    $ $ $ $ $ $ $ $ $ $ $ $ $ $ $ $ ($)
Saturday  $ $ $ $ $ $ $ $ $ $ $ $ $ $ $ $ ($)
Sunday    $ $ $ $ $ $ $ $ $ $ $ $ $ $ $ $ $

Evan looked at the picture. It started to make sense. He needed to make seventeen dollars on Friday, seventeen dollars on Saturday, and seventeen dollars on Sunday. And somewhere over the three days, he needed to make two *extra* bucks in order to earn fifty-three dollars by Sunday evening.

Evan felt his heart jump in his chest. He had done it. He had figured out fifty-three divided by three. That was a *fourth-grade* problem. That was *fourth-grade* math. And he hadn't even started fourth grade! And no one had helped him. Not Mom, not Grandma, not Jessie. He'd done it all by himself. It was like shooting the winning basket in double overtime! He hadn't felt this good since the Lemonade War had begun.

But seventeen dollars a day? How was he going to do that? Yesterday he'd made forty-five dollars, but that was because he'd had help (and free supplies) from his friends. They weren't going to want to run a lemonade stand every day. Especially on the last days of summer vacation.

He needed a plan. Something that would guarantee good sales. The weather was holding out, that was for sure. It was going to hit 95 degrees today. A real scorcher. People would be thirsty, all right. Evan closed his eyes and imagined a crowd of thirsty people, all waving dollar bills at him. Now where was he going to find a lot of thirsty people with money to spend?

An idea popped into Evan's head. *Yep!* It was perfect. He just needed to find something with wheels to get him there.

It took Evan half an hour to drag his loaded wagon to the town center—a distance he usually traveled in less than five minutes by bike. But once he was there, he knew it was worth it.

It was lunchtime and the shaded benches on the town green were filled with people sprawling in the heat. Workers from the nearby stores on their half-hour lunch breaks, moms out with their kids, old people who didn't want to be cooped up in their houses all day. High school kids on skateboards slooshed by. Preschoolers climbed on the life-size sculpture of a circle of children playing ring-around-the-rosey. Dogs lay under trees, their tongues hanging out, *pant, pant, pant.*

Evan surveyed the scene and picked his spot, right in the center of the green where all the paths met. Anyone walking across the green would have to pass his stand. And who could resist lemonade on a day as hot as this?

But first he wheeled his wagon off to the side, parking it halfway under a huge rhododendron. Then he crossed the street and walked into the Big Dipper.

The frozen air felt good on his skin. It was like getting dunked in a vat of just-melted ice cream. And the smells—*mmmmmm.* A mix of vanilla, chocolate, coconut, caramel, and bubblegum. He looked at the tubs of ice cream, all in a row, carefully protected behind a pane of glass. The money in his pocket tingled. He had plenty left over after buying five cans of frozen lemonade mix with his earnings from yesterday. What would it hurt to buy just one cone? Or a milk shake? Or maybe both?

"Can I help you?" asked the woman behind the counter.

"Uh, yeah," said Evan. He stuck his hand in his pocket and felt all the money. Bills and coins ruffled between his fingers. Money was meant to be spent. Why not spend a little?

"I, uh . . ." Evan could just imagine how good the ice cream would feel sliding down his hot throat. Creamy. Sweet. Like cold, golden deliciousness. He let his mind float as he gazed at the swirly buckets of ice cream.

The sound of laughter brought him back to earth in a hurry. He looked around. It was just some girls he didn't know at the water fountain. But it had *sounded* like Megan Moriarty.

"Can you please tell me how much a glass of lemonade costs?"

"Three dollars," said the woman.

"Really?" said Evan. "That much? How big's the cup?"

The woman pulled a plastic cup off a stack and held it up. It wasn't much bigger than the eight-ounce cups Evan had in his wagon.

"Wow. Three bucks. That's a lot," said Evan. "Well, thanks anyway." He started to walk to the door.

"Hey," said the woman, pointing to the ice cream case. "I'm allowed to give you a taste for free."

"Really?" said Evan. "Then, uh, could I taste the Strawberry Slam?" The woman handed him a tiny plastic spoon with three licks' worth of pink ice cream on it. Evan swallowed it all in one gulp. *Aahhh*.

Back outside, he got to work. First he filled his pitchers with water from the drinking fountain. Then he stirred in the mix. Then he pulled out a big blue marker and wrote on a piece of paper, "$2 per cup. Best price in town."

He'd barely finished setting up when the customers started lining up. And they didn't stop. For a full hour, he poured lemonade. *The world is a thirsty place,* he thought as he nearly emptied his fourth pitcher of the day. *And I am the Lemonade King.*

(Later, Evan would think of something his grandma said: "Pride goeth before a fall.")

When Evan looked up, there was Officer Ken, his hands on his hips, looking down on him. Evan gulped. He stared at the large holstered gun strapped to Officer Ken's belt.

"Hello," said Officer Ken, not smiling.

"Hi," said Evan. Officer Ken did the Bike Rodeo every year at Evan's school. He was also the cop who had shown up last fall when there was a hurt goose on the recess field. Officer Ken was always smiling. *Why isn't he smiling now?* Evan wondered.

"Do you have a permit?" asked Officer Ken. He had a very deep voice, even when he talked quietly, like he did now.

"You mean, like, a bike permit?" That's what the Rodeo was all about. If they passed the Rodeo, the third-graders got their bike permits, which meant they were allowed to ride to school.

"No. I mean a permit to sell food and beverages in a public space. You need to get a permit from the town hall. And pay a fee for the privilege."

Pay the town hall to run a lemonade stand? Was he kidding? Evan looked at Officer Ken's face. He didn't look like he was kidding.

"I didn't know I needed one," said Evan.

"Sorry, friend," said Officer Ken. "I'm going to have to shut you down. It's the law."

"But . . . but . . . there are lemonade stands all over town," said Evan. He thought of Jessie and Megan's lemonade stand. When he'd wheeled by with his wagon more than an hour ago, their stand had looked like a beehive, with small kids crowding around. He had read the sign over their stand: FREE FACE-PAINTING! NAIL-POLISHING! HAIR-BRAIDING! What a gimmick! But it sure looked like it was working. "You know," said Evan, "there's a stand on Damon Road right now. You should go bust them."

Officer Ken smiled. "We tend to look the other way when it's in a residential neighborhood. But right here, on the town green, we have to enforce the law. Otherwise we'd have someone selling something every two feet."

"But—" There had to be some way to convince Officer Ken. How could Evan make him understand? "You see, I've got this little sister. And we've got a . . . a . . . competition going. To see who can sell the most lemonade. And I've *got* to win. Because she's . . ." He couldn't explain the rest. About fourth grade. And how embarrassed he was to be in the same class as his kid sister. And how it made him feel like a great big loser.

Evan looked up at Officer Ken. Officer Ken looked down at Evan. It was like Officer Ken was wearing a mask. A no-smiling, I'm-not-your-buddy mask.

Then Officer Ken shook his head and smiled and the mask fell off. "I've got a little sister, too," he said. "Love her to death, *now,* but when we were kids—" Officer Ken sucked in his breath and shook his head again. *"Hooo!"*

Then the mask came back, and Officer Ken looked right at Evan for ten very stern seconds.

"Tell you what," said Officer Ken. "I *do* have to shut you down. The law's the law. But before I do, I'll buy one last glass of lemonade. How's that sound?"

Evan's face fell. "Sure," he said without enthusiasm. He poured an extra-tall cup and gave it to the policeman.

Officer Ken reached into his pocket and handed Evan a five-dollar bill. "Keep the change," he said. "A contribution to the Big Brother Fund. Now clean up your things and don't leave any litter behind." He lifted his cup in a toast as he walked away.

Evan watched him go. *Wow,* he thought. *I just sold the most expensive cup of lemonade in town.*

Evan stared at the five-dollar bill in his hand.

It was funny. Two days ago, he would have felt as rich as a king to have that money in his hands. It was enough to buy two slices of pizza and a soda with his friends. It was enough to rent a video and have a late night at someone's house. It was enough to buy a whole bagful of his favorite candy mix at CVS.

Two days ago, he would have been jumping for joy.

Now he looked at the five dollars and thought, *It's nothing*. Compared to the one hundred dollars he needed to win the war, five dollars was *nothing*. He felt somehow that he'd been robbed of something—maybe the happiness he should have been feeling.

He loaded everything from his stand into the wagon, making sure he didn't leave a scrap of litter behind. He still had a glassful of lemonade left in one pitcher, not to mention another whole pitcher already mixed up and unsold, so he poured himself a full cup. Then, before beginning the long, hot haul back to his house, he found an empty spot on a shaded bench and pulled his earnings out of his pockets.

He counted once. He counted twice. Very slowly.

He had made sixty-five dollars. The cups and lemonade mix had cost nine dollars. When he added in his earnings from Wednesday and Thursday, he had one hundred and three dollars and eleven cents.

*Now* that's *enough*, he thought.

# Chapter 8
# Going Global

**global** (glō′bəl) adj. Throughout the world; refers to expanding one's market beyond the immediate area of production.

On Saturday morning, Jessie slept in. And even when she opened her eyes—at 9:05!—she still felt tired. *How can I wake up tired?* she wondered as she buried her face in her pillow and dozed off.

Five minutes later she was awake for real, remembering why she was so tired. Yesterday's lemonade stand had been the hardest work of her life. Face painting, hair braiding, nail polishing—it had sounded like such a good idea. Jessie had been sure that every kid in the neighborhood would line up to buy a cup of lemonade.

But that was the problem. Every kid *had* lined up for lemonade—and then wanted face painting *and* hair braiding *and* fingernail polishing *and* toenail polishing. One boy had asked for face paintings on both cheeks, both arms, and his stomach. One girl begged for lots of little braids with ribbons woven in. And the nail polishing! They all wanted different colors and decals, and it was impossible to get them to sit still long enough for the polish to dry.

"We're going to run out of lemonade," Megan had said to Jessie at noon, as the line stretched all the way to the street.

"Pour half-cups instead of full ones," whispered Jessie. "It has to last."

Jessie and Megan had each made twenty-four dollars on lemonade, but they'd worked eight hours to do it. At the end of the day, they'd agreed: A good idea, but *not worth it!*

After breakfast, Jessie pulled out her lock box and sat on her bed. She kept the box hidden in her closet on a shelf under some sweaters. She kept the key in a plastic box in her desk drawer. The plastic box was disguised to look exactly like a pack of gum. You would never know it was hollow and had a secret sliding panel on its side.

Jessie unlocked the box and opened the lid. First she took out the three torn slips of paper. There was one for *value-added* and one for *goodwill*. There was also a new one that Jessie had added last night:

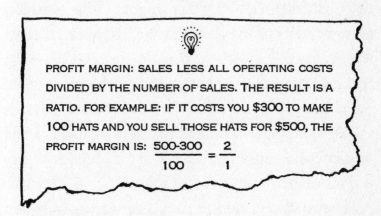

PROFIT MARGIN: SALES LESS ALL OPERATING COSTS DIVIDED BY THE NUMBER OF SALES. THE RESULT IS A RATIO. FOR EXAMPLE: IF IT COSTS YOU $300 TO MAKE 100 HATS AND YOU SELL THOSE HATS FOR $500, THE PROFIT MARGIN IS: $\dfrac{500-300}{100} = \dfrac{2}{1}$

Jessie lined up all three scraps of paper on the bed beside her. She wasn't sure why she was saving these words, but she felt like they belonged in her lock box.

Next, she took out her lemonade earnings. Every day, Megan had squealed over how much money they'd made. But every day, Jessie had known: *It's not enough. It's not going to be enough to win.*

Jessie counted the money. So far, she had earned forty dollars. It was a lot of money. But it wasn't nearly enough. She still needed to earn sixty more dollars. And today was Saturday. Only two more selling days before she and Evan counted their earnings on Sunday night. How was she going to sell enough lemonade to earn sixty dollars in two days?

She couldn't. That was the problem. No kid could earn a hundred dollars in just five days by selling lemonade. The *profit margin* was too small. She knew because she'd used her calculator to figure it out last night.

The numbers said it all. There was no way two girls in one neighborhood could sell 375 cups of lemonade. Nobody wanted *that* much lemonade, no matter how hot the day was.

Jessie looked at the money in her lock box and the page of calculations on her desk. Any other kid would have quit. But Jessie wasn't a quitter. (On

Profit margin for 1 can of lemonade (8 cups):

## Sales

8 cups @ 50¢/cup = (8 × .50) = $4.00

## Operating costs

Lemonade cost = $1.25

8 paper cups cost = $.15

Total operating costs = $1.40

## Number of Sales

8 cups = 8 sales

$$\text{Profit margin} = \frac{\$4.00 - \$1.40}{8}$$

$$= \frac{\$2.60}{8} = \frac{.325}{1}$$

So this means that for every 1 cup of lemonade sold, we earn about 32¢. I get half the profit, and Megan gets half the profit. That means I earn about 16¢ for every cup we sell.

I need to earn $60 to beat Evan.

$60 = 6000¢ (because 60 × 100 = 6000)

So how many times does 16 go into 6000?

6000 ÷ 16 = how many cups I need to sell = 375

I need to sell 375 cups of lemonade! I am DOOMED!!

good days, Jessie's mom called her *persistent*. On bad days, she told her she *just didn't know when enough was enough*.)

Jessie reached for *Ten Bright Ideas to Light Up Your Sales*. It was on her bedside table, right next to *Charlotte's Web*. Jessie's hand hovered. She looked longingly at Wilbur and Fern watching Charlotte hanging by a thread.

But this was war, and she couldn't stop to read for fun.

She grabbed the booklet and opened it to Bright Idea #6.

An hour later, she had a new scrap of paper stashed in her lock box and a whole new page of calculations on her desk. It might work. It *could* work. But she and Megan would have to risk every-thing—*everything* they'd earned over the past three days. And Jessie would have to be braver than she had ever been in her whole life.

Jessie carried her lock box and calculations downstairs. She went into the kitchen and pulled down the school directory, scanning the names of all the third-grade girls from last year. She knew them all—from Evan, from recess, from the lunchroom. Knew who they were. Knew their faces. Which ones were nice. Which ones were not so nice. But she didn't *really* know any of them. Not enough to call them up. Not enough to say, "Want to do something today?" Not enough to ask, "Would you like to have a lemonade stand with me?"

These girls were going to be her classmates. Jessie felt her face grow hot and her upper lip start to sweat. What was it going to feel like to walk into that classroom on the first day of school with all those eyes looking at her? Would they stare? Would they tease? Would they ignore her, even if she said hi?

Jessie looked at the names, then slammed the directory shut. She couldn't do it. She just wasn't brave enough.

Evan walked into the kitchen and grabbed an apple from the fruit bowl. A cloud of fruit flies rose up in the air and settled again. Evan inspected the apple and then bit into it, without washing it first.

Jessie wanted to say something but held her tongue. She looked at him and thought, *It is* never *going to feel normal, not talking to Evan.*

"Hey," she said.

Evan raised his apple to her, his mouth too stuffed to talk.

"So, is Paul coming over today?" she asked.

Evan shook his head, munching noisily.

"Well, is anyone coming over?" Jessie was curious to see what the enemy was up to today. Yesterday, Evan's smile had told her plenty: He had sold a lot of lemonade. A *lot*. But what was he going to do today?

Evan shrugged his shoulders. He swallowed so hard it looked like he was choking down an ocean liner.

"But you *are* setting up a stand, right?" asked Jessie.

"Nah. I'm good," said Evan, looking closely at his apple. "I'm just gonna take it easy today." He took another enormous bite and walked out of the kitchen and down the basement stairs.

Take it easy? How could he take it easy? You didn't take it easy when you were in the middle of a war.

Unless.

Unless he had already won the war.

Could that be possible?

It was impossible!

There was no way Evan had earned a hundred dollars in just three days of selling lemonade. *No way*.

Jessie's mind skittered like one of those long-legged birds on the beach. Had he? Could he? Were her calculations wrong? Was there some other way? Had she overlooked some detail? Some trick? Was she missing something?

Jessie flipped open the school directory. Maybe he had a hundred dollars. Maybe he didn't. She couldn't take a chance. She started putting pencil check marks next to the names of girls she thought might work out.

She'd gone over the list twice when the doorbell rang. It was Megan.

"I've got a new idea," said Jessie.

"Awww, not more lemonade," said Megan, sinking onto the couch in the family room. "I'm tired of selling lemonade. And it's just too hot. I practically had sunstroke yesterday painting all those faces."

"We're done with that," said Jessie. "No more extra services. Doesn't pay off. But here's an idea—"

"Forget lemonade! Let's go to the 7-Eleven," said Megan. "Is Evan home? We could all go."

"No. He's not home," said Jessie, eyeing the door to the basement. She needed Megan to be on board with her plan. She needed Megan to make the phone calls. "Look. This is great. And *we* don't need to sell the lemonade."

Jessie laid out all the details. She showed Megan the new scrap of paper.

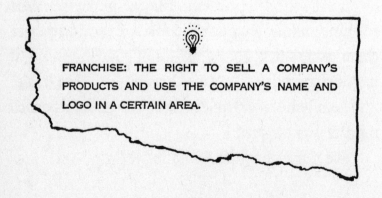

FRANCHISE: THE RIGHT TO SELL A COMPANY'S PRODUCTS AND USE THE COMPANY'S NAME AND LOGO IN A CERTAIN AREA.

Then she showed Megan her page of calculations. At first Megan buried her head under a pillow, but then she poked her head out like a turtle and started to listen for real.

"That sounds like a pretty good plan," she said. "But is it really going to work?"

Jessie looked at her calculations. She'd done them twice. "It should," she said. "I really think it should." She frowned, suddenly not so sure of herself. "It's a big up-front investment. And a lot of work organizing everybody. But once they're set up, we should just be able to sit back and watch the money roll in. The key is spreading everybody out so there'll be plenty of customers. We'll need at least ten girls. Fifteen would be better."

"That's the whole fourth-grade class," said Megan, looking doubtful. "How are we gonna get them to do this?"

"Well, you could phone them all up," said Jessie. She handed Megan the school directory, open to the third-grade page.

"Me?" said Megan. "Why me?"

"Because they know you," said Jessie.

"They know you, too."

"Yeah, but they *like* you."

Megan shook her head. "Not all these girls are my friends."

"Even the ones that aren't your friends, they still like you. *Everybody* likes you, Megan."

Megan looked embarrassed. "Oh, everybody likes you, too," she said.

"No, they don't," said Jessie. "They really don't." There was an uncomfortable silence between the two girls. Then Jessie shrugged her shoulders and said, "I don't know why those girls in my class last year didn't like me. I'm hoping this year will be better."

Megan tapped her fingers on her knees. "You're nervous, huh? About fourth grade?" she asked.

Jessie thought hard. "I'm worried that I won't make any new friends," she said. "You know, that all the kids will think I'm just some puny second-grader and that"—she took a deep breath—"I don't belong."

Megan looked up at the ceiling for a minute. "Do you have an index card?" she asked.

"Huh?"

"I need an index card," said Megan. "Do you have one?"

Jessie went to the kitchen desk and got an index card. She handed it to Megan. Megan started to write something on the card.

"What are you doing?" asked Jessie.

"I'm writing a comment card," said Megan. "That's something you're going to miss from third grade. We did it every Friday. We each got assigned a person, and you had to write something positive about that person on an index card. Then it got read out loud." She folded up the card and handed it to Jessie.

Jessie unfolded the card and read what Megan had written.

You're a really nice person and you have good ideas all the time. You're fun to be with and I'm glad you're my friend.

Jessie stared at the index card. She kept reading the words over and over. "Thanks," she whispered.

"You can keep it," said Megan. "That's what I did. I've got all my comment cards in a basket on my desk. And whenever I'm feeling sad or kind of down on myself, I read through them. They really help me feel better."

Jessie folded the index card and put it in her lock box. She was going to save it forever. It was like having a magic charm.

"So, how about I make half the phone calls and you make the other half?" said Jessie.

"Okay," said Megan, jumping up from the couch.

It was surprising how many almost–fourth-grade girls had absolutely nothing to do three days before school started. In less than an hour, Jessie and Megan had thirteen lemonade "franchises" signed up for the day.

The rest of the day was work, but it was fun. Jessie and Megan attached the old baby carrier to Megan's bike, then rode to the grocery store and spent every penny of their earnings on lemonade mix—fifty-two cans. They actually bought out the store. The four bags of cans filled the carrier like a boxy baby. They also bought five packages of paper cups. When they got back to Megan's house, Jessie tucked the receipt in her lock box, right next to her comment card. Jessie liked receipts: They were precise and complete. A receipt always told the whole story, right down to the very last penny.

```
              Salisbury Farms
       Your Neighborhood Grocery Store
              232 Central Ave.
            09/01/07   11:42AM


Store  23              Trans   246
Wkstn  sys5002         Cashier  KD68VW
Cashier's Name         James
Stock Unit Id          SIAJAMES
Phone Number           800-555-1275


Tastes Right Lemonade
       (52 @ 1.25)                  65.00

Pixie paper Cups
       (5 @ 2.85)                   14.25

Subtotal                            79.25
Tax                                  0.75
Total                               80.00

Cash                                80.00
Change due
   Cash                              0.00

Number of items sold: 57

  Get all your back-to-school supplies
           at Salisbury Farms.
           Happy Labor Day!
```

Then they tossed construction paper and art supplies into the carrier and started making the rounds.

First stop, Salley Knight's house. She was ready for them with a table, chair, and empty pitcher all set up. Jessie mixed the lemonade, Megan quickly made a "Lemonade for sale—75¢ a cup" sign, and they left Salley to her business. The deal was that Salley got to keep one-third of the profits and Jessie and Megan got to keep the rest.

After they'd set up all thirteen lemonade stands, each with enough mix to make four pitchers of lemonade, Jessie and Megan hung out at Megan's house, baking brownies and watching TV. Then they hopped on their bikes again and made the rounds.

Jessie and Megan stopped in front of Salley's house first. The lemonade stand was nowhere to be seen.

"Whaddya think is going on?" asked Megan. Jessie had a bad feeling in her stomach. Something must have gone wrong.

They rang the doorbell. Salley came to the door.

"Hurry," she said, grabbing their arms and pulling them inside. "My mom goes totally mental when the AC is on and the door is open."

"Where's your stand?" asked Jessie nervously, feeling goose bumps ripple up her arms because of the suddenly cool air.

Salley waved her hand. "Done," she said. "I sold out in, like, half an hour. It's so darn hot. We made twenty-four dollars, besides tips. Do I get to keep the tips?"

"Sure," said Jessie. Tips! She'd forgotten about those on her calculations page. Salley handed Jessie some crumpled bills and an avalanche of coins: eight dollars for Jessie and Megan, *each*.

"You wanna stay and have some ice cream?" Salley asked.

"Okay," said Megan. "And we brought you a thank-you brownie. You know, for being part of our team." That had been Bright Idea #9.

After a bowl of The Moose Is Loose ice cream, Jessie and Megan headed out. The story was the same at every girl's house: The lemonade had sold out quickly and the money just kept rolling in.

"I can't believe we made—how much did we make?" squealed Megan once they got back to her house.

"One hundred and four dollars each. *Each!*" shouted Jessie. She couldn't stop hopping from one foot to the other.

"I've never seen so much money in my life!"

Jessie was already running numbers in her head. Subtracting the eighty dollars that she and Megan had spent on lemonade and cups, each girl had made a profit of sixty-four dollars. If they increased the number of franchises from thirteen to twenty-six, they could each make one hundred and twenty-eight dollars in one day. If they ran the twenty-six franchises every day for one week, they could each make eight hundred and ninety-six dollars! Jessie pulled out a piece of paper and scribbled a graph.

The sky was the limit!

Megan pretended to faint when Jessie showed her the graph. "What are you going to do with your money?" she asked from the floor.

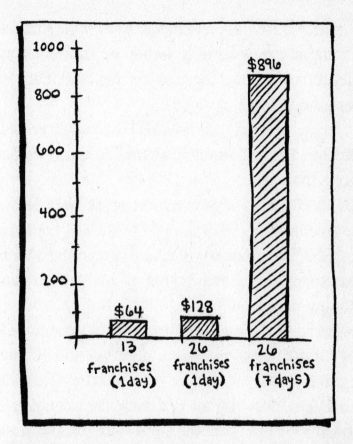

*Win the war!* thought Jessie. Oops. She couldn't say *that* to Megan. Megan didn't even know about the Lemonade War. After all, Megan *liked* Evan.

Jessie suddenly wondered, *If Megan knew about the war, whose side would she be on?*

All at once, Jessie felt as if Evan were a hawk, circling above, waiting to swoop down and snatch Megan away. Oh, she was so mad at him! He deserved to lose *everything*.

*Is one hundred and four dollars enough to win?* wondered Jessie. Surely Evan couldn't have earned more than *that*. Still . . . better safe than sorry. She would work all day tomorrow, Sunday, selling lemonade.

"So?" said Megan. "What are you gonna do with the money?" She was kicking off her sneakers and fanning herself with a magazine.

Jessie said, "I'm going to donate all my money to the Animal Rescue League."

Megan stopped waving the magazine. "Oh, that is *so* nice of you. I want to donate my money, too." She dropped the magazine and started shoving her money toward Jessie. "Here. Give mine to the Animal Rescue League, too. On the card, just put both our names."

The money came at her so fast, Jessie didn't know what to say. There it was. Two hundred and eight dollars. Two hundred and eight dollars! All in her hands.

She had won. She had really and truly won the Lemonade War.

"Just promise me one thing," said Megan. "No lemonade stand tomorrow! Okay?"

"O-*kay,*" said Jessie. She didn't need a lemonade stand on Sunday if she had two hundred and eight dollars today!

"My dad said tomorrow's the last day before the heat breaks," said Megan. "So we're going to the beach for the whole day. Wanna come?"

"Sure!" said Jessie.

"Maybe Evan wants to come, too?" said Megan.

Jessie shook her head. "No. Evan's busy all day tomorrow. He told me he's got plans."

Megan shrugged. "Too bad for him."

"Yep," said Jessie, thinking of all that money. "Too bad for him."

# Chapter 9
# Negotiation

**negotiation** (nǐ-gō′shē-ā′shən) n. A method of bargaining so that you can reach an agreement.

Evan looked up from the marble track he was building when Jessie walked in the front door. She looked hot. She looked sweaty. She looked . . . happy. Really happy. Like she'd just gotten an A+. Or like . . . like she'd just won a war.

"What are you smiling for?" asked Evan, holding a marble at the top of the track.

"No reason." Jessie put her hands on her hips and stared at Evan. She looked like one of those goofy yellow smiley faces—all mouth.

"Well, quit looking at me, would ya? It's creepifying. You look like you're going to explode or something." Evan dropped the marble into the funnel. It raced through the track, picking up speed around the curves. It passed the flywheel, sending the flags spinning, then fell into the final drop. When it reached the end of the track it went sailing through the air like a beautiful silver bird.

And fell short.

The marble landed on the ground, instead of in the bull's-eye cup.

Evan muttered under his breath and adjusted the position of the cup.

"Raise the end of the track," said Jessie. "You'll get more loft."

Evan looked at her angrily. The marble had fallen into the cup the last ten times he'd done it. Why did it have to fall short the one time *she* was watching? "Don't tell me what to do," he said. Why was she smiling like that?

"I didn't tell you what to do," she said. "I just made a suggestion. Take it or leave it." She turned to walk up the stairs. "Grumpminster Fink," she tossed over her shoulder.

Evan threw a marble at her disappearing back but missed by a mile. Well, he hadn't really been aiming anyway; he just wanted that feeling of throwing something. He'd been feeling the need to throw something these past four days.

Grumpminster Fink. That was the name of a character he'd made up when he was six and Jessie was five. That was back when Mom and Dad were fighting a lot and Evan and Jessie just had to get out of the house. They'd scramble up the Climbing Tree—Evan had his branch, Jessie had hers—and wait it out. Sometimes they had to wait a long time. And once, when Jessie was thirsty and impatient and cranky, Evan had said, "Be quiet and I'll tell you a story about Grumpminster Fink."

Grumpminster Fink was a man who was cranky and mean and made everybody miserable. But deep down, he wanted people to love him. It's just that every time he tried to do something nice, it turned out all wrong. Evan had made up a lot of stories about Mr. Fink in that tree. But after Dad left, there just weren't any more stories to tell.

No one in the whole world, besides Jessie and Evan, knew about Grumpminster Fink. And Evan hadn't thought about him in years.

"Hey!" he said sharply. He heard Jessie stop at the top of the stairs, but she didn't come down.

"Do you want to call this whole thing off?" he asked.

"What?" she shouted.

"This . . . this . . . Lemonade War," he said.

"Call it off?"

"Yeah," he said. "Just say nobody wins and nobody loses."

Jessie walked down the stairs and stood with her arms crossed.

Evan looked at her.

He missed her.

He had spent the whole day—the third to last day before school started—by himself. It stunk. It totally stunk. If Jessie had been around—and they hadn't been fighting with each other—they could have played air hockey or made pretzels or built a marble track with twice as many gizmos that launched the marble into the bull's-eye cup every time. Jessie was very precise. She was good at getting the marble to go into the cup.

"Whaddya say?" he asked.

Jessie looked puzzled. "I don't know . . ." she said, frowning. "You see, Megan kinda, well, she . . ."

Evan felt his face go hot. Megan Moriarty. Every time he thought of her his throat got all squeezed and scratchy. It was like the allergic reaction he had if he accidentally ate a shrimp.

"You told Megan Moriarty about—*everything?*" he asked, feeling itchy all over.

"No. Well . . . what 'everything'?" asked Jessie. Evan thought she looked like a fish caught in a net.

"You did." And suddenly Evan knew exactly why Jessie had been smiling when she walked in the door. And why she didn't want to call off the war. She had done it. Again. She had figured out some way to show the world just how stupid he was. Like the time he'd come home with 100 percent on his weekly spelling quiz—the *only* time he'd ever gotten every word right—to find that Jessie had won a statewide poetry-writing contest. He'd thrown his paper into the trash without even telling his mom. What was the point?

Evan didn't know how, but somehow Jessie'd found a way to earn more than one hundred and three dollars. She was going to beat him. And Megan Moriarty knew all about it. And she would tell everyone else. All the girls would know. Paul would know. And Ryan. And Adam and Jack.

Scott Spencer would know. *Can you believe it? He lost to his little sister. The one who's going to be in our class. What a loser!*

"You know what?" he said, pushing past her. "Forget it! Just forget I said anything. The war is on. O-N. Prepare to die."

# Chapter 10
# malicious mischief

**malicious mischief** (mə-lĭsh′əs mĭs′chĭf) n. The act of purposely destroying the property of someone else's business.

Jessie was all in knots. Evan was madder than ever at her, and she couldn't figure out why. He had said, "Do you want to call off the war?" and she had said, "Sure, let's call off the war." Or *something* like that. That's what she'd meant to say. That's what she'd *wanted* to say.

But what had she *really* said? She'd mentioned Megan. Oh! She'd almost spilled the beans about Megan giving her the $104. But she hadn't! She'd kept her mouth shut, just in time.

Jessie smiled, remembering that.

So why had Evan acted like that? What was the matter with him?

Jessie lay down on her bed. The world was a confusing place, and she needed Evan to help her figure it out. If this is what fourth grade was going to be like, she might as well just give up now.

And there was something else that was tying her up in knots. That two hundred and eight dollars—it wasn't *really* hers. Megan had given it to her to make a donation. She hadn't given it to Jessie the way Evan's friends had given their money to him. (That still made her so mad when she thought about it. Oh, she wanted to get even with him for saying she didn't have friends!) So even though it looked like she had two hundred and eight dollars in her lock box, only half of that was money she could honestly call her own.

Still . . . if push came to shove and she needed it all to win—

Sure, she'd use it all! This was a war!

But if she pretended that all the money was hers—

*Hey, what if Evan has even more than that?*

So if she lost, even *with* Megan's money—

*Gulp!*

Jessie hadn't thought of that. If she lost, even with two hundred and eight dollars. If she lost. *Oh my gosh. Winner takes all.* She would lose all of Megan's money to Evan. How could Jessie explain that to her friend? *You see, I took all the money you earned to help rescue animals and I lost it to my brother, who's going to buy an iPod.* Megan would hate her. All the girls who were friends with Megan would hate her. And Evan already hated her. So that was that. Goodbye, fourth grade.

She couldn't use Megan's money to try to win the bet. It was too risky. But did she have enough to win on her own?

Jessie felt desperation rise in her throat. How much money did Evan have? She had to find out.

Jessie tiptoed upstairs to the attic office. She listened at the closed door. Her mother was on the phone. Then Jessie snuck downstairs. Evan was watching TV in the family room. Like a whisper, she crept back upstairs. And into Evan's room.

There was a strict rule in the Treski house: No one was allowed in anyone else's room without an *express invitation*. That was the term. It meant that Jessie had to say, "Evan, can I come into your room?" and Evan had to say, "Yes," before she put even one toe over the line.

So even though Evan's door was wide open, just crossing the threshold was a direct violation that carried a fine of one dollar. But that was the least of Jessie's concerns.

She snuck over to Evan's bookshelf and picked up a carved cedar box—Evan's chosen souvenir from the family summer vacation. The orange-red wood of the box had a scene etched into the top: a sailboat sailing past a lighthouse while gulls flew overhead. The words "Bar Harbor, Maine" were painted in the sky. The box had brass hinges and a clever latch. What it didn't have was a lock.

Jessie flipped open the lid, immediately smelling the spicy, sharp scent of the wood. She couldn't believe her eyes.

Her hands started pawing through the bills. Dozens of them. There was a ten and a bunch of fives and more ones than she could count. She sat on Evan's bed and quickly sorted out the money.

Evan had one hundred and three dollars and eleven cents.

Eighty-nine cents less than she had.

Eighty-nine cents. He could sell one lousy cup of lemonade tomorrow and beat her. And there was nothing she could do about it because she'd be at the beach.

*I can't let him win,* she thought. *I can't.* She had gotten to the point where she couldn't even remember what had started the whole war. She couldn't remember why it had been so important to win in the first place. Now she just had to win.

She messed up the money and stuffed it back into the box.

That night in bed, she lay awake trying to think of some way to stop Evan from selling even a single glass.

Sometimes in the dark, dark thoughts come.
Jessie had a very dark thought.

The next morning was Sunday, and the rule in the Treski house was that everyone could sleep in as late as he or she wanted. But Jessie awoke to the sound of the electric garage door opening. She sat up in bed and checked the clock: 8:00 a.m. Then she looked out her window just in time to see Evan pedaling away on his bike, his backpack on his back. She quickly dressed and hurried down to the kitchen.

Her mom was making scrambled eggs and toast. "Hi, Jess. Want some?" she asked, pointing with her spatula at the pan of sizzling eggs.

"No, thanks," said Jessie.

"I washed your blue bathing suit last night. It's hanging in the basement. What time are the Moriartys picking you up?"

"Nine o'clock," said Jessie. "Mom, where did Evan go?"

"He went to the store to buy some lemonade

mix." Jessie's mom scooped the eggs onto a plate and put the pan in the sink. When she turned on the faucet, the pan hissed like an angry snake. A great cloud of steam puffed into the air and then disappeared. "What's going on, Jess? What's with all the lemonade stands and you and Evan fighting?"

Jessie opened the pantry cupboard and pulled out a box of Kix. "Nothing," she said. She watched the cereal very carefully as she poured. She didn't want to look at her mother right then.

Mrs. Treski got the milk out of the refrigerator and put it on the counter next to Jessie's bowl. "It doesn't seem like nothing. It seems like there's a lot of bad feeling between the two of you."

Jessie poured her milk slowly. "Evan's mad at me." *And he's going to be a whole lot madder after today*, she added in her head.

"What's he mad about?" asked Mrs. Treski.

"I dunno. He called me a baby and said I ruin everything. And . . ." Jessie felt it coming. She tried to hold it back, but she knew it was coming. Her shoulders tightened up, her chest caved in, and her mouth opened in a howl. "He said he hates me!" Tears poured out of her eyes and dropped into her cereal bowl. Her nose started to run and her lips quivered. With every sob, she let out a sound like tires squealing on a wet road.

For the whole time Jessie cried, her mother wrapped her in a hug. And then, like a faucet turned off, Jessie stopped.

She had told the truth; she really *didn't* understand why Evan was so angry. Even before the Lemonade War he had been mad, and Jessie still didn't know why.

"Better?" asked Mrs. Treski.

"Not much," said Jessie. She wiped her nose with her paper napkin and started eating her cereal. It was soggy, but thankfully not salty.

"Don't you think it would be a good idea to find out what he's mad about?" asked Jessie's mom. "You're never going to stop being mad at each other until you both understand what the other person is feeling."

"I guess so," said Jessie.

"It can be hard. Sometimes it's even hard to know what you're feeling yourself. I mean, how do you feel about *him?*" asked Mrs. Treski.

Jessie didn't have to think long. All the insults and anger, the confusion and fighting, seemed to converge in a single flash of white-hot feeling. "I hate him! I hate him for saying all those mean things. And for not letting me play. I hate him just as much as he hates me. More!"

Mrs. Treski looked sad. "Can we have a sit-down about this tonight? After you get back from the beach?"

"No," said Jessie, remembering the spit vow. Evan would be mad if he knew that she had worried Mom with their fighting. And then he'd spill the beans about the terrible thing she was about to do. Jessie didn't want her mom knowing anything about that. "We'll work it out ourselves, Mom. I promise. Evan and I will talk tonight."

"I'm sorry I've been working so hard," said Mrs. Treski. "I know it's a lousy end to the summer."

"It's okay, Mom. You gotta work, right?"

"Yes. No. I don't know. I promise I'll be finished

by dinnertime tonight. That way we can all go to the fireworks together." Jessie's mom looked out the window. "I hope they don't get canceled because of weather. They're saying scattered thunderstorms this evening."

Jessie and her mom finished breakfast without saying much else.

"I'll clean up," said Jessie. She liked to do dishes, and she wanted to do something nice for her mom.

While she cleaned, she thought about the terrible plan she had come up with last night. It was mean. It was really mean. It was the meanest thing she had ever imagined doing.

*I'm not going to do it,* she decided. *I hate him, but I don't hate him* that *much.*

She was putting the last glass in the dishwasher when Evan walked in. His backpack was bulging.

"I thought you were going to the beach for the whole day," he said.

"Megan's picking me up in half an hour." She thought she saw Evan stiffen up. *Good.* "What's in the backpack?"

"Not much," he said, dumping out the contents

onto the kitchen table. Cans of lemonade mix rolled all over. Jessie tried to count, but there were too many. Fifteen? Twenty?

"Holy macaroni! How many cans did you buy?"

"Thirty-two." Evan started to stack the cans in a pyramid.

"But, but, you don't need that much. Even to win, you don't need that much. That's, that's—" She did the calculations in her head. "That's two hundred and fifty-six cups of lemonade. If you sell them at fifty cents apiece—"

"A dollar. I'm going to charge a dollar apiece."

Jessie felt like her head was going to explode. "You'll never sell it all," she said. "There isn't a neighborhood in town that will buy two hundred and fifty-six cups in one day." *Too much lemonade. Not enough thirsty people,* she thought.

"I'm going to roll! Like the ice cream truck! I'm going to mix it all up in the big cooler and wagon it from street to street. The high today is going to be ninety-four degrees. It might take me all day, but I'll sell every last drop. *Two hundred and fifty-six smackers!*

And then tonight, Juicy, we count our earnings. Don't forget: Winner takes all!"

"But you don't need two hundred and fifty-six dollars to win!" she shouted.

Evan stood tall and said in that gravelly voice that all the boys imitated, "I don't play to win. I play to *pul-ver-ize*."

Oh! What an idiot! Jessie couldn't believe her brother could be such a jerk. She watched as Evan put together his rolling lemonade stand in the garage. The big cooler was something Mrs. Treski had bought a few years back when she was in charge of refreshments for the school Spring Fling. It looked like a giant bongo drum with a screw-off top and a spigot at the bottom. Evan loaded it into the wagon, then poured in the mix from all thirty-two cans. He used the garden hose to fill the cooler to the top, then dumped in four trays of ice cubes. With a plastic beach shovel, he stirred the lemonade. The ice cubes made a weird rattling noise as they swirled around in the big drum. Using the shovel like a big spoon, he scooped out a tiny bit and tasted it. "Perfect!" he announced, screwing the top on tightly. Then he went into the basement to make his Lemonade-on-Wheels sign.

Without a moment's hesitation, Jessie sprang into action.

First she got out a large Ziploc bag from the kitchen drawer, the kind that you could freeze a whole gallon of strawberries in if you wanted to. Then she held it, upside down and wide open, over the fruit bowl. She gave the bowl a solid knock. Jessie was surprised how easy it was to catch the fruit flies that floated up from the bowl. It was like they wanted to die!

She filled that bag and two more with flies, then hurried to the garage. She unscrewed the top of the big cooler. Holding the first bag upside down, she unzipped it, expecting the flies to fall down into the lemonade. They didn't. They stayed safe and dry in the bag. It was like they wanted to live!

"Too bad for you, you stupid flies," said Jessie as she plunged the bag into the lemonade. Under the surface, she turned the bag inside out, swishing it back and forth so that all the flies were washed off into the lemonade. She emptied all three bags of flies into the big cooler, then hunted around until she found two green inchworms and a fuzzy gypsy moth caterpillar. She tossed them into the cooler. Then she threw in a fistful of dirt, for good measure. She was just about to screw the top back on when she heard Evan coming up the basement stairs. There wasn't time to get the top back on! He would see the bugs and the whole plan would be ruined!

Jessie ran to the steps and shouted, "Evan, Mom wants to see you in her office. Right away!"

"Aw, man," muttered Evan as he started to climb the second set of stairs.

Jessie quickly screwed on the cap, grabbed her blue bathing suit from the basement, then went upstairs to her room. On the way, she passed Evan coming down.

"Mom did *not* want to see me," he said, annoyed.

Jessie looked surprised. "That's what it sounded like. She yelled something down the stairs. I thought it was 'Get Evan.'" Jessie shrugged. "So I got you."

From her bedroom window, she watched Evan rolling down the street with his Lemonade-on-Wheels stand. He was like one of those old-time peddlers, calling out, "Lemonade! Git yer ice-cold lemonade here!" as he walked. For one lightning-brief second, Jessie felt a stab of regret. She could see how hard he was straining to pull the heavy cooler. She knew what it was like to stand in the hot sun selling lemonade. But the feeling was snuffed out by the hurricane of anger she felt when she remembered Evan's gravelly voice: *"pul-ver-ize."*

Jessie switched into her bathing suit, packed up her beach bag, and said a quick goodbye to her mother as the Moriartys pulled into the driveway.

"What a great day for the beach," said her mother. "Have fun. And be home in time for the fireworks, okay?"

The fireworks. Yep. Jessie imagined there would be some fireworks tonight.

## Chapter 11
# A TotaI LosS

**total loss** (tōt′l lôs) n. Goods so damaged that there's no point in repairing them (or they can't be repaired at all).

The first cup was an easy sell.

The second cup, too.

It was on the third cup that a little girl, about six years old, said, "Ew, there's a bug in my drink."

Then her brother said, "There's one in mine, too."

"Gross," said an older boy on a skateboard. "There are, like, three in mine. I want my money back, man," he said, dumping his lemonade on the ground.

The mother of the little girl and boy looked into

their cups carefully. "I think you need to check your lemonade, honey," she said to Evan.

Evan unscrewed the cap and everyone looked in. The surface was swimming with dead bugs: fruit flies, worms, and a soggy brown caterpillar.

"Oh my goodness," said the mother.

The boy started spitting on the ground like he was going to die. The girl started wailing. "Mommy! I drank bugs. I have bugs in my tummy!"

Evan couldn't believe his eyes. How did this happen? Did they crawl in somehow? They couldn't have. He had screwed the lid on tightly. He was sure of it. And anyway . . . one or two bugs crawling in— maybe. But fifty dead fruit flies and two inchworms and a caterpillar? It just wasn't possible.

Evan was burning with embarrassment as everyone looked at him and his buggy lemonade. Frantically, he reached into the cooler and started to scoop out the dead bugs with his hands.

"Uh, sweetheart," said the mother, "you can't sell that lemonade."

"I'll get them all," said Evan. "I'll get every last one out."

"No, dear. You really can't. You need to dump it out," she said.

Evan looked at her like she was crazy. Dump it out? *Dump it out?* He'd spent forty dollars of his hard-earned money on that lemonade and another dollar for the cups. He wasn't going to dump it out.

"I'll do it at home," he said.

"No. You should do it here, I think. I need to be sure it's all disposed of properly."

Evan looked at her. He didn't know her, but he knew her type. Boy, did he know her type. She was the kind of mother who thought she was the mother of the whole world. If you were on a playground and she thought you were playing too rough, she'd tell you. If you were chewing gum in line at the 7-Eleven, she'd say, "I sure hope that's sugarless." Mothers like that never minded just their own business. Or just their kids' business. They thought they had to take care of every kid in the kingdom.

"It's too heavy for me to dump," he said. "I'll take it home and my mom can help."

"*I'll* help," said the busybody mother of the world. "All we need to do is tip it a little." She

145

grabbed one handle of the big cooler. Evan had no choice but to grab the other handle. Together they tipped and the lemonade poured out of the top of the cooler.

They poured and poured and poured. The lemonade sparkled in the sunlight, like a bejeweled waterfall, and then disappeared without a trace, soaking into the parched September grass. As the last sluice of lemonade slipped out of the cooler, a slick of mud poured out.

"Oh my goodness," said the mother.

Evan couldn't believe it. He couldn't believe how quickly his victory had turned to defeat. It was just like the lemonade. It had disappeared into the grass, leaving nothing behind. A total loss.

The mother smiled sympathetically as Evan returned her two dollars. The skateboard dude had already skated off with his refund. There was nothing to do but go home.

Evan walked slowly, dragging the wagon with the empty cooler rattling inside.

With every step he took, the wagon handle

poked him in the rear end. Step. Poke. Step. Poke. He felt like someone was nudging him forward.

*"Evan, Mom wants to see you in her office. Right away!"*

That had been weird. His mom had had no idea what he meant. "I didn't call you. I didn't call anyone," she had said. "I've been on the computer."

*"Evan, Mom wants to see you."*

He had been coming up the stairs. Jessie had been in the garage. She had looked anxious. *"Right away!"* she had said.

Evan stopped walking. He stared at the empty cooler. Then he started to run. The wagon bounced crazily along the uneven sidewalk. Twice it tipped over. *What did it matter?* thought Evan angrily. *There's no lemonade to spill.*

By the time he got home, he had it all figured out. He looked in the kitchen trash and found the three Ziploc bags, inside out and sticky with lemonade. He shook the fruit bowl and noticed how few fruit flies took to the air. If he'd had the right materials, he would have dusted the cooler for fingerprints. But there was really no need for that.

He knew what he would have found: Jessie was all over this one.

"That RAT! That lousy rotten stinking RAT of a sister!" he shouted. He went back to the garage and kicked the wagon. He knocked the cooler to the floor. He tore up his Lemonade-on-Wheels sign into a dozen pieces.

He was going to lose. She had a hundred dollars (he was sure of it) and he had just sixty-two left. Tonight, before the fireworks, when they counted their money, she would be the winner and he would be the loser.

Winner takes all.

Loser gets nothing.

It was so unfair.

Evan stomped upstairs to his room. He slammed the door so hard, it bounced open again. When he went to close it, he was staring across the hallway, straight into Jessie's room. He could see her neatly made bed covered in Koosh pillows, the poster of Bar Harbor from their trip to Maine this summer, and her night table with *Charlotte's Web* at the ready.

Evan crossed the hall, then paused at Jessie's door. There was the rule about not entering. Well, *she'd* broken the rules first. (Even though there wasn't really a rule about fruit flies and lemonade, it was clearly a dirty trick.) Evan walked in and went straight to Jessie's desk drawer.

There was the fake pack of gum. Inside, the key. Did she really think he didn't know where she hid it? He'd seen her slip the key inside the box when he was passing by on his way to the bathroom. Jessie was smart, but she wasn't very smooth. He'd known for months where the key was hidden. He just hadn't bothered to use it.

Until now.

It took him a while to find the lock box. He checked the bureau drawers first and then under Jessie's bed. But finally he found it hidden in her closet. Again, not very smooth.

Evan carried the key and the lock box back to his room and sat on the bed. He put the key in the lock and opened the top. Then—the moment of truth—he lifted out the plastic change tray.

There were a whole bunch of scraps of paper on top, and there was a folded index card, too. Evan moved these aside and found a ten-dollar bill paper-clipped to a birthday card. Under that was an envelope labeled "Pre-War Earnings" with four dollars and forty-two cents inside it. That was the money Jessie had had before the Lemonade War began. She'd kept it separate, just like she promised. Next to it was a fat envelope labeled "Lemonade Earnings." Evan opened the envelope.

Inside, the bills were arranged by ones, fives, and tens. All the bills were facing the same way, so that the eyes of George Washington, Abraham Lincoln, and Alexander Hamilton were all looking at Evan as he counted out the cash.

Two hundred and eight dollars.

There it was. The winning wad.

Evan thought of how hard he'd worked that week, in the blazing sun, in the scorching heat. He thought about the coolerful of lemonade pouring into the grass. He thought about handing over his sixty-two dollars and eleven cents to Jessie and how she'd smile and laugh and tell. Tell everyone that she had won the Lemonade War. The guys would all shake their heads. *What a loser*. Megan would turn away. *What a stupid jerk*.

Evan slammed the lid of the lock box shut. He stuffed the envelope in his shorts pocket. He was *not* going to let it happen!

He wasn't planning to keep the money. Not for good. But he wasn't going to let her have it tonight. When it came time to show their earnings, he'd have sixty-two dollars and eleven cents and she'd have *nothing*. He'd give her the money back tomorrow or maybe the day after that, but *not tonight*.

He suddenly felt a desperate need to get out of the house as fast as he could. He shoved the lock box back into Jessie's closet and the key back into the fake pack of gum.

"Hey, Mom," he shouted, not even waiting for her to answer back. "I'm going to the school to see if there's a game. 'Kay?"

# Chapter 12
# waiting period

**waiting period** (wāt′tĭng pĭr′ē-əd) n. A specified delay, required by law, between taking an action and seeing the results of that action.

Jessie wanted to have fun. She really did. But it seemed like the more she tried, the less she had.

First, the drive to the beach took two and a half hours because of traffic. Jessie felt the car lurching. Forward, stop. Forward, stop.

"Memo to myself," said Mr. Moriarty. "Never go to the beach on the Sunday of Labor Day weekend. Especially when there's been a heat wave for more than a week."

In the back seat, Jessie and Megan played license

plate tag and magnetic bingo and twenty questions, but by the end of the car ride, Jessie was cramped and bored.

Then the beach parking lot was full, so they had to park half a mile away and walk. Then the beach was so crowded that they could hardly find a spot for their blanket. Then Megan said the water was too cold and she just wanted to go in up to her ankles. She kept squealing and running backwards every time a gentle ripple of a wave came her way.

What fun was that? Sure, the water was cold! It was the North Shore. It was *supposed* to be cold. That's why it felt so good on a hot day like this. When Jessie and Evan went to the beach, they would boogie board and bodysurf and skimboard and throw a Screaming Scrunch Ball back and forth the whole time. They loved to stay in the water until their lips turned blue and they couldn't stop shaking. Then they'd roast themselves like weenies on their towels until they were hot and sweating again, and then they'd go right back in. Now *that* was fun at the beach.

Megan liked to build sandcastles and collect

shells and play sand tennis and read magazines. *That's all fine,* thought Jessie. *But not going in the water? That's crazy.*

The ride home was itchy and hot. Jessie had sand in all the places where her skin rubbed together: between her toes, behind her ears, and between the cheeks of her bottom. And somehow she'd gotten sunburned on her back, even though Mrs. Moriarty had smeared her all over with thick, goopy sunscreen twice. Jessie didn't even have the patience for ten questions, let alone twenty.

But Megan didn't get that Jessie didn't feel like talking. She kept trying to get her to take a quiz in a teen magazine. If Evan had been there, he would have kept quiet. Or maybe hummed a little. Jessie liked it when Evan hummed.

As they turned onto Damon Road, Megan asked, "Are you feeling sick?"

In fact, she was. For the past half-hour, Jessie had been imagining walking in the door and facing Evan. And she'd been feeling sicker and sicker with every mile that brought her closer to home.

# Chapter 13
# crisis management

**crisis management** (krī′sĭs măn′ĭj-mənt) n. Special or extraordinary methods and procedures used when a business is in danger of failing.

"Sucker!"

"Oh, man. You were *schooled!*"

"*Pre*-school, baby!"

For the third time that afternoon, Scott Spencer had gotten the drop on Evan, dribbling around him and then hitting the easy lay-up. So the guys were giving him the business, even the ones on his own team. It was Evan, Paul, and Ryan against Kevin Toomey, Malik Lewis, and Scott. Evan wished that

Scott hadn't shown up, but he had, and they needed the sixth guy for three-on-three since Jack had gone home to ask his mom if they could all swim at his house. So what was Evan supposed to say?

Anyway, Evan was three times the ball handler that Scott was and everyone knew it. So it was all in fun.

But it didn't feel like much fun to Evan.

"What's up, man?" Paul asked.

Evan dribbled the ball back and forth, left hand, right hand, and then through his legs. "Hey, it's hot," he said.

"Yeah, it's hot for all of us," said Paul. "Get your game on, dude."

But Evan couldn't get his moves right. He was a half-step behind himself. And every time he moved, the envelope slapped against his thigh like a reprimand.

"Speaking of hot," said Ryan. Everyone turned to look. Jack was coming up the path, running at a dead-dog pace.

"Oh, please, God," said Paul. "Let her say yes."

As soon as he was in range, Jack shouted, "She said yes!"

"What's up?" asked Scott.

"Jack asked his mom if we could all go swimming in his pool," Kevin said.

"Hey, Jack," shouted Scott. "Can I come, too?"

"Yeah, sure," said Jack, who'd stopped running toward them and was waiting for them to join him on the path.

*Oh, great,* thought Evan. But he wasn't about to turn down a dunk in a pool just because Scott Spencer would be there.

Nobody wanted to go home for suits and towels. Kevin, Malik, and Ryan were wearing basketball shorts anyway, so they could swim in those. "We've got enough suits at the house," said Jack. "My mom saves all our old ones."

At the house, Evan changed into one of Jack's suits. He wrapped up his underwear and shirt inside his shorts and put the bundle of clothes on the end of Jack's bed next to all the other guys' piled-up clothes. It felt good to drop the heavy shorts with the envelope stuffed in the pocket. Then, just to be sure, he put his shoes on top of his pile of clothes. He didn't want anything happening to that money.

They played pool basketball all afternoon, even though the teams were uneven. Mrs. Bagdasarian brought out drinks and cookies and chips and sliced-up watermelon. Every time one of them went into the house to use the bathroom, she shouted, "Dry off before you come in!" but she did it in a nice way.

Then, just when Evan thought the afternoon couldn't get any better, it did. Scott had gone into the house to go to the bathroom. A few minutes later he came out dressed, his hair still dripping down his back.

"I gotta go," he said, jamming his foot into his sneaker.

"Did your mom call?" asked Ryan.

"Nope, I just gotta go," he said. "See ya." He ran out the gate.

"Great," shouted Evan. "Now the teams are even." And they went back to playing pool hoops. Evan didn't think about Scott Spencer for the rest of the afternoon.

He didn't think about Scott Spencer until he went into Jack's bedroom to change back into his clothes and noticed that his shoes were on the floor and his shorts weren't folded up.

# Chapter 14
# Reconciliation

**reconciliation** (rĕk′ən-sĭl′ē-ā′shən) n. The act of bringing together after a difference, as in to reconcile numbers on a balance sheet; resolution.

"Come on, you two," Mrs. Treski called up the stairs. "If we don't go now, there won't be any room on the grass."

"We're coming," shouted Evan, sticking his head out of his room. Jessie was sitting on his bed, and he was trying to get her to go to the fireworks. She had her lock box on her lap and a mulish look on her face.

"Just say it's a tie," said Evan. "C'mon, Jess. This

160

whole thing is stupid and you know it."

"It's not a tie unless it's a tie," said Jessie, knowing she sounded like a brat but not able to stop herself. "How much have you got?"

"Mom's waiting," said Evan. "Put your dumb box away and let's go to the fireworks."

"How much have you got?"

Evan tensed up his fingers as if he were strangling an invisible ghost. "Nothing! Okay? I've got nothing. Look." He turned the pockets of his shorts inside out.

Jessie looked skeptical. "You can't have *nothing*. You must have made *something*."

"Well, I had expenses. So I ended up with nothing. Okay? Are you happy? You win." Evan sat on the edge of the bed, looking at the floor.

Jessie felt her heart sink. "You spent *all* your money on mix for your Lemonade-on-Wheels stand?" Jessie asked. "All of it?"

Evan nodded. Jessie felt like crawling under the bed and never coming out. "It didn't pay off so good?" she whispered.

"There were a few bugs in the system," said Evan. *That's a joke Jessie would have loved,* he thought. Before the war. Now it was all just money and numbers and bad feelings. There was no room for laughing.

"Oh," said Jessie, her voice the size of an ant. She stared down at the box in her lap. "I've got—"

She opened the lid of the lock box, took out the change tray, and pushed aside all the scraps of paper she had collected and the comment card from Megan. She stared. "Wait a minute. This isn't my money." She picked up a handful of wrinkled, bunched-up bills. Evan lay down on the bed and covered his head with his pillow. Jessie counted the money quickly. "Sixty-two dollars and eleven cents? Where'd this come from?"

"Imamummy," said Evan from underneath the pillow.

"What?" said Jessie. "Take that dumb pillow away. I can't understand what you're saying." She hit the side of his leg for emphasis.

"It's my money!" he shouted, still through the

pillow. "It was a hundred and three dollars, but then I spent forty-one dollars for the Lemonade-on-Wheels stand. So now it's just sixty-two."

"Your money? But where's my money?"

Evan pulled the pillow away from his face. His eyes were closed. His nose pointed at the ceiling. He folded his arms across his chest like a dead man. "I took it."

"Well, give it back," said Jessie. This time she hit the side of his leg for real.

"I can't. It's gone." He lay as still as a three-day-old corpse.

"Gone? Gone where?" Jessie was shrieking now. Never in her life had she worked so hard to earn money. Never in her life had she had more than one hundred dollars in her hand. Never in her life had she had a friend who trusted her like Megan had.

"I don't know. It was in my shorts pocket. And then I played basketball with the guys. And then we went to Jack's house to swim. And I took off my shorts and borrowed a suit. And when I went back to change, the money was gone." He sat up and faced his sister. "I'm *really* sorry."

In a real war you fight. You fight with your hands and with weapons. You fight with anything you've got because it's a matter of life and death. Jessie felt the loss of her hard-earned money like a death, and she ripped into Evan with all the power in her body. She punched him. She kicked him. She threw her lock box at him. She wanted to tear him up into little pieces.

Evan didn't try to pin her, though it would have been easy to do. Part of him just wanted to lie on the bed and take it. Take it all. For being the one who started the whole thing by saying, "I hate you." For making Jessie feel so rotten about herself just because Evan felt so rotten about himself. For taking Jessie's money and losing it to Scott. Just for being so stupid.

But Jessie was really going at it, and if he didn't protect himself at least a little, he was going to end up in the emergency room and that would upset his mom. So he kept his hands up in front of his face, just enough to keep Jessie from gouging out his eyes. But he never once tried to hit her back. He was done fighting.

Finally Jessie ran out of gas. She lay down on the bed and tried to make her brain work. Her body was so worn out that her brain felt like the only part of her that *could* work.

"One of your friends stole my money?" she asked.

"I think it was Scott Spencer," said Evan. "He went upstairs to go to the bathroom. And then he came down all in a hurry and said he had to go home. After that, I went upstairs and the money was gone."

"He's such a jerk," said Jessie.

"The biggest," said Evan. "If he gets an Xbox, I'll *know* it was him."

"It was a lot of money," said Jessie, feeling tears start to spring from her eyes and run down her face.

"It *was,*" said Evan. "I couldn't believe how much when I saw it. You're really something, you know that? Earning all that money selling lemonade."

*Thanks,* thought Jessie, though she couldn't say the word. "Why'd you do it, Evan?" she asked. She meant *Why'd you take the money? And why'd you act so mean? And why'd you start this whole war in the first place?* There were too many questions.

"I was mad at you for putting the bugs in my lemonade," he said.

"Well, I was mad at you for saying you wanted to pulverize me," she said.

"I only did that because you were hanging out with Megan and I felt totally left out."

"Well, how do you think I felt when you wouldn't let me hang out with you and stupid Scott Spencer?"

"Well, I was mad at you because . . . because . . ."

Jessie sat up and looked at Evan. Evan looked at the wall.

"Because I don't want you in my class this year," he said.

"Because I'll embarrass you," she said solemnly.

"Because I'll embarrass *myself*," said Evan. "I never have the right answer in math. And I read slower than everyone when I read out loud. And I make mistakes. All the time. And now with you in

166

the class, it's going to be worse. They'll all say, 'Wow, he's even dumber than his little sister.'" Evan's shoulders slumped and his head hung low.

"You're not dumb," said Jessie.

"I know you don't *think* I am," he said. "And that stinks, too. That you're going to *see* how dumb I am in school."

"You're not dumb," said Jessie again. "You made a hundred and three dollars and eleven cents selling lemonade in just five days."

"Yeah, but you made two hundred and eight dollars! You see? You're my little sister, and you're twice as smart as me."

Jessie shook her head. "Half that money is Megan's. She just gave it to me to give to the Animal Rescue League. I only made a hundred and four dollars."

Evan unslumped. "Really?" Jessie nodded yes. "So you made a hundred and four and I made a hundred and three?"

"And eleven cents," said Jessie.

"So it was really a tie?" said Evan.

"No," said Jessie. "I won. By eighty-nine cents."

"But, I mean, c'mon," said Evan. "After all that, it was *practically* a tie."

"No," said Jessie. "It was close. But I really won."

"Wow, we pretty much tied," said Evan.

Jessie decided to let it go. For the first time in four days, she didn't care about who had more and who had less. Besides, she was waiting to see how long it took before Evan figured *it* out.

Not long.

"Holy crud!" he said suddenly. "I lost Megan's money, too? A hundred and four dollars of her money? Oh, CRUD." He threw himself back on his bed and covered his face with both arms. Neither of them said anything for a long time. Finally Jessie broke the silence.

"I'm really sorry I put the bugs in your lemonade."

"Thanks," said Evan. "I'm sorry I took your and Megan's money."

"We shouldn't have done any of this," Jessie said, waving her hand at the money on the bed.

"It ruined the end of summer."

"Yeah, the whole summer's been crud," said Evan.

"Not the *whole* summer. Just the last five days. Remember we went to Bar Harbor? And we swam at the pond?" Jessie couldn't stand Evan thinking their whole summer together had been crud.

"Yeah, but I think the last five days kind of cancels all that out," said Evan. "I can't believe I have to tell Megan Moriarty—"

"She likes you," said Jessie.

Evan sat up, surprised. "Really?"

"Yeah," said Jessie. "I don't get it either. But she's always asking what you're doing and if you can play and stuff. Why do you think she does that?"

"Cool," said Evan, smiling. "So you guys are friends?"

"Yeah," said Jessie. "We're good friends."

"Okay then. So she'll be coming over here to play and stuff. Right? That's cool."

"You're weird," said Jessie.

"Yes, I am," said Evan.

There was another long silence. The late-summer light in Evan's one-window room had faded to black, but neither one of them wanted to turn on a light. It was nice sitting there, just the two of them, in the cooling darkness. An afternoon breeze had kicked itself into a gusty wind, and the shade on the window tapped out a steady beat that was pleasant and reassuring.

"This war was stupid," said Jessie.

Evan nodded in the dark.

Just then they heard the sound of thunder booming in the distance. Then more and more until the whole house shook.

"The fireworks!" shouted Jessie.

"Oh, snap!" shouted Evan.

Jessie and Evan raced down the stairs. At the bottom, they found their mother sitting on the last step, watching the sky through the sliding screen door.

"Why didn't you call us?" said Evan.

"We're missing the fireworks!" said Jessie.

"Oh, I figured whatever the two of you were talking about was more important than a fireworks show." Mrs. Treski turned to look at her kids. "Did you work it out?"

Evan and Jessie nodded just as a roman candle exploded in the sky.

"Not a bad seat," said Mrs. Treski, patting the step. "Enjoy."

For twenty minutes, the night sky was alive with wagon wheels, party-colored dahlias, and whistling glitter palms. Evan, Jessie, and Mrs. Treski sat watching, silent but for the occasional "Oohhh" and "Aahhh" that seemed to escape from their lips like hissing air from an overblown tire.

When the last of the fireworks bloomed and then faded, Evan, Jessie, and Mrs. Treski sat in the darkness, waiting. No one said anything for several minutes. And then Jessie whispered, "It's over."

Yes. It was over.

"Wait," said Evan. "What was that?"

"What?" asked Jessie, straining her ears.

"Listen."

In the distance, a boom and a rattle.

"More fireworks," said Evan, staring up at the dark sky.

"Where? I don't see them," said Jessie.

All of a sudden the sky split in two as lightning sliced the night. An explosion of thunder rolled through the house, rattling the windows and pictures on the walls. Rain poured from the sky as if a gigantic faucet had been twisted on.

"Yow!" shouted Mrs. Treski, leaping up from the step. "Battle stations!"

Every window in the house was wide open, so Evan, Jessie, and Mrs. Treski ran from the top floor to the bottom, shutting windows and sopping up puddles. The rain came down with the fury and impatience of a two-year-old having a tantrum. As he closed the window in his room, Evan could hear the gurgle of the gutters choking on the downpour.

"One thing ends, another begins," said Mrs. Treski, meeting Jessie and Evan on the stairs. She raised her index finger, like a wise philosopher. "Fireworks. Rainstorm."

Jessie raised her index finger. "Summer. School."

Evan raised his index finger. "War. Peace."

Then they laughed because it was silly—the three of them acting like wise philosophers, standing on the stairs.

That night, before she closed her door, Jessie whisper-shouted to Evan, who was already in bed, "Hey. I've got an idea. About getting Megan's money back."

# Ten Tips For Turning
## By Jessie and

**FIRST PRIZE**

### Tip #1
*Location:* It all starts with where you put your lemonade stand.

### Tip #2
*Advertising:* Make your lemons stand out in a crowd.

### Tip #6
*Business Regulations:* Be sure you know your local lemon laws.

### Tip #8
*Franchises:* How thirteen lemons can earn more than one.

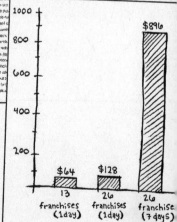

1000
800 — $896
600
400
200 — $64   $128

13 franchises (1 day)   26 franchises (1 day)   26 franchise (7 days)

# Lemons Into Loot
## Evan Treski

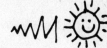

### Tip #3
*Underselling:* Cheap! Cheaper! Cheapest lemons in town!

### Tip #5
*Value-added:* Giving your lemons that something extra.

### Tip #4
*Goodwill:* How to make people love your lemons.

### PROFIT AND LOSS STATEMENT

Expenses:

| | |
|---|---|
| 52 cans of lemonade | $65.00 |
| 5 packages of cups | $14.25 |
| Tax on cups | $0.75 |
| TOTAL EXPENSES: | $80.00 |
| | |
| Gross sales: | $312.00 |
| Total profit: | $232.00 |
| | |
| Jessie's gross: | $104.00 |

### Tip #7
*Profit Margin:* How to calculate the limits of your lemons.

### Tip #9
*Going Mobile:* Take your lemons on the road.

### Tip #10
*Employee Appreciation:* Don't be a sour boss—always say thank you to your workers.

# BROTHER AND SISTER WIN ANNUAL LABOR DAY CONTEST

This year's winners in the annual Rotary Club Labor Day Contest open to all town residents ages 8–12 are Jessie (age 8) and Evan (age 10) Treski of 81 Parsons Road. The brother-and-sister team created an impressive poster that described their entrepreneurial efforts as purveyors of lemonade.

"It was hot, so we decided to sell lemonade," said Evan. "And then Jessie had the great idea of taking everything we learned and making it into a poster for the contest."

The award-winning poster included ten tips for running a successful lemonade stand, a profit-and-loss statement, business definitions, and a chart that tracked franchise profits.

"We've had other entries in other years that described businesses," said Jack Petrocini, president of the local chapter of the Rotary Club. "But never anything with this much detail. We were very impressed."

Jessie and Evan will share the $100 prize money. Will they use it to start up another business? "No," said Jessie. "We kind of need a break from running a business, because of school starting."

Both Jessie and Evan are fourth-graders at Hillside Elementary School.

# Jessie and Evan's Money Plan  PRIVATE!

$100    (prize money)
$ 62.11 (Evan's lemonade money)
$ 10    (Jessie's birthday money)
—————————
$ 172.11

**$104**
Megan's
donation to
the Animal
Rescue
League

**$34.05**
Evan's
iPod
fund

**$34.06**
Jessie's
Animal
Rescue
League
fund

# The Lemonade Crime

by
Jacqueline
Davies

Houghton Mifflin Harcourt
Boston New York

For C. Ryan Joyce
*in loco parentis* to many—
and one, in particular

# Contents

## Chapter 1
# Fraud

**fraud** (frôd), *n*. The crime of deceiving someone for personal or financial gain; a person
who pretends to be something that he or she
is not.

"No fair!" said Jessie. She pointed to the four chocolate chip cookies that her brother, Evan, was stuffing into a Ziploc bag. They were standing in the
kitchen, just about ready to go to school—the fourth
day of fourth grade for both of them, now that they
were in the same class.

"Fine," said Evan, taking out one cookie and
putting it back in the cookie jar. "Three for you.
Three for me. Happy?"

1

"It's not about being happy," said Jessie. "It's about being fair."

"Whatever. I'm outta here." Evan slung his backpack over his shoulder, then disappeared down the stairs that led to the garage.

Jessie walked to the front-room window and watched as her brother pedaled down the street on his bike. She still didn't have her bike license, so she wasn't allowed to ride to school without a parent riding along. That was just one of the bad things about skipping third grade and being the youngest kid in the fourth-grade class. Everyone else in her class could ride to school, but she still had to walk.

Jessie went to the refrigerator and crossed off another day on the lunch calendar. Today's lunch was Chicken Patty on a Bun. Not her favorite, but okay. With her finger, she tapped each remaining day of the week and read out loud the main dish: Deli-Style Hot Dog (*barf*); Baked Chicken Nuggets with Dipping Sauce; Soft-Shell Tacos; and, on Friday, her favorite: Cinnamon-Glazed French Toast Sticks.

Saturday's box was empty, but someone had used a red marker to fill in the box:

| Saturday |
| --- |
| Yom Kippur |

Jessie put her hands on her hips. Who had done that? Probably one of Evan's friends. Adam or Paul. Messing up her lunch calendar. Probably Paul! That was just like him. Jessie knew that Yom Kippur was a very serious Jewish holiday. She couldn't remember what it was for, but it was definitely serious. You were *not* supposed to write the word *par-tay!* after Yom Kippur.

"Jessie, are you all ready?" asked Mrs. Treski, walking into the kitchen.

"Yep," said Jessie. She picked up her backpack, which weighed almost as much as she did, and

hefted it onto her shoulders. She had to lean forward slightly at the waist just to keep from falling backwards. "Mom, you don't have to walk me
to school anymore. I mean, I'm a fourth-grader,
you know?"

"I know you are," said Mrs. Treski, looking on
the garage stairs for her shoes. "But you're still just
eight years old—"

"I'll be nine next month!"

Mrs. Treski looked at her. "Do you mind
so much?"

"Can't I just go with Megan?"

"Isn't Megan always late?"

"But I'm always early, so we'll even out."

"I suppose that would be okay for tomorrow. But
today, let's just walk together. Okay?"

"Okay," said Jessie, who actually liked walking to
school with her mother, but wondered if the other
kids thought she was even more of a weirdo because of it. "But this is the last time."

It took them less than ten minutes to get to
school. Darlene, the crossing guard, held up her

gloved hands to stop the traffic and called out, "Okay, you can cross now."

Jessie turned to her mother. "Mom, I can walk the rest of the way myself."

"Well," said Mrs. Treski, one foot on the curb, one foot in the street. "All right. I'll see you when school gets out. I'll wait for you right here." She stepped back up on the curb, and Jessie knew she was watching her all the way to the playground. *I won't turn around and wave,* she told herself. *Fourth-graders don't do that kind of thing.* Evan had explained that to her.

Jessie walked onto the playground, looking for Megan. Kids weren't allowed in the school building until the bell rang, so they gathered outside before school, hanging on the monkey bars, sliding down the slide, talking in groups, or organizing a quick game of soccer or basketball—if they were lucky enough to have a teacher who would let them borrow a class ball before school. Jessie scanned the whole playground. No Megan. She was probably running late.

Jessie hooked her thumbs under the straps of her backpack. She had already noticed that most of the fourth grade girls didn't carry backpacks. They carried their books and binders and water bottles and lunches in slouchy mailbags. Jessie thought those bags were stupid, the way they banged against your knees and dug into your shoulder. Backpacks were more practical.

She wandered toward the blacktop where Evan and a bunch of boys were playing HORSE. Some of the boys were fifth-graders and tall, but Jessie wasn't surprised to find out that Evan was winning. He was good at basketball. The best in his whole grade, in Jessie's opinion. Maybe even the best in the whole school. She sat down on the sidelines to watch.

"Okay, I'm gonna do a fadeaway jumper," said Evan, calling his shot so the next boy would have to copy him. "One foot on the short crack to start." He bounced the ball a few times, and Jessie watched along with all the other kids to see if he could make the shot. When he finally jumped, releasing the ball as he fell back, the ball sailed through the air and made a perfect rainbow—right through the hoop.

"Oh, man!" said Ryan, who had to copy the shot. He bounced the ball a couple of times and bent his knees, but just then the bell rang and it was time to line up. "Ha!" said Ryan, throwing the ball sky high.

"You are so lucky," said Evan, grabbing the ball out of the air and putting it in the milk crate that held the rest of the 4-O playground equipment.

Jessie liked Evan's friends, and they were usually pretty nice to her, so she followed them to stand in line. She knew not to get in line right behind Evan. He wasn't too thrilled about having his little sister in the same classroom with him this year. Mrs. Treski had given Jessie some advice: *Give Evan some space,* so that's what she was doing.

Jessie looked across the playground just in case Megan had appeared, but instead she saw Scott Spencer jumping out of his dad's car. "Oh, great!" muttered Jessie. As far as Jessie was concerned, Scott Spencer was a faker and a fraud. He was always doing something he wasn't supposed to behind the teacher's back, and he never got caught. Like the time he cut the heads off the daffodils that were growing in the art room. Or when he erased stars from the blackboard so that his desk group would win the weekly Team Award.

When Scott got to the line, he cut right in front of Jessie and tapped Ryan on the back of the shoulder. "Hey," he said.

"Hey," said Ryan, turning and giving him a nod.

"Excuse me," said Jessie, poking Scott in the arm. "The end of the line is back there." She jerked her thumb behind her.

"So what?" said Scott.

"So you can't just cut in front."

"Who cares? All we're doing is going into school."

"It's a line," said Jessie. "The rule is you go to the end of the line."

"Who cares what you say?" said Scott, shrugging and turning his back on her. The line was starting to move forward. Scott punched a couple more boys on the arm and said hey to them. Some of the boys said hi back, but Jessie noticed that Evan kept looking straight ahead.

"Man, am I late," said Scott to Ryan. He was grinning from ear to ear. "I couldn't stop playing my new Xbox 20/20."

"You got a 20/20?" asked Ryan.

Paul turned around. "Who did? Who got one?"

"He says he did," said Ryan, pointing to Scott.

"No way," said Paul. "That's not even out yet."

"Well, you can't get it in a store," said Scott. "But my mom knows people in Japan."

Jessie looked toward Evan, who was at the front of the line. She could tell that he hadn't heard what Scott said, but more and more boys in line turned around to hear about the 20/20. It was the newest game system, with surround-sight goggles and motion-sensing gloves. The line in front of Jessie started to bunch up.

When Jessie got to the door of her classroom, Mrs. Overton was standing there, saying good morning to each student as the line filed in.

"Mrs. Overton, Scott Spencer cut in front of me this morning." Jessie was no tattletale, but Scott needed to learn a thing or two about rules.

Mrs. Overton put a hand on Jessie's shoulder. "Okay, Jessie. I'll watch tomorrow to make sure it doesn't happen again, but for now, let's just let it go."

*Perfect!* thought Jessie as she walked to her desk and took down her chair. *Scott Spencer gets away with something again.*

After putting her chair on the floor, she walked out into the hall to hang her backpack in her locker. She tore off a corner of a page from her Writer's Notebook and quickly wrote a note on it. Then, as she passed Evan's desk on the way to her own, she slipped the note into his hand. She didn't see him open it and read it, but by the time she sat down at her own desk, she could tell that he had. Evan was staring at Scott Spencer, and you could practically see bullets coming out of his eyes.

Scott Spencer got an Xbox 20/20. Where do you think he got the money for that???

11

# Chapter 2
# **Revenge**

**revenge** (rĭ-vĕnj′), *n.* The act of causing pain or harm to another person because that person has injured you in some way.

Evan crushed the note in his hand. Suddenly he didn't feel like laughing and joking around with his friends. Suddenly he wanted to punch his fist through the wall.

Here's why: Evan was more certain than ever that Scott had stolen money from him. It had happened just last week. Right in the middle of that heat wave. Right in the middle of the lemonade war with Jessie. They'd all been at Jack's house. All the guys—Paul and Ryan and Kevin and Malik and Scott—were playing pool basketball. Evan had $208 in the pocket of his shorts. *Two hundred and eight dollars!* It was more money than he'd ever seen in his whole life. He'd left his shorts folded on the bed in Jack's bedroom while they all went swimming. But then Scott got out of the pool to go to the bathroom. And a minute later, he came running out of the house, saying he had to go home right away. And when Evan went back in the house to get dressed, the money was gone.

It had been the worst feeling in Evan's entire life.

Once upon a time, about a million years ago, Scott and Evan had been friends. Sort of. Evan used to play at Scott's house a lot, and once in a while Scott would play at Evan's, although Scott said his house was better because there was more stuff to do. One time, Evan even went overnight to Scott's beach house on the Cape. The Spencers had plenty of money because Scott's mom was a lawyer at one of the biggest law offices downtown and his dad ran a financial consulting business out of their home.

But things had cooled off since then. Way off. The truth was, Scott was kind of a pain to be around.

The way he bragged, the way he cheated at games, even stupid little games like Go Fish or Operation. Who cared about winning a game like Go Fish? And the way he kept things locked up—like the snacks at his house! He kept Yodels and Ring Dings locked in a metal file cabinet in his basement. If Evan thought about it, he had to admit that he really couldn't stand the kid. And now he had a reason to hate him.

"Morning work, Evan," said Mrs. Overton, tapping the work sheet on his desk as she walked by. Evan turned back to his own desk and studied the Daily Double math problem in front of him. All the other kids in the class were working on the same problem, and Evan could tell that some of them had already finished. Normally this would have made him tense, but this morning, he couldn't even concentrate enough on the problem to get that *uh-oh* feeling inside of him.

*I'd get an Xbox. The new one.* That's what Scott had said last week, just before the money disappeared from Evan's shorts. They were trying to figure out how much money they would make from a lemonade stand and what they would buy if they got rich. Suddenly rich.

And now he had an Xbox. Scott Spencer had a 20/20, and Evan was sure he'd bought it with the money he'd stolen from Evan's pocket. Evan felt like lifting his head and howling.

*Sh-sh-sh-sh-sh-sh-sh*. A sound like a rattlesnake ready to strike shimmied through the classroom. Evan looked up. Mrs. Overton was shaking the big African *shekere* she used to get everyone's attention. The beads draped around the hollowed-out gourd made a rustling, rattling sound.

"Okay, Paper Collectors," said Mrs. Overton, "please gather the Daily Doubles and put them on my desk." Every week, the students in 4-O were assigned a job. Some of the jobs were serious, like Paper Collector and Equipment Manager and Attendance Monitor, and some of them were silly, like Chicken Dresser (the person who chose an outfit for the rubber chicken that sat on Mrs. Overton's desk) and Goofy Face Maker (the person who made a face that all the kids in 4-O had to copy at the end

16

of the day on Friday). "Everyone else, come over to the rug for Morning Meeting."

Evan looked back down at the blank math problem in front of him. The only thing he'd written on his page was his name. He handed the paper to Sarah Monroe, then walked over to the rug in the corner and dropped onto the floor, his back up against the bookcase.

"Evan, sit up, please," said Mrs. Overton, smiling at him. "No slouching in the circle." Evan crossed his legs and sat up properly.

First, they went around the circle and every person had to say hello to the person on the right and the person on the left, but in a different way. When it was his turn, Evan said *"konichiwa"* to Adam, who was sitting next to him. Evan liked saying the Japanese word. It made him feel like he was kicking a ball around inside his mouth. Jessie used sign language to say hello to Megan. Scott Spencer said "Whassup?" to Ryan, which made everyone in the class laugh. Everyone except Evan.

Then Mrs. Overton turned to a fresh page on the

Morning Board. A wild goose had landed on the playground yesterday morning, and that was the topic for discussion. Mrs. Overton wanted to know what the kids knew about geese in particular and migrating birds in general. So they took turns until every single one of them had written a fact on the easel. Evan wrote, *Some birds fly for days.* He was going to add *when they migrate,* but he was pretty sure he'd mess up the spelling of the word *migrate,* so he left off that part.

When they'd finished talking about geese and migration, Mrs. Overton capped the Magic Markers and said, "Would anyone like to share something with the class before we go back to our desks?" About half the kids raised their hand, but no one's hand went up faster than Scott Spencer's.

"Scott?" said Mrs. Overton. Evan slumped back against the bookcase. He did not want to hear what Scott had to share with the class.

"I got an Xbox 20/20," Scott said, looking around at all the other kids.

Immediately, the class exploded with noise.

Twenty-seven fourth-graders started talking at once. Mrs. Overton had to shake her *shekere* for nearly ten seconds to get the kids to quiet down.

"Holy rubber chickens!" said Mrs. Overton. The kids in 4-O laughed. "I can tell you're all interested in Scott's new game box. Let's have three questions for Scott about his share, and then we'll move on to the next person."

Mrs. Overton called on Alyssa first.

"What's so great about a 20/20?" she asked.

"Are you kidding?" said Paul. "You put on these goggles, and the TV goes totally 3-D."

"Paul, remember to raise your hand if you want to talk," said Mrs. Overton.

Scott nodded his head. "Yeah, it's like you're really *in* the jungle," said Scott. "Or in a car chase. Or wherever the game goes. And the controls are the gloves you wear. It's how you move your fingers, like this." Scott held out his hands and showed how he moved them in different ways to make things happen in the game. Ryan shook his head as if he couldn't quite believe it.

Mrs. Overton looked at all the hands that were still raised. "Question number two? Jack?"

"What games do you have?" asked Jack. All the boys and even some of the girls had turned their bodies so that the whole circle was facing Scott.

"So far I've got Defenders, Road Rage, and Crisis. And then I've got a whole bunch that are in Japanese, and I have no idea what they are."

The class started to whisper and talk again until Mrs. Overton called for the last question before moving on. "Jessie?"

Evan sat up a little, wondering what his little sister would ask. The first few days of school, Jessie had hardly said a word. Now everyone in the class turned to hear what she had to say.

"How much did it cost?" she asked.

Evan smiled. Leave it to Jessie to ask the one thing that everyone wanted to know but didn't dare ask.

"Jessie, that's not an appropriate question," said Mrs. Overton.

Jessie's forehead wrinkled up. "Why not?"

"We don't talk about money in class," said Mrs. Overton.

"We do in math," said Jessie. "All the time."

"That's different," said Mrs. Overton. "What I mean is, we don't ask each other how much things cost. It isn't polite. Okay, let's move on. Evan, do you have something you'd like to share with the class?"

Evan had raised his hand, and now he dropped it. "Since Jessie's question didn't count, can I ask the third question?"

Mrs. Overton paused for a minute. Evan could tell that she wanted to move on to a different topic, but she also wanted to follow the rules of Morning Meeting. "Okay," she said. "That seems fair."

Evan turned to Scott and looked him right in the face. That feeling came over him, the same one he'd had when he read Jessie's note. It was like a giant steamroller. Evan almost never got angry or jealous, but now he wanted to reach across the room and grab Scott and shake something out of him.

"Who bought it?" he asked. "You or your parents?"

Scott jutted his chin out, like he did when he was challenging Evan on the basketball court. "*I* did. All my own money."

The class erupted again, and Mrs. Overton didn't bother with the *shekere*. She just held her hands up and said, "4-O!" When they quieted down, she said, "Scott, it's very impressive that you saved your money for something you wanted to buy. Now let's move on."

But Evan couldn't move on. He couldn't listen to Salley tell the class about the trip she'd taken to her grandparents' house. Or even to Paul talk about the nest of snakes he'd found in his backyard. He couldn't hear anything or see anything. That feeling was all over him, through him, inside him. That feeling of wanting to shake something out of Scott. And now he knew what it was he wanted.

Evan wanted revenge.

# Chapter 3
# Eyewitness

**eyewitness** (ī'wĭt'nĭs), *n*. A person who actually sees something happen and so can give a first-person account of the event.

Jessie stood in the doorway, one foot inside the classroom, one foot outside on the playground. All the other kids had run outside. Everyone except Evan and Megan. They were staying inside to finish their Daily Double.

Jessie didn't want to go outside if Megan and Evan weren't there. She still didn't know most of the fourth-graders—not enough to know who was friendly and who wasn't—and she knew she'd probably say the wrong thing to the wrong person. And people would laugh. Or be mean. Or just give her one of those looks—those looks she never understood—and then turn their backs on her.

Maybe Jessie could stay inside and read her Independent Reading book instead. It was worth asking.

She walked back to her desk and pulled out *The Prince and the Pauper*. It was a book her grandmother had given to her. Twice, actually. First, Grandma sent it at the beginning of the summer with a note that said, *Jessie, I loved this book when I was your age.* Then a month later she'd sent another copy of the same book with a note that said, *This book made me think of you, Jessie. Hope you enjoy it!*

Jessie had laughed and said, "I hope she forgets and sends me my birthday money twice!" But Mrs. Treski didn't laugh. She frowned and shook her head and went to the phone to give her mother a call, just to see how she was doing.

"Mrs. Overton?" said Jessie. Evan had gone to the boys' room, and Megan was in the hall getting a drink of water, so the room was empty except for Jessie and her teacher.

"Yes, Jessie?" Mrs. Overton looked up from her desk, where she was reading over what the students had written in their Writer's Notebooks that morning. Jessie had written about the fireworks that she and Evan and her mother had watched from their house on Labor Day. She'd used lots of long words, like *kaleidoscope* and *panorama,* and vigorous verbs, like *exploded* and *cascading.* She thought her paragraph was pretty good.

Jessie heard Evan and Megan laughing in the hallway. That stopped her, the way they were laughing together. She didn't want them to see her, staying inside with the teacher during recess. She was pretty sure that Evan would say, "That's not what fourth-graders do." So she mumbled, "Uh, nothing," and carried her book back to her desk.

"You should go outside, honey," said Mrs. Overton. "You don't want to miss all of morning recess. Right?"

"Right," said Jessie faintly. She hurried to the back door, the one that opened right onto the playground. When she turned to close the door behind her, she saw Evan and Megan walking into the classroom from the hallway. They both looked pretty happy, considering that they were missing recess *and* had to do math.

Outside, a handful of girls were sitting at the picnic table, folding origami flowers. Some of the fourth-graders were swinging and sliding on the Green Machine. About eight or nine were playing kickball. All of Evan's friends—Paul and Ryan and Adam and Jack—were shooting baskets, along with Scott Spencer. Where should Jessie go? She wondered if the boys were still talking about the 20/20 so she drifted over to the basketball hoop. She sat down on the grass and pretended to concentrate on her book, but really she was listening to the boys' conversation. Jessie overheard Paul ask Scott, "How'd you save up that much?" They weren't playing a real game, just shooting free throws from the line.

"Lots of ways," said Scott. Paul bounce-passed the ball to Scott, and he took his shot. And missed. Jessie was glad to see that.

26

"Like what?" asked Adam.

"I did a lot of chores around the house."

"There's no way you saved up that much money from doing chores," said Adam.

"I did, too," said Scott. Now he held on to the ball and dribbled it in place. Ryan held up his hands for it—it was his turn to shoot—but Scott wouldn't give it up. "What're you saying?"

"I'm saying what I said," said Adam. "There's no *way* you saved up that much money just from chores."

*What he's saying,* thought Jessie, *is that you stole all our lemonade money from Evan, and everybody knows it!* If only someone had seen him take it. If only there'd been an eyewitness—like the crime shows on TV! Then Scott wouldn't have gotten off . . . scot-free.

A shadow fell across the page of her book. Jessie looked up, and there was David Kirkorian standing next to her.

Jessie still didn't know a lot of the fourth-graders, but David Kirkorian was legendary throughout the school. Everyone said he had all kinds of weird collections at his house. He kept a jar of peach pits on his dresser, and he added a new one every time he ate a peach. He had a box full of shoelaces from every shoe he'd ever worn. He even had a large brown envelope filled with his own toenail clippings. At least, that's what everybody said, though Jessie was pretty sure that no one had actually seen the envelope.

"You're not allowed to read outside during recess," said David.

"I never heard of that rule," said Jessie.

"Just because you don't know a rule doesn't mean it isn't a rule." David started picking at one of his fingernails, and Jessie wondered if he collected those, too.

"That's the dumbest rule I ever heard."

"No, it's not," said David. "You could get run over sitting here. You're not even paying attention. A ball could conk you on the head. You could *die*."

He started to walk off in the direction of the duty teacher. Jessie felt her face getting hot. What was David going to say to the duty teacher?

Jessie stood up and hurried toward the school building. She would say that she had a stomachache. She would go to the nurse. Mrs. Graham always let you lie down for a couple of minutes before sending you back to your class. It was a good place to rest and be quiet. A good place to think. And Jessie had a lot of thinking to do. Not just about rules and recess. But about how unfair it was that Scott always escaped punishment—and what she could do to change that.

"Toenail collector," Jessie muttered under her breath as she hurried inside.

# Chapter 4
# Hearsay

**hearsay** (hîr′sā′), *n.* Quoting someone else's words when that person is not present to say whether those words are true; rumor. Hearsay is not allowed as evidence in a court of law.

"So, you get it?" asked Megan, leaning back in her chair. "They're the same. See?"

The math problem was about symmetry. There were five different shapes drawn on the page, and for each one, Evan had to figure out if the shape was symmetrical or not. If it was, he had to draw the line of symmetry. Megan had already done the first one to show him how.

But Evan was having a hard time thinking about symmetry when he was sitting right next to Megan Moriarty.

"That one's easy," said Evan, trying to sound cool. "Everybody knows that hearts are symmetric."

"Not all hearts," said Megan. "Look at this one."

"Well, that's just freaky," said Evan.

The next three shapes weren't too hard, and Evan was able to draw the line of symmetry for each one.

But the last one had him stumped, and Megan finally had to let him in on the trick: the shape wasn't symmetrical at all.

"It looks like it should work," said Megan, "but it never does, no matter where you draw the line. Jessie showed me that. She's a math genius, huh?"

Evan didn't say anything. Having a sister who was smart enough to skip a whole grade was like having a best friend who was a basketball star. It made you look bad by comparison.

"Hey, Evan?" said Megan, dropping her voice and leaning in even closer. They both looked over at Mrs. Overton, who was talking on the class phone. Evan could smell the coconut shampoo Megan used on her hair. It made him think of ice cream at the Big Dipper. "How do *you* think Scott Spencer got the money for that 20/20?"

The nice, floaty feeling leaked out of Evan. "Scott Spencer? Huh!" said Evan.

"I know what you mean," said Megan, sitting back and twirling her hair. "He always acts so nice when the teacher's around, but then he's really mean in the halls."

"Yeah, that's Scott," mumbled Evan.

"You know," said Megan, leaning in again. "Scott once told me his mother makes ten dollars a *minute*. Do you believe that?"

Evan thought of the Spencers' house and the vacations they took every year—skiing and the Caribbean and even Europe—and he didn't doubt it for a second. "Sure," he said. "You should see where he lives."

"I heard he has a new TV that's as big as the whiteboard." Megan pointed to the large whiteboard at the front of the room.

"Probably," said Evan. "You wouldn't think a kid like that would steal things."

Megan's eyes opened wide. "Does he really steal? Alyssa told me he does. She said he took her charm bracelet out of her locker and then pretended he'd found it on the playground. Just to impress her. But I don't know if that's true."

Evan was dying to tell her that Scott had stolen

$208 from him—but he couldn't. "He stole lunch money from Ryan once. And he took a candy bar from the Price Chopper. He steals lots of things."

Megan looked at him closely. "Did you see him take the money or the candy bar?" she asked.

Evan shook his head. "No, but Ryan said—"

"That's just a rumor, then," said Megan. "You can't believe everything you hear. That's what my parents always say."

"If you knew him like I do, you'd think it was true, too."

"Maybe," said Megan. "But I don't listen to rumors. People probably say things about me that aren't true! And about you, too!"

Evan wondered if that was so. What would people say about him? Did his friends talk about him behind his back? He didn't like to think about that.

But what Megan said got him thinking about the missing money. Evan never actually saw Scott take the money, but he had told everyone—Paul and Ryan and Adam and Jack—that Scott had taken it.

And they'd all believed him, because . . . well, because it was true! Evan was sure of it.

"You have to know Scott," Evan said, shaking his head again. But he could hear his mother's voice: *Rumors are like pigeons. They fly everywhere and make a mess wherever they go.*

# Chapter 5
# Accused

**accused** (ə-kyōōzd'), *n.* A person who has been charged with a crime or who is on trial for a crime.

Jessie and Megan were walking to school, and they were late. Jessie had called Megan at 7:00 that morning, and again at 7:30, and then at 7:55 *and* 8:10, but Megan had still been late leaving her house. ("I was late because you kept calling me," she grumbled on the way out the door.) *Ten whole minutes late.* So now they were half running, half walking, trying to get to school before the bell rang.

Normally, Jessie wouldn't have minded missing the before-school time on the playground, but today she had things to do. On the playground. Before school. With no grownups around.

"C'mon, c'mon," she said to Megan. Megan's legs were longer than Jessie's, but Megan was slow because her mailbag kept banging into her knees.

"Why do we need to get there so early?" asked Megan. She was loping along, about ten feet behind Jessie.

"You'll see when we get there. Keep running, keep running."

"Better hurry, girls," said Darlene when they got to the crosswalk. "I heard the first bell." Jessie and Megan speed-walked across the street. Running wasn't allowed.

"Oh, no!" said Jessie when they rounded the corner and caught sight of the playground. "They're already lining up. Come *on!*"

By the time Jessie and Megan ran onto the blacktop, the entire fourth grade was lined up, waiting for the signal to file into school. The girls should have gone to the end of the line, but Jessie marched right up to the middle, where Scott Spencer was trying to knock Paul's baseball cap off his head. Evan was standing farther up, bouncing the class basketball. He was Equipment Manager this week, which meant he was responsible for bringing in all the playground stuff—balls, jump ropes, Frisbees.

"Hey," said Scott, noticing Jessie. "The end of the line is back *there!*"

"So?" said Jessie, rummaging in her backpack.

"So no cutting," said Scott. "Isn't that the *rule?*" Even Jessie could tell he was making fun of her.

"I'm not cutting," said Jessie, pulling a piece of paper from her backpack and holding it out in front of her. "I'm serving you with a warrant for your arrest."

A few of the boys in front of Scott turned around, and some of the girls at the end of the line moved up so they could see, too.

"You're what?" asked Scott.

"Here, take it," said Jessie, shoving the piece of paper closer to him. Scott reached out and grabbed it like he was going to rip it to shreds.

"That's it!" shouted Jessie. "You touched it. That

means you've been served. Now you have to appear in court." Jessie was pretty sure she knew what she was doing. She had been reading a booklet called "Trial by Jury: The American Legal System in a Nutshell." It was one of the public service booklets that her mom wrote as part of her business as a public relations consultant.

Scott immediately dropped the paper on the ground like it was on fire. "You can't do that!"

"Oh, yes I can," said Jessie. "If you touch it, that means you've been served. You can't get out of it now."

"Get out of what? What are you even talking about?" By now, everyone in the line had turned to watch. Evan had stopped dribbling the basketball, but he didn't leave his spot in line.

Jessie picked up the arrest warrant from the ground and read it out loud. She had written it using the calligraphy pen her grandmother had given her for her last birthday.

# Warrant for the Arrest of Scott Spencer

Scott Spencer, you are hereby charged with the crime of stealing $208 from the pocket of Evan Treski's shorts on September 5th of this year.

On Friday, you are to appear in court to plead your case. There, a Jury of your Peers will decide if you are guilty or not. If you are found guilty, your punishment

She got as far as that when Scott interrupted.

"You gotta be kidding me," he said, crossing his arms and laughing. "You're joking, right?"

Jessie shook her head. Not a single person in the fourth-grade line was talking. Everyone was watching Jessie and Scott. She continued reading, "'If you are found guilty—'"

"Are you saying," said Scott, his eyes narrowing and a scowl appearing on his face, "that I stole money?"

Jessie took a deep breath. She knew it was a big deal to accuse someone like that.

"Yes, I am," she said. There were murmurs among the fourth-graders.

"What about *you?*" asked Scott, turning toward Evan and taking a few steps forward. He reached out to poke Evan in the chest, but Evan swatted his hand away before it ever touched him. "Are *you* saying I stole your money?"

Jessie looked at Evan. He dribbled the basketball twice, then held it in his hand, staring at it. Suddenly, Jessie realized that she should have talked to Evan before doing any of this. He was the one who'd been the victim of the crime. He was the one who would still have to play with Scott every day at recess. He was the one who would have to testify against him in a court of law.

But it was too late now. Everyone was watching them. Everyone was waiting to see what would happen next.

Evan dribbled the ball again. One, two, three. Jessie knew that he was thinking. Evan thought with his whole body, not just his brain.

"That's what I'm saying," he said quietly. "I'm saying you stole the money from me."

The line of fourth-graders had twisted into the shape of a large, sloppy C with both ends watching what was happening in the middle.

Now that Evan had accused Scott of stealing, the line started to fall apart entirely as kids pulled in close to hear what Scott would say next.

But it was Jessie who spoke first. "'If you are found guilty, your punishment will be that you have to give your new Xbox 20/20 to Evan Treski.'"

"No way!" said Scott, but he could barely be heard over all the noise that the fourth-graders were making. Everyone had an opinion about the fairness of the punishment.

"Hey," said Ryan. "What happens if he's found not guilty?"

Jessie shook her head. "He won't be."

"I will, too, you twerp!" said Scott. "And when I am, here's what's going to happen. Both of you"—he pointed at Jessie and Evan—"are going to stand up in Morning Meeting and tell everyone, including Mrs. Overton, that you told lies about me and that I didn't take anything from anyone. And then you're going to apologize to me. In front of *everyone*."

"4-O!" Mrs. Overton was standing in the doorway, a look of dismay on her face. "What kind of a line is this?"

The kids scrambled back to their places, and those at the front started the morning march into the classroom. But Evan, Jessie, and Scott still faced each other.

"Is it a deal?" asked Scott.

"Deal," said Evan, and turned his back on them to head inside.

"I'll even put it in writing," said Jessie. She waved the arrest warrant in front of Scott. Then she picked up her backpack and hurried to the end of the line, smiling.

Soon, justice would be served.

# Agreement of Atonement following the Trial of Scott Spencer

If Scott Spencer is found GUILTY in a court of law of the crime of stealing $208 from the pocket of Evan Treski's shorts on September the 5th of this year, he will give his Xbox 20/20 to Evan Treski to keep forever.

If Scott Spencer is found NOT GUILTY in a court of law of the crime of stealing $208 from the pocket of Evan Treski's shorts on September 5th of this year, Evan and Jessie Treski will stand up in Morning Meeting on Monday and will tell the entire class that Scott Spencer did not steal $208 from the pocket of Evan Treski's shorts on September 5th of this year, and they will apologize to him for telling lies.

*Evan Treski*

*Jessie Treski*

*Scott Spencer*

## Chapter 6
# Impartial

**impartial** (ĭm-pär′shəl), *adj*. Treating everyone the same; not taking sides in an argument; fair and just.

At recess, Jessie didn't waste any time. Evan watched as she pulled index cards, one by one, out of a big envelope. All the fourth-graders crowded around.

"You're the plaintiff," she said to Evan, and handed him a green index card that said PLAINTIFF on it. "That means you're the victim of the crime." Evan studied the card, then stuck it in his back pocket. A kids' court sounded like a crazy idea to him. A crazy Jessie idea. But he was used to those, and this one might get him a new Xbox 20/20, not to mention the satisfaction of proving Scott's guilt in front of everybody. For that, he was willing to give it a try.

"I'm Evan's lawyer," said Jessie, and she gave herself a purple index card that said LAWYER FOR THE PLAINTIFF.

Then she turned to Scott. "You're the defendant, which means you're the one who's on trial." She gave him a yellow index card that said DEFENDANT on it.

Then she started to hand out five orange index cards.

"Hey!" shouted Scott. "Don't I get a lawyer?"

"Hold on! You'll get one in a minute," said Jessie sharply. She continued handing out cards.

"I want Ryan," said Scott.

"Sorry," said Ryan, holding up an orange card. "I'm a witness."

"Then I want Paul."

"He's a witness, too," said Jessie, handing Paul the last orange card. "Everyone who was at Jack's house on the day of the crime is a witness."

"Well, then who's going to be *my* lawyer?" asked Scott, crumpling his DEFENDANT card.

Jessie ignored his question. She held up a purple card. "Megan, you're on the jury," she said. Evan's heart jumped. There was one vote he could count on.

"When's the trial?" said Megan.

"After school," said Jessie. "On Friday."

Megan shook her head. "I think we're going away this weekend."

"You can't miss the trial!" said Jessie. Evan wanted to shout the same thing, but he kept his mouth shut.

"I'll talk to my mom," said Megan. "Maybe we can leave later. But you'd better give this card to somebody else." She handed the purple card back to Jessie.

"Oh, all right," said Jessie, sounding disappointed. "Take one of these." She handed Megan a white card that said AUDIENCE on it.

It only took Jessie another minute to hand out the twelve JURY cards and the rest of the AUDIENCE cards. All the audience members were girls because all the witnesses were boys and the jury, as Jessie explained to everyone, had to be fifty-fifty.

Evan looked around. It was weird, the way all the kids were going along with Jessie's idea. Didn't they know this was all fake? And how did Jessie know all this legal stuff? How did she always know things he didn't know?

Jessie rounded up the six girls who held white audience cards. Then she turned to Scott. "You can pick anybody from the audience to be your lawyer. Technically, we don't even need the audience. No offense," said Jessie, turning to the girls.

"I don't want a girl lawyer," said Scott.

"Suit yourself," said Jessie, shrugging. "But don't come back and complain you weren't offered legal counsel."

"A bunch of girls!" said Scott. "Some offer! I'll be my own lawyer. I'll defend myself." He turned to Jessie. "And I'll beat you at it, too!" he said. That was just like Scott, thought Evan. Always thinking he was the best. Always the kid who had the best stuff. Who took the best vacations. Who had everything.

"Good," said Jessie. "Defend yourself." There was just one more index card in her envelope. Evan watched as she pulled it out slowly. The card was red. It had one word on it.

Jessie looked around like she was making a very important decision, but Evan knew she'd already decided who would get that red card. Jessie never left anything until the last minute.

"The judge is going to be . . . David Kirkorian."

There was dead silence.

Then Paul shouted out, "Are you kidding me?"

"He can't be a judge!" said Ryan. "He collects human bones!"

"I do not!" said David, turning bright red but stepping up to Jessie and taking the card out of her hand.

Then everyone started talking at once. David, meanwhile, held up the red card and shouted, "Ha, ha! I'm the judge! I'm the judge!" They made so much noise, the duty teacher came over to see what was going on with class 4-O. That quieted everyone down. Nobody wanted the duty teacher getting involved. One of the unspoken rules on the playground was *Never tell the duty teacher what's really going on.*

"Why him?" asked Paul after the duty teacher walked away.

"Because he's the only one in the whole class who's *impartial,*" said Jessie. "He's not friends with Evan or Scott. He'll be fair. He won't play favorites. And that's the most important thing about a judge. A judge has to treat everyone the same."

David held up the red card in one hand and placed the other one over his heart. "I solemnly swear that I'll be a fair judge," he said.

"Good," said Jessie.

But Evan couldn't believe it. Who was going to listen to a kid like David Kirkorian?

For Evan, the day went downhill from there. All afternoon in class, they worked on things that Evan hated: math fact drills, spelling rules, and writers' workshop. Then Mrs. Overton discovered that one of the jump ropes was missing from the 4-O milk crate, and that was Evan's fault because he was Equipment Manager.

But the thing that really slam-dunked the day right into the garbage can, the thing that changed it from a crummy day into absolutely one of the top ten worst days of his life, happened after school.

Evan was strapping on his bike helmet when Adam walked up to him at the rack and pulled out his bike. "You want to come over?" asked Evan.

"Can't," said Adam. "I promised my mom I'd help her get the house ready for Yom Kippur."

"Is that today?" asked Evan, clicking the buckle under his chin.

"It starts Friday night, but my mom wants me to clean up my room today and do some other stuff, too."

Evan knew that Yom Kippur is a holiday where the grownups don't eat all day. It was supposed to help them think about their sins, but Evan couldn't figure that out. When he was hungry, he couldn't think about anything except what he was going to eat next.

"You want to come to the break-fast party?" asked Adam. The Goldbergs always ate a big meal at sunset when the holiday fast was over.

"Sure," said Evan. He'd been to lots of Friday

night dinners at Adam's and Paul's houses. He liked the candles and even the prayers he didn't understand, but mostly he liked the food: challah bread, roasted chicken, and applesauce cake.

"Are you going to go the whole day without eating this year?" asked Evan. Last year, Adam had bragged that he was going to fast next year for Yom Kippur.

Adam shrugged. "I might try." Then he looked down at his bike and bounced the front wheel a couple of times on the hard blacktop. "Look. Uh. There's something I've been meaning to say to you. You remember how over the summer, Paul and Kevin and me, we ditched you in the woods that time?"

"Yeah," said Evan, wondering why Adam was bringing up something that had happened months ago. Evan had been really mad back then, but now it was over.

"Well, I'm really sorry. And I hope you'll forgive me." Evan looked confused. Adam shrugged. "Dude. It's Yom Kippur. The Day of Atonement. You have to go around and ask people to forgive your sins."

Evan laughed. "You're such an idiot!" He shoved Adam. Adam grinned, faked like he was going to throw a punch, then got on his bike, and rode away.

Evan was just about to push off on his bike when he saw Ryan and Paul walking together toward the path. He rode across the blacktop and crossed in front of them right before they came to the fence. Before Evan could say anything, Paul slung his arm around him, nearly knocking him off his bike. "Hey, Evan, I totally owe you one. Thanks for taking the blame, you know, when Charlie got off his leash."

"Yeah, sure. No big deal," said Evan, shrugging. Evan and Paul did that all the time for each other: swapping the blame so that they wouldn't get in trouble with their own parents. Parents always went way easier on other people's kids than they did on their own.

"You want to come over?" Evan said to Paul and Ryan, balancing on his bike without pedaling forward.

Paul shook his head. "No, we're going to Scott's."

Evan slammed his feet to the ground and stared at the two of them.

"He said we could try out the 20/20," said Ryan. "It's supposed to be awesome. You should come, too."

Evan felt like he'd been sucker-punched. "No way!" he shouted. He stared at Paul and then Ryan with an expression that said, *Traitor!* but neither one of them said anything in return. Finally, Evan said quietly, "I can't believe you're going over to his house."

Paul shrugged. "He didn't do anything to us."

"Some friend you are," said Evan.

"C'mon, Evan," said Paul. "You don't even know for sure that he took the money . . ."

"I know!" said Evan.

"You should come," said Ryan. "Everyone's going over there after school."

A picture came into Evan's mind of the whole fourth-grade class marching over to Scott's house. All his friends. And where would he be? He'd be at home, with his little sister. "Who?" he asked. "Everyone, who?"

"All the guys," said Paul. "You know, me and Ryan and Jack and Kevin. All the guys."

"Not Adam," said Evan, thinking to himself that at least he had one friend who was loyal.

"Well, he's gotta help his mother with some stuff," said Ryan, "but then he's coming over after that. Like in an hour."

Evan shook his head in disbelief. His best friend. Stabbing him in the back. He yanked his handlebars away from Paul and Ryan and rode off without saying another word.

## Chapter 7
# Due Diligence

**due diligence** (dōō dĭl′ə-jəns), *n*. Taking the time and making the effort to do a reasonably good job at something; the opposite of negligence.

"Can we take a break now?" asked Megan, sitting up on her knees. She held the blue marker in her hand as if it were a lighted candle. Her fingers were covered with ink in all colors, and she had a pencil stuck through the base of her ponytail.

Jessie was lying on her stomach with her whole box of colored pencils spread out in front of her. There was no way they could take a break now! The trial was tomorrow. There was still so much left to do.

She'd already interviewed the five witnesses who were going to testify—Paul, Ryan, Kevin, Malik, and Jack—to find out exactly what they remembered about the day of the crime when they were at Jack's house. She'd written out index cards for David Kirkorian that told him exactly what he was supposed to say during the trial.

WHEN THE TRIAL BEGINS:

You bang your gavel and say:
"All rise! Court is in session.
The Honorable David P.
Kirkorian presiding."

IF SOMEBODY TALKS WHO'S
NOT SUPPOSED TO:

You say: "Order in the court!
Order in the court! If you're not
quiet, I will hold you in
contempt!"

WHEN YOU SWEAR IN A WITNESS:

You say: "Do you swear to
tell the truth, the whole truth,
and nothing but the truth?"

Now she was finishing up coloring the map that showed where each person would stand or sit during the trial. And she still had to write her closing argument!

Jessie felt—for the first time in her life—as if she was about to take a test and she hadn't studied long enough.

"Let's just work a little longer," she said. "Are you almost done with the nametags?"

Megan showed Jessie the twelve jury nametags,

the five witness nametags,

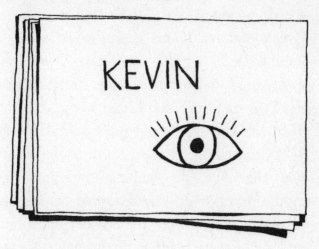

and the judge's nametag.

"Those are good," said Jessie. "Now you just have to do the ones for the audience."

Megan groaned. "This is why Evan calls you Obsessie Jessie."

Jessie hated that nickname. She hated all nicknames! Why had Evan told Megan about that?

"I am not obsessed. I just work hard. It's called *due*"—she thought for a minute, but couldn't come up with the name—"something." She scrounged under the papers that were scattered on the floor and found "Trial by Jury," the booklet her mother had written. She started flipping through the pages.

"But we've been doing this for hours!" wailed Megan. "I want to go outside."

"Due diligence!" said Jessie. "That's what it's called. Doing your job so that later, no one can blame you and say you didn't work hard enough."

"Well, due diligence is BORING!" said Megan. She picked up the ruler that Jessie had been using to draw straight lines on her map and began to balance it upright in the palm of her hand. She was pretty good at it. Jessie was impressed.

Suddenly, Megan asked, "Do you think you can really prove that Scott stole Evan's money?"

Jessie felt her throat close up for an instant.

That was the question she was most afraid of. That was the question that had kept running through her mind last night as she lay in bed, trying to fall asleep.

"I don't know. I'd better be able to." Jessie imagined standing up in front of the whole class and apologizing to Scott. It made her feel like throwing up.

Megan put the ruler down and flopped onto the floor, spreading her arms and legs out like a starfish. She picked up the map Jessie had drawn that showed where everyone would be in the courtroom.

The courtroom wasn't a "room" at all. It was the grassy part of the school playground—the part that was farthest away from the building and the blacktop and was shaded by a row of large elm trees. Jessie had drawn exactly where they would set up the milk crates and the jump ropes and the balls and who would sit where. Everybody's name was marked with some kind of symbol.

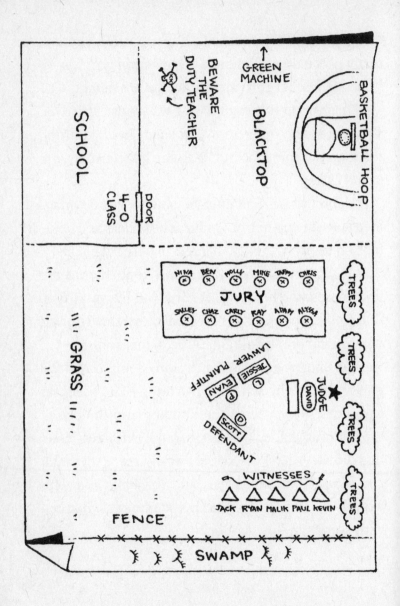

Megan stared at the map. "It's like I can almost imagine the whole thing happening," she said. "There's just one thing." She turned the paper one way, then the other. "It's not symmetrical. See?"

Jessie looked at the map. What was Megan talking about?

"It's supposed to be balanced, right? Everything even. But look." Megan pulled the pencil out of her ponytail and drew a light, dotted line down the middle of Jessie's drawing.

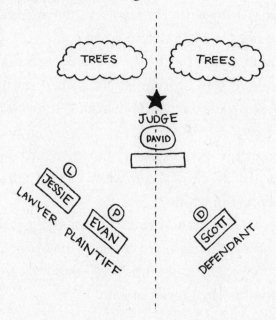

"Scott doesn't have a lawyer," she said. "The sides aren't even, so it's really not, you know, *fair.* I mean, to Scott."

"Well, it's his own fault," said Jessie. She'd worked too hard on her map to hear any criticism of it.

"But still," said Megan. "Isn't it the law that everyone gets to have a lawyer if they get arrested? Even if you're poor and even if no one likes you. And even if everyone thinks you're guilty. You get to have a lawyer. That's how they always do it on TV."

Jessie shrugged. "He wants to defend himself. You're allowed to do that in a real court."

Megan shook her head. "He only said that because there was no one left to pick. I mean, no boys." She looked at the map again. "It just doesn't seem right."

"What are you saying?" Jessie wished people would just be clear about what they meant. "Are you saying I'm wrong?"

Megan crossed her arms. "All I'm saying is that it isn't fair if Evan has a lawyer and Scott doesn't. And you know it, Jessie. You know it better than anyone else. You're—the Queen of Fair."

Another nickname! Was it an insult? The way Megan said "the Queen of Fair" didn't sound like an insult. But Jessie wasn't sure. Sometimes someone said something one way and meant it exactly the opposite. That was called *sarcasm,* and Jessie always missed it, like a pitch thrown too fast, leaving her swinging at nothing but air.

Outside, Jessie could hear the steady bouncing of a basketball in the driveway. Evan. Shooting hoops. Did he even know how hard she was working—for *him?*

Then the bouncing stopped, and she heard a car pull into the driveway. Megan heard it, too. "That's my mom," she said. "Gotta go." Megan had a dentist appointment at four o'clock.

For the first time ever, Jessie was glad to see Megan go.

# Chapter 8
# Defense

**defense** (dĭ-fĕns'), *n.* The argument presented in a court of law to prove the innocence of the accused; (in sports) the act of protecting your goal against the opposing team.

It wasn't hot enough to sweat, but Evan was sweating. Two wide rivers ran down the sides of his face, and every time he spun he could feel droplets flying off the tips of his hair.

He was going to get this shot right even if it killed him.

He'd been working on it all afternoon. Actually, he'd been working on it all month. It was a turn-around jumper from the top of the key. A good fifteen feet from the basket, and he was shooting with his left hand. That's what all the greats could do— shoot with their weak hand and still make the basket. Evan's dad used to say to him: "Work from your weak side, and no one will be able to defend against you."

Evan turned his back to the basket and planted his feet on the painted lines of the driveway. He dribbled once, dribbled twice, dribbled three times, then—like a rocket shooting off its launching pad, he sprang into the air and pivoted his whole body around. Even as his body was falling back to the ground, he got off the shot, falling away from the basket as the ball sailed toward the pole and—

*missed.*

Sometimes he made it; sometimes he didn't. About one time out of every ten he made the shot. Evan wanted to flip that around so that only one time out of every ten he *missed.* It was a killer shot. If he had that kind of shot in his pocket, he could beat anyone on the court.

Dribble once, dribble twice, dribble three times . . .

"Hey, Evan."

Evan straightened up and looked toward the street. Megan was riding her bike toward him. She came to a sliding stop, then hopped off her bike before walking it across. Evan shook to get some of the sweat out of his eyes. Then he ducked his head and wiped his face on the sleeve of his T-shirt. Girls do not like sweat.

"I thought you had a dentist appointment," he said as she pushed her bike onto the driveway.

"It was short. Just a checkup," she said. "Is Jessie still in there?" Megan nodded her head in the direction of the house.

"Yeah. Still getting ready for The Big Day." Evan was dreading the trial. Every fourth-grader was going to be there—on the playground after school tomorrow—and what if Jessie couldn't prove that Scott Spencer was guilty? She wasn't a real lawyer. And could Evan really count on his friends? It seemed like every day this week Paul and Ryan had gone to Scott's house after school. Maybe by the time of the trial, all the guys would be on

Scott's side. Evan imagined standing up in front of the whole class and apologizing to Scott. He dribbled the ball, as if he could drum that idea out of his head.

"Wow," said Megan. "She gets kind of like . . ."

"Obsessed," said Evan. Then again, he thought about what *he'd* been doing all afternoon. How many times had he practiced that shot? One hundred? Two hundred? And he planned to keep going until it got too dark to see the basket. So maybe it ran in the family.

As if she was reading his thoughts, Megan asked, "You been out here the whole time?"

"I'm working on a shot. You want to see?"

Megan shrugged and smiled, and Evan decided that meant yes. He set his feet and started his dribbling rhythm. *Please let it fall, please let it fall, please let it fall,* he said in his head as he bounced the ball on the blacktop.

But it didn't. It *ka-thunked* off the backboard and ricocheted toward the street. Evan had to run fast to save it from rolling into the road.

"That was close," said Megan. "You're really good."

Evan shook his head as he dribbled the ball back to the center of the paint. "Close doesn't count in basketball. You either make the shot or you don't."

"Well, it was better than I could have done," she said. "And I'm the best shooter on my team."

Evan raised his eyebrows. "You play basketball?"

"And soccer," she said. "But I'm better at basketball."

"Really? Can you make a three-pointer?"

Megan laughed. "Sometimes."

"So, let's see," said Evan. He tossed the ball to her, and she dribbled across the driveway so that her feet were just outside the three-point line.

Evan watched as Megan handled the ball, watched the way her ponytail bounced back and forth and her bracelets danced up and down her arm.

"Okay, here goes," she said. "Don't hold your breath, though." She lifted the ball over her head, then sent it sailing through the air like water shooting out of a garden hose. It landed right in the basket.

"Awesome!" said Evan. He scooped up the bouncing ball and made an easy lay-up. "You want to shoot some? We could play HORSE. Or one-on-one, if . . . " Evan thought about defending against a girl, and his stomach turned over on itself. How did you defend against someone without ever touching them?

"Can't," said Megan, looking down the road. "I'm going over to someone's house."

"Whose?" asked Evan, bouncing the ball back and forth between his legs. He was a pretty good shooter, but he was a great ball handler. When he made it to the pros, he'd probably be a point guard. Sure, they didn't get all the glory, but point guards ruled the court.

Megan waved her hand up the street, but didn't say a name as she strapped on her bike helmet.

Evan stopped dribbling. "Whose house?"

Megan kicked the pedal on her bike so that it spun backwards, the gears making a whirring sound like insects on a summer night. "Scott's. He said I could try out his 20/20."

An elbow to the face, that's how her words felt. Evan squeezed the ball between his hands. "Are you like, *best friends* now?"

Megan gave him a look. "You don't have to be best friends to go to someone's house."

"Yeah, well, it sure looks like everyone is suddenly Scott's best friend." It seemed as if the 20/20 was all anyone talked about anymore. Scott was always the center of attention. And now. Now Megan was going over there, too. Evan scooped up the basketball and threw it hard against the garage door. It made a loud, angry, rattling sound as it hit. He threw it again. "All any of you care about is that stupid 20/20." Suddenly Evan realized that Scott didn't need a lawyer. He already had the best defense in town: the 20/20. Nobody would say Scott was guilty if it meant losing the chance to play with the coolest game system ever invented.

"Oh, c'mon," said Megan. "I bet you're dying to try it out, too."

Evan didn't respond. He just kept banging the ball against the garage door.

Megan pushed off on her bike and called out, "See you in school."

When she was halfway down the street, Evan shouted after her, "See you in *court!*"

# Chapter 9
# Bona Fide

**bona fide** (bō′nə fīd), *adj*. From the Latin, meaning "good faith," genuine, signifying "the real thing."

Jessie was hanging upside down on the Green Machine, her knees hooked over a monkey bar. This, she decided, was going to be the best Friday ever. After school, everyone would gather on the playground for the trial—even Megan, who had talked her mother into leaving later for their trip. Mrs. Overton had already given them permission to use the playground equipment after school. Jessie had her map. She had her note cards. She had practiced her closing argument at least twenty times. Evan had even listened to her practice and had given her some good tips on how to make the speech better. *Today is going to be great,* she thought.

At that moment, Scott Spencer walked over and stuck his face right next to hers.

"My *mom's* going to be my lawyer," he said.

"What?" said Jessie. She grabbed hold of the bar and flipped herself onto the ground. Everybody knew that Scott's mom was a big-time lawyer who worked downtown. Jessie had heard a million times about how fancy her office was. Scott said you could see the whole city from her office window. Sometimes her name was even in the newspaper.

"That's right. My mom. She's going to mop up the floor with you. She's going to bury you alive!"

Jessie squinted her eyes at Scott. "She's taking a day off from work?"

"No," said Scott, sneering at Jessie. "But she said she'd leave early. I told her it was important, and she said she'd be here."

"Well—she—can't," said Jessie, stammering. "It's for kids only. No grownups allowed."

"Are you saying I can't have a lawyer?"

"I didn't say that," said Jessie. But she was stuck, and she knew it. Everybody has the right to legal counsel. It was on page two of "Trial by Jury." It was the law. "Fine," she said, pressing her lips together. "But she'd better not be late."

Jessie remembered those words that afternoon as she ran around the playground, madly trying to set up the courtroom so the trial could start on time.

Thank goodness Mrs. Overton had let them use the playground equipment without asking any questions. She had made it clear that it was Evan's responsibility to bring everything back when they were done playing. Even though it was Friday afternoon and school was over for the day, he was still technically the Equipment Manager until Monday morning.

By quarter to three, Jessie had carried all the equipment outside and set up the milk crate under the elm trees, standing it up on end so that it looked like a podium. On top of the crate she placed the pile of index cards that told David Kirkorian *exactly* what he was supposed to say, then she called David over. He was holding a real wooden gavel in one hand and a brown paper bag in the other.

"Look what I borrowed from my dad," said David, waving the gavel. "It was a gag gift, and he said we could use it."

"What's in there?" asked Jessie, pointing to the bag.

David reached into the bag and pulled out a bunched-up ball of black cloth. He slipped it over his head. The cloth puddled at his feet. "It's my brother's graduation robe," he said. "I know it looks big, but just wait." He stepped behind the podium so that the milk crate covered all the extra fabric dragging on the ground. Jessie had to admit, it made him look like a real judge. And when he banged the gavel on a block of wood he'd brought, Jessie felt maybe she really could count on David Kirkorian to do his part.

In front of the milk crate, Jessie placed two basketballs, one for Evan to sit on and one for Scott. Jessie's "chair" was the dodge ball, and she set it up right next to Evan's. Should she set up the other dodge ball for Scott's mother to sit on? She couldn't imagine a grownup sitting on a ball the way kids did, so she left the second dodge ball in the crate. Off to one side, she stretched out the jump ropes to form a box on the grass where the jurors would sit, and on the other side she put down a squiggly jump rope that marked where the witnesses would stand while they waited to testify. There were only six people in the audience, so Jessie figured that they could just sit behind the three Frisbees that she had carefully placed on the grass.

"It looks great!" said Megan, walking over to Jessie.

Jessie looked around. For the first time, she could actually *see* the courtroom. It wasn't just a picture in her head. It wasn't just a map drawn on a piece of paper. It was a bona fide court. The real deal.

She nodded, a single butterfly tickling the inside of her stomach. "So far, so good."

# Chapter 10
# Trial by Jury

**trial by jury** (trī′əl bī jo͞or′ē), *n.* A legal proceeding in which the guilt or innocence of a person accused of a crime is decided by a group of his or her peers, rather than by a judge or panel of judges.

Evan looked around and felt as though he'd dropped into an alternate universe.

First of all, he was sitting on a basketball, which felt strange.

Second, here was his sister, acting like she was the leader of the free world. Jessie could sometimes be bossy at home, but Evan was used to seeing her on the sidelines at school. On the edge of whatever was happening on the playground. Eating quietly at a cafeteria table. Sitting with her hands in her lap at the all-school assemblies.

Suddenly she was the leader. And it was weird.

Evan stared at the twelve kids sitting in the jury box, and that was weird, too. If he looked at each kid, one at a time, all he saw were the faces of kids he'd known for most of his life. Nothing new. But when he looked at them all together, standing in the box that Jessie had made out of jump ropes, they looked different. Even Adam, his best friend in the world, seemed almost unfamiliar. They were the jury—the ones who would either hand him a new Xbox 20/20 or make him stand up in class and apologize in front of everybody. Suddenly, they didn't seem like the kids he'd known forever. They had turned into something much bigger.

Evan's eyes traveled across the courtroom: to the witnesses all standing together behind the line of the jump rope, to the audience waiting patiently for the trial to begin, and to David Kirkorian standing at his milk-crate podium.

And that was the weirdest thing of all. Every single one of the fourth-graders had shown up after school and put on a nametag. (Okay, so Malik had taped his nametag to his butt, but he was still standing in the witness box, ready to testify.) Everyone was waiting to do whatever Jessie told them to do. It was as if all of a sudden there was a whole new set of rules at school, and everyone—*everyone*—had agreed to follow them.

Even Scott Spencer was sitting on his basketball. He had his knees spread wide, and he was drumming a beat on the ball. *Chook-uh-ta-chook, chook-uh-ta-chook, chook-uh-ta-chook.* He had that look. That Scott Spencer look. The look in his eyes that seemed to say, *It's all good. It's all cool. It's all mine.*

That was the thing about Scott Spencer. Somehow, some way, he always managed to spin things so that everything worked to his advantage. Evan remembered the time they were in first grade, playing in Scott's basement playroom. Scott's mom was at work. His dad worked at home, like Evan's mom did, but his office was all the way at the other end of the house, and it was soundproof! Evan remembered how they used to play a game of seeing who could make enough noise to get Mr. Spencer to come out of his office. They practically had to set off a bomb to get him to come out!

So that day, they were playing pick-up sticks for pennies, betting a penny on every game. At first Scott was winning, and Evan had lost about seven cents. But then Evan started catching up, and then he was ahead, and Scott owed him eleven whole cents, which seemed like a lot of money back then. "Hey, let's get a snack," said Scott, and they could have gone all on their own to get something out of the kitchen, but instead Scott went to his dad's office and asked him to bring them something in the playroom. And of course when Scott's dad saw that they were betting pennies, he ended the game and made Evan return everything he'd won. "Betting isn't allowed in this house," he'd said. But Evan had thought to himself, *Losing, that's what's not allowed*.

Evan looked at Scott. Evan wasn't a fighting kid.

He'd only gotten in two fistfights in his whole life, and one of them had been with Adam, his best friend! Both those fights had been fast and furious, and then they'd been over. No hard feelings. Apologies all around. Everyone agreeing not to fight anymore.

Why couldn't it be that way with Scott? What was it about him that made Evan's blood boil? That turned one thing into another—a fight about some missing money into a full-blown trial by jury? Evan opened his mouth to say something to Scott—

Which is exactly when David K. picked up the gavel, banged it on the block of wood, and read from the top index card, "All rise! Court is in session. The Honorable David P. Kirkorian presiding."

# Chapter 11
# Perjury

**perjury** (pûr′jə-rē), *n*. Purposely telling a lie in a court of law after taking an oath to tell the truth and only the truth.

"Will the lawyer for the prosecution please step forward?" said Judge Kirkorian. The defense lawyer, Scott's mother, still hadn't arrived, but they couldn't wait any longer. About half the jury had to be home by four o'clock.

Jessie stood up and addressed the court. She made her voice sound strong. "Ladies and gentlemen of the jury, for my first witness, I call Jack Bagdasarian."

Jack walked up to the podium, and David told

him to put his right hand over his heart and raise his left hand in the air.

"Do you swear to tell the truth, the whole truth, and nothing but the truth?" asked David.

"I do," said Jack, standing straight as a pole.

"You may proceed," said David, turning to Jessie.

Jessie walked up to Jack. "Mr. Bagdasarian," she said. "Where were you on the day of Sunday, September fifth?"

"What do you mean?" asked Jack. "Is that the day Scott stole the money?"

"Hey! I didn't steal the money!" yelled Scott.

"Says you!" shouted Malik, and everybody began yelling.

"Call for order," Jessie hissed at David, who was just standing there, watching it all, like it was a movie on television.

David shuffled through his index cards until he found the right one. Then he banged the wooden gavel on the block of wood. "Order in the court! Order in the court! If you're not quiet, I will hold you in"—he looked more closely at his card—"contempt!" David waved the card and added, "That means you'll get sent home. And when you come to school on Monday, we won't tell you what happened, either."

Everybody got really quiet then.

Jessie turned to her witness again. "September fifth was the day everyone went to your house to swim," she said. "Can you tell the court what you remember about that day?"

So Jack told the story: They'd all been playing basketball on the playground—Evan and Jack and Paul and Ryan and Kevin and Malik—but it was really hot, and they decided they wanted to swim at Jack's house. So Jack had gone home to ask his mom if it was okay, and when he came back to the playground, Scott was there, too, so then they'd all gone back to Jack's house.

"And then what happened?" asked Jessie, pacing back and forth in front of the podium. She was holding a pencil and carrying her Writer's Notebook tucked under her arm. It made her feel more official.

"We played pool basketball," said Jack. "I've got one of those floating hoops, so we just goofed around and stuff."

"Did Evan swim in his own bathing suit or did he borrow one from you?" asked Jessie.

"I think he borrowed one," said Jack. "Yeah, I'm pretty sure he did. And so did Scott."

"So both Evan and Scott changed into borrowed bathing suits at your house. Is that correct?"

"Yep," said Jack, bobbing his head up and down.

"And where did they put their regular clothes when they went swimming?" asked Jessie, pointing her finger at Jack so that the jury would know she was getting to the good part.

"In my room, I guess. That's where everyone puts their shoes and socks and stuff at my house, 'cause if you leave anything downstairs, the dog gets it."

"So let me be clear on this point," said Jessie, standing directly in front of Jack. "Evan's shorts— and whatever was in his pockets—were in *your* room. And Scott's shorts—and whatever was in his pockets—were also in your room. Is that correct?"

"Yeah. I already said that."

Jessie turned to the jury. "I just want to make sure that everyone knows that fact. Evan's and Scott's shorts were in the same room." She turned back to Jack. "One more question for you, Mr. Bagdasarian. Did anyone get out of the pool and go inside?"

"Well, sure," said Jack, laughing. "I mean, jeez, we were drinking like ten gallons of lemonade and eating watermelon slices. You can't hold *that* in forever."

The courtroom burst into laughter, but David banged his gavel so loudly that everyone quieted right down. Nobody wanted to get sent home before there was a verdict.

"Did *Scott* go into the house?" asked Jessie.

"Uh-huh," said Jack.

"Did he go in *alone?*"

"Yeah."

"And how long was he in the house *alone?*"

"I don't know," said Jack, shrugging.

"Long enough to run upstairs and steal an envelope filled with money out of Evan's shorts?" asked Jessie.

"Sure," said Jack. "He was in there for a while. And I know he went into my room, because he came down dressed."

"Dressed?" asked Jessie. "Why did he do that?"

"He said he had to go, right away."

"But did he say why?"

"No. Just said he had to go."

"Did he leave in a hurry?"

"You should have seen him. He went tearing out of there. I don't think he even had both shoes on when he left."

"I don't suppose you happened to check his pockets before he left, did you?"

"Uh, no," said Jack.

"Too bad," muttered Evan. Jessie looked over at her brother. He didn't look happy.

"That will be all," said Jessie.

"The witness is excused," said David in his serious judge voice, and when Jack didn't move, he added, "You may step down."

"Step down?" asked Jack, looking at the ground.

"You may go back to the witness area," said David, and he gave Jack a look that made Jack close his mouth and do what he was told.

Jessie called up the witnesses one by one, and each boy said the same thing: Scott had gone into the house to use the bathroom, came out a while later dressed, and then rushed out the door. Hearing the story five times made it seem like it was the absolute truth.

Jessie was feeling good. So good, she decided to call Evan to the stand. She hadn't planned out any questions to ask him, but that didn't matter. Everyone liked Evan, and Jessie knew it was a good strategy to put a likable witness on the stand.

But when she said, "For my next witness, I call Evan Treski to the stand," Evan shot her a furious look. He walked up to the judge's podium like he was walking to the gallows. When he turned to face the court, he had both thumbs hooked in his back pockets, and his shoulders were hunched forward. What was wrong? thought Jessie. They were going to win!

"Mr. Treski," Jessie began. "Can you please tell the court where you were on the afternoon of September fifth?"

"We already know that!" shouted Taffy Morgan, who was sitting in the second row of the jury box. "Ask him something *different!*"

"Yeah!" shouted Tessa James from the audience. "Ask him where he got all that money from. That's what I want to know."

Ben Lesser shouted out the same thing: "Ask him that!" And Nina Lee echoed, "Yeah, ask him that!"

Slowly, Jessie felt her face turning hot. That was the *last* question she wanted to ask Evan while he was on the stand. If the jury found out that Evan had stolen that money from her—it would be all over. Some of the kids in the jury box started to chant, "Ask him! Ask him!"

"Order in the court!" shouted David. When everyone quieted down, he said to Jessie, "That's a good question. Why don't you ask him that?"

"He's *my* witness," said Jessie, "and I get to make up the questions." Jessie knew the rules: She was the lawyer, and nobody could make her ask her witness a question she didn't want to ask. "I'll ask what I want, and I don't want to ask that."

"What?" said Scott. "Have you got something to hide?"

"Leave her alone," said Evan.

"Yeah, leave me alone," said Jessie, looking from David to Scott to Evan.

"Fine," said Scott, crossing his arms and looking smug. "Don't ask him. I'll just have my mom ask him where he got the money."

"Your mom's not even here," said Jessie angrily. "And I bet she won't show up, either."

Scott jumped up to his feet and looked like he was going to take a swing at Jessie. "She will, too. She's just late, that's all. 'Cause she's a *real* lawyer, with *real* work to do. Not like you! You faker!"

"Order in this court, or I will throw you both out!" shouted David. He even stepped in front of the podium and swung his gavel over his head like he was going to bean someone with it. Then he turned to Jessie and said, "You might as well ask

Evan the question, Jessie. He's going to end up answering it anyway."

And Jessie knew he was right.

She'd really made a mess of this. And she'd been feeling so good. So confident. So sure of herself.

"Mr. Treski," she said, "where did you get the money—the two hundred and eight dollars—that you had in your pocket on that day?"

You could have heard a pin drop—except that a pin wouldn't have made any noise at all because of the grass. But it was *quiet* in the court. Even the birds seemed to fall silent as if they were waiting to hear the answer.

Evan mumbled something, and Jessie had to ask him to repeat what he said.

"I took it from your lock box," said Evan, looking at her like he wanted to squash her like a bug.

Nobody said a word. Everyone stared at Evan, and Evan stared at Jessie.

"You *stole* it?" asked Paul, his eyes wide with surprise.

"Man, you never told us *that* part of the story," said Adam, shaking his head.

"Wow. You stole money from your little sister?" said Scott, smiling for the first time all afternoon. "That is *low*."

Jessie looked down at the ground. She knew that Evan was staring at her with a look that said, *I wish you'd never been born.*

"Excuse me?" said a voice from the audience. Jessie turned. It was Megan, and she was raising her hand, like she was in class.

"The bench recognizes Megan Moriarty," said David.

"The bench can't recognize someone from the audience," said Jessie. "The audience isn't allowed to talk during a trial. This is all wrong."

"Well," said David. "I'm the judge, so I get to decide. Megan!"

"Was that my money, too?" Megan asked. She looked straight at Evan. "Was half of that two hundred and eight dollars mine from the lemonade stand?"

Jessie's mouth fell open, but no sound came out. Evan dropped his head into his hands.

Things were coming out in this trial that Jessie had never expected to come out. Like the fact that

Evan had stolen the money from Jessie before Scott stole the money from Evan. Or the fact that half the money he'd lost had been Megan's money. And just because Evan had planned to return the money to Jessie a day later—and she'd forgiven him for taking it in the first place—and just because Jessie and Evan had worked really hard to earn back all of Megan's money so that she'd *never know* she lost it—those facts didn't seem to matter much at all. In the eyes of everyone, it looked like Evan was a thief. A lying thief.

All of a sudden, words started to fly out of Jessie's mouth. "He didn't steal it," she said. "*I* told him to take the money. I gave it to him for safekeeping. He *didn't* steal it." Jessie turned to Megan. "It's my fault your money got stolen."

Evan looked at her. Megan looked at her. Scott looked at her. Everyone in the courtroom stared at Jessie. And all Jessie could think was that she had just told a lie in court. And everyone knew it.

# Chapter 12
# Sixth Amendment

**Sixth Amendment** (sĭksth ə-mĕnd′mənt), *n.* The part of the U.S. Constitution that explains the rights of anyone who is accused of a crime and brought to trial, including the right to legal counsel.

Jessie whispered, "The prosecution rests," and she and Evan went back to their seats. Evan kept his eyes nailed to the ground. He didn't trust himself to look at Jessie. If he did, he knew that all his anger was going to spill over like lava pouring out of a crack in the earth's crust. He'd been humiliated—in front of the entire fourth grade. And even though he knew that Jessie hadn't done it on purpose, it was still *all her fault*. If she hadn't called him as a witness. If she hadn't made David the judge. If she hadn't given Scott Spencer that stupid arrest warrant in the first place, none of this would have happened.

David banged his gavel three times. "Will the lawyer for the defense please step forward?"

Evan saw Scott twist his head around and look at the parking lot. "We gotta wait a couple more minutes," said Scott, matter-of-factly. "My mom's not here yet."

"If she doesn't come," said Paul, "does Scott have to forfeit?"

David flipped through his cards. "Jessie? Does Scott forfeit if his mom doesn't come?"

"Here she is!" shouted Scott, jumping up from his ball. "I told you! I told you!" He turned to Jessie. "Now you're going to see how it's done by a *real* lawyer. She's going to make you look like a fool!" Scott ran off to the parking lot, where a large gray SUV was pulling up to the curb.

Evan watched as Scott ran up to the car and leaned in at the open window, talking with his mom. Scott turned around and pointed at all the kids, sitting in the courtroom. Evan could just barely see Mrs. Spencer, her hands on the wheel, the engine of the car still running. Then Scott stepped back from the car, and it drove away.

Scott came walking back and sat down on his basketball. He shrugged, but Evan could tell it was an act. "She can't stay," said Scott. "She's got a big meeting. Real stuff, not kids' stuff." He shrugged again and looked straight ahead at David, avoiding everyone else's eyes.

"So . . . ?" said David. "What do we do now?" Everyone in the courtroom turned to Jessie, who had been keeping quiet ever since she sat down.

Evan looked at Jessie. She wasn't smiling, and that surprised him. After all, this meant they won, right? At least, that's how it worked in basketball. If the other team didn't show up or didn't have enough players, then they forfeited the game, and that meant your team won automatically. Usually, Evan hated forfeit games, even if it meant winning. He'd rather play and lose than win by forfeit. But this time, Evan would take a win any way he could get it. The image that had been haunting him for days—of standing up at Morning Meeting and apologizing to Scott—began to fade, and a new one took its place: Evan playing with his new Xbox 20/20—with all his friends over at *his* house.

Jessie said, "David, you say, 'Will the lawyer for the defense please step forward,' and then Scott says—well, whatever he wants to say in his own defense, and then he says, 'The defense rests,' and that's it."

"And then the verdict!" said Salley Knight, who was in the jury box. "Then we vote and give the verdict!"

"Right," said Jessie, glumly.

What was her problem? wondered Evan. They were sure to win if Scott had no defense lawyer.

"Ahem." David cleared his voice. "Will the lawyer for the defense please step forward?"

Everyone turned to look at Scott, but it was a

voice from the back of the courtroom that broke the silence.

"That would be me." Megan stood up from the audience and walked to the front of the courtroom.

*What?*

At first Evan thought he must have heard wrong.

Did Megan Moriarty just say that she was going to defend Scott Spencer?

"You can't do that," said Evan, jumping up from his seat. "You're . . . you're . . ." He wanted to shout, *You're supposed to be on my side, not his!,* but he couldn't say that. Not in front of the whole fourth grade.

"Hey!" shouted David, banging his gavel once. "Order in the court. Plaintiff, sit down. If you keep making a disturbance, I'll have you thrown out of court!"

"Oh, right! Like you could!" said Evan, but he sat down on his basketball anyway.

"Jessie," said David, holding up his watch. "It's three-thirty. I've got to go in ten minutes. Is this allowed?"

Jessie nodded her head. "Yes. It's . . . fair."

Evan couldn't believe it. Was this really happening? Was the girl he was *in love with* about to destroy his one and only chance for revenge against his sworn enemy?

Megan turned to Scott. "Do you still not want a girl lawyer?"

Once again, Scott shrugged. "You're all I got. I guess it's okay."

"All right," said Megan. "This won't take long. Can I call my first witness?"

David nodded, and Megan moved to the front of the courtroom.

# Chapter 13
# Circumstantial Evidence

**circumstantial evidence** (sûr′kəm-stăn′shəl ĕv′i-dəns), *n.* Indirect evidence that makes a person *seem* guilty. For example, if a suspect is seen running away from the scene of a crime, a jury might assume that he's guilty of the crime, even though no one saw him commit it.

Megan started with Jack. She asked him three simple questions and told him to answer with just one word: *yes* or *no*.

"Jack, did you ever see the money in Evan's shorts pocket?"

"No."

"Did you see Scott Spencer take anything out of Evan's pocket?"

"No."

"Since that day, have you ever seen Scott Spencer carrying around two hundred and eight dollars?"

"No."

Then, one by one, she called Kevin, Malik, Ryan, and Paul to the witness stand and asked the same three questions. Their answers were all the same—*no*.

Listening, Jessie felt miserable—but she was impressed. In less than five minutes, Megan had unraveled her whole case against Scott Spencer. The truth was, nobody had actually *seen* anything that day at the pool. It was all just guessing about what had happened to Evan's money.

The whole time Megan was asking the witnesses questions, Jessie worried that Megan was going to call Evan to the stand for cross-examining. She knew that Evan would rather pull his hair out, one strand at a time, than get back up on that witness stand. But instead Megan called a different witness—one that even Jessie didn't expect.

"My last witness," Megan said to the jury, "is Scott Spencer."

Scott Spencer had been slouching forward, sitting on his ball, his elbows resting on his knees, his eyes on the ground. Now he straightened up and squared his shoulders. He looked as surprised as anyone to hear his name called out in court.

"I don't want to," he said. He looked defiantly at Megan and then at David, as if he was going to challenge both of them to a fight.

David pointed his gavel at him. "Well, you have to. You've got to do what your lawyer says."

Jessie was fairly certain that this wasn't true. She thought she remembered a rule that said you didn't have to testify against yourself in court, but she wasn't positive, so she didn't say anything.

Scott stood up, shoving his basketball with his heel so that it rolled a few feet toward the back of the courtroom. He walked to the podium and put his right hand over his heart and raised his left.

"Do you swear to tell the truth, the whole truth, and nothing but the truth?" asked the judge.

"Yeah," said Scott, but he said it long and low, like the word was being pulled out of his mouth on a rope.

"I just have one question," said Megan, "and it's an easy one." She put her hands on her hips and faced him straight on. "Did you really pay for your new Xbox 20/20 with your own money?"

"What?" said Scott, like he couldn't believe what he'd just heard. He turned to David K. "I'm not going to answer that. I don't have to answer that question."

"Yes, you do!" said David. "Or I'll hold you in contempt." He banged his gavel sharply once to let Scott know that he was serious.

Jessie looked at Scott and knew exactly how he felt. *Everyone* was staring at him.

"Well—I—" Not a single person made a sound. Even the branches of the elm trees stopped moving, the gentle rustling of the leaves dying down to silence.

"Remember," said Megan quietly. "You're under oath."

Scott made a sour face. "*No.* I didn't. You happy?" He smirked at Megan. "My parents bought it for me."

Everybody started shouting then. "I knew it! I knew it!" said Adam. David had to whack his gavel about ten times to get 4-O to quiet down. "The witness is excused! Closing arguments! The prosecution goes first! Hurry up!"

Jessie stood up. This was supposed to have been her big moment.

"I wrote a really great closing argument," she said, pulling some index cards from her back pocket, "but I guess we don't have time for it. So I'll just say this."

She walked over to the jury box. Twelve pairs of eyes stared right back at her. Some of the jurors, like Adam and Salley, she knew well enough, but most of them she hardly knew at all. Now they were all looking at her. Everyone in the jury box was waiting to hear what she had to say.

"Ladies and gentlemen of the jury," she began.

"The facts are the facts. The money was in Evan's shorts, safely folded up in Jack's room. Scott went into Jack's room and then went running home, like a guilty crook. When Evan went upstairs, his shorts were unfolded and the money was gone. It doesn't take a genius to solve this crime. In the end, it comes down to who's telling the truth. So think of all the years you've known Evan Treski and all the years you've known Scott Spencer, and ask yourself this: Who do *you* believe?"

Jessie stuffed her index cards back in her pants pocket. She hadn't even gotten to use them. And she'd spent all that time writing a really great closing argument. This trial was nothing like what she'd thought it would be.

"Okay, done," said David. "Now, the closing argument for the defense. *Fast,* Megan."

Megan stood up and walked to the jury box. "Here's the thing," she said. "You can't convict Scott, because there's absolutely no proof. It's all just us imagining what happened. We don't know for sure, because nobody *saw* anything, and the money never turned up, so . . . we just don't know. And I guess we'll never really know what happened that afternoon." Megan looked at David. "That's it," she said.

"Done!" shouted David, banging his gavel again. "Jury, make your decision!"

"My mom's here!" said Salley Knight, noticing a car parked in the parking lot.

"So's mine," said Carly Brownell.

"Jury! Huddle up!" shouted Adam. All twelve members of the jury formed a tight circle, their heads bowed together, their backs to the courtroom.

Jessie stood up, then sat down, then stood up again. She felt that dangerously bubbly feeling she sometimes got in her stomach. She started to think: If she had to throw up, where would be the best place to do it? Behind the podium? By the trees? Could she make it to a bathroom in time? She wished she could talk to Evan, but one look at him told her she'd better stay clear. His mouth was clenched so tight, it looked like he would bite through his own teeth.

"Break!" shouted Adam, clapping his hands together loudly. The jury huddle broke up, and Jessie saw Adam quickly scribble something on a slip of paper, then hand the paper to David.

"All rise to hear the verdict of the jury," said David. Everyone stood.

Jessie felt her breath catch in her throat. She tried to swallow, but it was as if the muscles in her neck were paralyzed. A picture swam into her head: standing up in front of the whole class and apologizing to Scott Spencer.

"My mom's coming over," said Carly, pointing to the parking lot. Jessie turned to see a tall woman wearing sunglasses and a baseball cap heading toward them.

"Hurry up!" said Adam.

"Okay," said David, his voice rising to a squeak. "I'm supposed to say all this official stuff, but I'll just read the verdict out loud! The verdict is—not guilty!"

"Yes!" shouted Scott Spencer, jumping in the air and double-pumping both fists over his head. "I win! Man, I cannot wait for Monday morning!"

But nobody else moved. And nobody else said a word.

Something had gone terribly wrong out here on the playground. In the shade of the elm trees, away from the scolding eyes of duty teachers and parents, the kids in 4-O had created a court all their own and followed all the rules—but somehow come out with the wrong answer. Jessie felt it, and so did everyone else. Jessie was sure of it.

"Are we done?" asked David, holding his gavel aloft. "Jessie?"

Jessie nodded.

"This court is adjourned," David said, and hit the gavel once on the wooden block, just as Carly Brownell's mother came up alongside her daughter.

"What are you kids playing?" she asked.

"Nothing," said Carly. She picked up her book bag and headed for the parking lot with her mother. David stuffed the black robe and gavel into his brown paper bag and headed for the path. About half of the other kids followed, but the rest of the fourth-graders stayed where they were.

All of a sudden, a voice sliced through the air. "This is *not* over!"

Evan was standing with the basketball in his hands. "You and me!" he said, poking Scott Spencer in the chest so hard, Scott took a step back. "On the court. The basketball court."

# Chapter 14
# Fighting words

**fighting words** (fī′ting wûrdz), *n*. Words that are so venomous and full of malice that they cause another person to fight back physically. Fighting words are not protected as free speech under the First Amendment.

"You're on," said Scott.

Nobody bothered to pick up any of the equipment. The jump ropes, the Frisbees, the milk crate, the extra balls were all left right where they were. Instead, all the kids of 4-O who hadn't gone home lined up on either side of the basketball court.

Evan dribbled the ball, trying to get that feeling of looseness that helped him play his best. "We'll play to seven by ones. Straight up. King's court. And you have to take it past the big crack to clear." Evan pointed to the wide crack in the blacktop that ran twenty feet from the basket. That was the line they always used to clear the ball for half-court games.

"Who's the ref?" asked Scott.

"No ref, no fouls," said Evan. "Just play. If the ball falls through the hoop, it's a point. If it doesn't, go home and cry to your mother. Okay?" Evan was practicing his crossover dribbling while he talked. He was starting to feel his rhythm. He looked at Scott standing at the top of the key. There it was, that look on Scott's face—the one that seemed to say, *Why bother? I always win.* More than anything else, Evan wanted to wipe that look off Scott Spencer's face, once and for all.

"Yeah, okay," said Scott. "But who goes first?"

"You," said Evan, shooting him a chest pass so fast that Scott didn't even have time to put his arms up. The ball hit him in the chest and fell at his feet.

Evan heard some of the kids laugh and noticed Megan crossing her arms and frowning. "Good start!" shouted Paul from the sidelines, as Scott picked up the ball and cleared it behind the line.

"Nice, Treski," said Scott. "Real nice."

Evan ran up to the clear line and got low, ready to defend.

Scott dribbled the ball, hanging behind the line. Then he faked left and drove right, blowing past Evan.

Scott was quick, but Evan was quicker. He came up from behind, and just as Scott was shooting the ball, Evan clawed it out of the air, whacking it so hard it smacked down on the blacktop. On the way, his hand smashed into Scott's face. Scott crumpled to the ground. Undefended, Evan took the easy shot and scored his first point.

"You can't do that!" said Scott. "You *mauled* me!" He sat on the blacktop, his legs sprawled, looking like he couldn't even get up.

Evan rebounded and dribbled toward the clear line. He put a hand up to his ear and pretended to concentrate hard. "Do you hear a whistle, Scott? I guess not, 'cause there isn't one. *Man up.*"

Scott jumped to his feet, and Ryan yelled out, "Faker!"

"One–nothing," called out Adam. "Evan's ball."

Evan didn't even bother to juke. He just plowed right into Scott, driving him to the blacktop before charging the basket for the easy lay-up.

"Oh, man!" shouted Ryan.

Megan shook her head. "Why even call it basket-ball if you're going to play like that?"

Evan watched as Scott started to get up slowly. But he had already cleared the ball at the line and was charging to the basket before Scott got on his feet. He made another easy lay-up, as pretty as a bird.

"Three–zip," shouted Adam.

"Scott," said Ryan. "C'mon, show a little backbone."

This time, when Evan started his move to the basket, Scott lunged at the ball. He stripped it from Evan's hands, but the ball went shooting out of bounds.

"Out," shouted Adam. "Evan's ball!" So Evan took it out again, and this time he faked left, right, left, so that Scott was leaning the wrong way when Evan finally made his move.

"It's basketball, Scott. Not freeze tag!" called out Kevin.

Evan slowly dribbled the ball back. Scott faced him across the line, scowling, with his hands on his hips. "None of this counts," said Scott. "This is dirt ball. This is trash. None of this counts."

"Why not?" said Evan, dribbling steadily. "You agreed. No fouls. You said okay. Right?"

He took a step past the clear line, still dribbling the ball slowly right in front of his body. Then Evan spread his hands out wide, the ball bouncing between the two of them, unprotected. "Go on, take it!"

When Scott made his move, trying to grab the ball out of the air, Evan was ready. Faster than an eagle diving, he snatched the ball back, made a spin move around Scott, and drove for the basket. He jumped as high as he could, and just barely managed to stuff the ball with both hands through the hoop.

"Slammed!" screamed Paul, doing a dance on the sidelines.

"This is gross," said Megan. "I'm going home." She picked up her mailbag and slung it over her shoulder. "Jessie, are you coming?"

"No," said Jessie in a small voice. She was sitting on the grass, her knees pulled up to her chest. "I'll stay." Megan nodded, then walked toward the parking lot. Evan noticed her leaving, but told himself, *Who cares?*

"Four–nothing," said Adam. "Hey, Evan. Wrap it up, would you? I have to get home."

Evan quickly ran the score up to six–nothing with a jump shot from mid-key and a little floater right in front of the basket.

All the guys on the sideline were screaming *Shutout, shutout!,* and Evan dribbled the ball in time to their chant. He glanced at Scott. Scott was breathing so hard, he looked like he might throw up. Both his knees and one of his elbows were bloody. *He's right,* thought Evan. *This isn't basketball. It's revenge ball.*

"You want the ball?" asked Evan. "Here. You can have it." He let the ball roll off the tips of his fingers so that it dribbled over to Scott. "Don't say I didn't show you mercy," said Evan as Scott picked up the ball and they swapped places, Evan switching to defense. "Go on, I'll even back off. I'll give you all the room in the world. You still can't make a basket against me."

Scott dribbled the ball slowly, and Evan could see that he was trying to come up with a strategy. There was no way he could push past Evan, because Evan had the weight, and there was no way he could speed past him, because Evan was faster. The only way Scott Spencer was going to get the drop on Evan was by tricking him. That's all Scott had, thought Evan. That's all Scott ever had.

Scott started dribbling slowly toward the basket. Evan moved into position, blocking the lane, but still giving Scott plenty of room. He kept his eyes locked on Scott's.

Suddenly, Scott's mouth dropped open. He stopped dribbling the ball and shouted, "Oh, my god! Jessie, are you okay?"

Evan spun around. Where was she? Was she on the Green Machine? Had she fallen? She was such a klutz. She could hardly walk across a room without tripping.

Evan's eyes had just caught sight of her—Jessie, sitting on the sidelines, the way she always did, her knees tucked up to her chin, watching the game intently—when he figured it out. But by then Scott was past him, driving to the basket. Evan almost got there in time to block the shot, but almost doesn't count. Scott's shot was rushed and weak. It circled the rim—and then fell through.

"I can't believe you fell for that, dog!" shouted Kevin.

"The oldest trick in the book," said Paul, shaking his head.

"Six–one," shouted Adam. "Scott's ball."

Scott took the ball and shrugged as he dribbled past Evan. "King's court, right?"

Evan had never in his life had a feeling like this. Not when he broke his leg. Not when his father left. Not even when Jessie put bugs in his lemonade. This was worse. This was stronger. This felt like everything to him.

So when Scott made for the basket, Evan came at him with both hands up, and it must have been the look on his face that made Scott freeze and lose half a step. That's all it took. Evan stripped the ball and headed for the top of the key.

He could have just dribbled to the basket and made the shot, and that would have been that. The game would have been over. And he would have won.

But no.

He wanted to make Scott pay. He wanted to make sure that when they told the story—for days, for weeks, for years—of how Scott Spencer got *crushed* on the basketball court, they would talk about the final shot that Evan Treski made.

So he headed for the top of the key and planted his feet so that he could make that beautiful turn-around jumper that he'd been practicing for months. He stood there, dribbling the ball, practically shouting out to Scott, *Yeah, come get me.* And when Scott did, Evan turned and threw an elbow that caught Scott right on the side of the face.

Scott went flying and landed hard on his rear end, his hands scraping along the blacktop. Evan didn't even look over to see if Scott was okay. He dribbled once, twice, three times, then jumped in the air, twisted his body, and let fly the ball.

Everyone watched as it sailed through the air and then swooshed through the hoop.

Nothing but net.

The ball dropped to the blacktop and bounced. Nobody made a move for it. Nobody said anything. Scott was still sitting on the ground, the blood on his hands a bright red. Evan was standing, his arms at his side. He felt like he'd been through a fistfight.

Scott got up slowly, picked up the basketball, and then drop-kicked it as hard as he could so that it sailed over the fence and disappeared into the swamp. Then he ran.

# Chapter 15
# Balance

**balance** (băl′əns), *n.* A device used for weighing that has a pivoted horizontal beam from which hang two scales. In statues and paintings, the figure of Justice is often shown holding a balance.

"Grandma, can you talk for a minute?" Jessie stuck a moshi pillow behind her head and cradled the phone to her ear.

"Sure, Jessie Bean. What's up?" Jessie's grandmother lived four hours away, so Jessie called her on the phone a lot.

"Everything's awful," said Jessie, picking at a corner of her bedroom wallpaper that was peeling. She explained to her grandmother about the trial yester-day and the basketball game and Scott kicking the ball into the swamp. She told her how Evan had to hunt for the ball for half an hour before finally find-ing it, and how he told all his friends to just go home, he'd find it himself, *just go home.* So they did. And how Evan and Jessie were left to look for the ball, and how Evan didn't talk the whole time they did.

"And today he's not even *eating,* or anything," said Jessie. "Did you know that it's Yom Kippur?"

"Yom Kippur, is that the one where the kids dress up?" asked Jessie's grandmother.

"No, that's Purim." Grandma was always mixing up things like that, things that sounded kind of the same, but were different. During their last phone call, she was talking with Jessie about the sequoia trees in California, but she kept using the word *sequester* in-stead. "Yom Kippur is the day when the Jewish peo-ple ask for forgiveness and they don't eat."

"Is Evan Jewish now?" asked Grandma.

"No, but he's not eating. He says he's not hun-gry," said Jessie.

"Sometimes that happens to me," Grandma said. "I practically forget to eat."

"But Evan's *always* hungry," said Jessie. "Mom says he's a bottomless pit."

"He'll eat when he's ready," said Grandma. "Let it go."

Jessie hated it when her grandmother said that. She was always telling Jessie to *let it go* and *be the tree*. Crazy yoga grandma. How could anyone be a tree?

"But . . . I want to do something to help," said Jessie.

"Why don't you bake cookies?" said Grandma. "That'll get him to eat. Right?"

"I don't think so," said Jessie. "Not this time." This was bigger than cookies. How could she explain to her grandmother how bad things were?

Jessie had believed in the trial. She had thought the truth would come out in court, and with truth would come justice.

But instead of truth in the courtroom, there had been lies, including hers. Instead of justice, there was a crime with no punishment. And now she and Evan

131

were going to have to stand up in front of the entire fourth grade and say that they had been wrong—even though Jessie knew that wasn't true.

"Grandma, it's so unfair," said Jessie. "I know Scott Spencer took that money. I know he's lying. And now it feels like I did all this work, just so he'd end up looking innocent!"

"Some things are beyond your control, Jessie," said her grandmother. "You need to learn to accept that. You can't run the whole world."

*I wish I did,* thought Jessie. The world would be a better place if she was in charge. But then . . . she thought of the terrible thing she'd done.

"Grandma," she blurted out. "I lied in court." She explained how it had happened. Her grandmother listened to the whole story without interrupting.

"Lying is wrong," Grandma said, "but at least you did it from a good place in your heart. You don't need to feel ashamed about loving your brother."

"I still feel really bad about it," said Jessie.

"That's good," said Grandma. "I'd be worried if

you didn't feel bad about lying. You *do* have control over that. Nobody can make you lie. So feel bad for a while, and always remember what you've learned, and then move on and be a better person. But don't beat yourself up, Jessie. You're only seven."

"Grandma! I'm eight!" said Jessie. How could her grandmother forget her age?

"Really?" said Grandma. "Are you sure?"

"I've been eight for almost a whole year. My birthday is next month."

"Good," said Grandma, "because I have a book I've been meaning to send you, and it will be the perfect birthday present."

"Grandma," said Jessie, her voice sounding a warning. "You're not going to send me *The Prince and the Pauper* again, are you?"

"No, Miss Smarty Pants! I remember I sent you that book—twice! You'll never let me forget that, will you?"

"Why do you forget things?" asked Jessie. "You didn't used to."

"Oh, Jessie Bean, I'm getting old." Her grandmother laughed quietly, and Jessie hugged the phone closer. "And that's something neither of us has any control over. Sorry to say."

Jessie heard the doorbell ring downstairs. She knew her mother wouldn't hear it all the way up in the attic office, and she was pretty sure that Evan wouldn't answer it, even if he did hear it. "Gotta go, Grandma," said Jessie. "There's someone at the door."

"Okay, Honey Bear. Be the tree! And bake cookies! I love you."

Jessie ran downstairs and opened the front door. There was Megan.

"Hi," said Megan.

Jessie lifted her hand in a short wave, but she didn't invite Megan in.

"I thought maybe you were mad at me," said Megan.

"Kind of," said Jessie. There was a short silence. "Why'd you do it?" Jessie hadn't wanted to believe that she was angry at her best friend, but now all the questions that she had tried to ignore since the trial came flooding into her brain. *Why'd you ruin all my hard work? Why'd you get Scott off the hook? Why'd you betray me and Evan?*

"I'm sorry, Jessie," said Megan. "I didn't want to make you mad, and I didn't want to mess up your trial, but the thing is, it wasn't really your trial. It was all of ours." Megan looked right at her. "You did this great thing, Jessie. You gave us a real court. Not some fake, dress-up, pretend thing. A real one. But in a real court of law, everyone has the right to a lawyer. So, somebody had to stand up for Scott. Otherwise, the trial would have been a great big fake."

Jessie didn't say anything, but she understood exactly what Megan was saying. Somewhere in the back of her brain, she'd known it all along. "I wanted to win," she said finally, feeling all over again the pain of losing. "But you're right. You did the right thing."

The two girls stood there, both looking at their feet. Why was it so hard to talk about feelings?

"I'm not mad at you anymore," Jessie said, knowing that it was mostly true and that by tomorrow it would be completely true.

Megan smiled. "See you on Monday, Jess." She hopped down the front steps.

"Hey, Megan?" called out Jessie. "Do you think Scott took the money?"

"Yep, I do," said Megan. She shrugged, and the look on her face seemed to say, *That's life.*

Jessie watched her friend walk down the street. It was a gorgeous end-of-summer-just-starting-to-be-fall day. The trees swayed in the breeze. The sky was the color of cornflowers. The sun felt good on her skin.

Jessie ran upstairs to her room and found the yoga book that her grandmother had given her the past Christmas. She flipped to page 48 and stared at the picture.

"Be the tree," Jessie murmured to herself. Slowly, she picked up her left foot and rested it on her right knee, finding and holding her balance for one blissful second.

## Chapter 16
# Amends

**amends** (ə-měndz′), *n.* Legal compensation (of money or other valuable assets) as a repair for loss, damage, or injury of any kind.

In his whole life, Evan had never gone this long without eating. And the weirdest thing of all was that he wasn't even hungry anymore. Sometime around two o'clock on Saturday afternoon, his hunger had just disappeared. Like turning off a light switch. He felt empty and light and a little buzzy in his head. But not hungry.

He hadn't even planned it. Yesterday, he'd come home and eaten his dinner, as usual. And then the sun went down and he thought about Adam and

Paul, and he wondered if they had started fasting and if they would make it all the way till tomorrow night. And then he wanted to see if he could do it. Go twenty-four hours without food. Just wanted to see what it was like, and if he had the strength to do it.

And that got him thinking about the Day of Atonement. The less he ate, the more he thought, until here he was, sitting on his branch of the Climbing Tree, way up high with the leaves whispering to him and the birds pecking for their last snack of the day and late-afternoon shadows beginning to stretch across the yard.

He began to think about his sins. And that was a hard thing to think about. Did he really have any sins? He didn't know. But there was one thing he did know. Right now, he felt lousy. And Evan knew that when he felt really bad, that usually meant he'd done something he regretted.

Evan regretted that whole basketball game. He wished he hadn't played like that. He wished Megan hadn't seen him play like that. Or Jessie. Or anyone. He wished he hadn't been such a jerk. The game kept playing over and over in his head, every perfect shot looping through his brain, and it made him feel sick. He was never going to know what had happened to that missing money, but crushing Scott on the basketball court wasn't going to change that.

Evan climbed down from the tree and went into the house. Jessie was in the kitchen with a mixing bowl and a bunch of ingredients spread out on the countertop: flour, sugar, butter, and eggs.

"What'cha makin'?" he asked as he walked through.

"Your favorite. Chocolate chip."

"Thanks," said Evan, grabbing his baseball hat from the front hall closet and heading for the door.

"Where are you going?" asked Jessie.

"Scott's."

"No!" said Jessie. "Don't do that."

"Quit worrying! Tell Mom where I went, okay?" Jessie followed him to the door. "And don't eat all the cookies before I get back," he shouted over his shoulder.

He didn't really have a plan. In the back of his

mind he figured a handshake and at least one "I'm sorry" were somewhere in his future. Beyond that, he didn't know what would happen.

Scott's house was a short bike ride away from Evan's, but his neighborhood was a world apart. The houses were huge and had fancy bushes planted in little groups and two-car attached garages and lawns that looked like they were edged with a razor blade. As Evan walked up the brick path to the front door, he noticed that the two large maple trees in the yard were beginning to turn. They would drop a lot of leaves next month, but Evan knew that Scott never had to rake because his family had a service that took care of the yard.

When the front door opened, Evan wasn't surprised to see Scott standing there. Evan could hardly ever remember Scott's parents answering the door.

He looked better than he had yesterday, that was for sure. Cleaned up, no blood, and he was wearing jeans, which covered up his knees. But the look on his face was the same—a look of hatred. Pure hatred beamed right at Evan.

"Hey," said Evan.

"What?" said Scott. "What do you want?"

Evan hadn't rehearsed what he was going to say, and now that he had Scott's angry face right in front of him, it was hard to come up with anything on the spot. He stood there for a minute, his mind a blank. What *had* he come here for?

And then he said the only thing he could think of. "I wanted to see your new 20/20."

That changed everything. Scott stopped scowling, and his arms loosened up. He waited just a second before saying, "Okay." Then he stepped back to let Evan through. That's how it had been, ever since they were little: Scott Spencer liked showing off his new toys.

Evan followed Scott down the flight of stairs to the finished basement, which was a combination playroom and family room. It was mostly the way that Evan remembered it: two couches, the computer desk, the file cabinet with the locked-up snacks, bins of toys and building things, sports equipment, the swinging chair that hung from the ceiling, an electronic keyboard, and a treadmill. The thing that caught his eye, though, was the new TV. It was enormous, the biggest flat-screen plasma that Evan had ever seen in his whole life.

"Wow!" said Evan.

Scott smiled. "Yeah, my dad bought that a few weeks ago. Cool, huh?"

Evan noticed the sleek white box hooked up to the TV. "Is that the 20/20?" he asked. "Wow, it's so small."

"Yeah, but watch what it can do."

Scott handed him two thick gloves that looked like hockey gloves, except that they were white, and a pair of heavy, dark goggles that wrapped all the way around his head. Evan took off his baseball cap and put the gloves and goggles on, then Scott pushed a button on the box. The next thing Evan knew, he was driving a car on a racetrack, with other cars whipping past him at about 120 miles per hour.

"Whoa!" shouted Evan.

"Turn to your right! With your gloves! Pretend you're holding a steering wheel and turn to your right!" screamed Scott.

Evan just barely missed crashing into the haystack barriers that protected the curves of the racetrack. He quickly grabbed hold of an imaginary steering wheel and got himself back on the road.

"Squeeze your right hand to go faster, and your left hand to slow down," said Scott, turning up the volume so that the roar of the racecars filled Evan's ears. Evan could practically smell the exhaust fumes.

For the next five minutes, Evan took the ride of his life. He had never, ever played on a game system that was so much fun. No wonder Scott couldn't stop talking about it.

"Scott. Scott!" yelled a voice from behind.

Evan turned and whipped off the goggles. Mr. Spencer was standing at the top of the stairs. Scott jumped to turn down the volume on the TV.

"I've been calling you for the last five minutes. Will you turn that thing down? Do you have any idea how loud it is?"

"Sorry, Dad," said Scott. "We were just playing Road Rage."

"Well, you're going to blow out the speakers on the TV, and then *you'll* be the one to buy me a new one. And don't think I won't hold you to that. I didn't spend five thousand dollars on a new TV just so you could destroy it with your video games. That's an expensive piece of equipment, and you need to learn how to treat it with respect. Now keep it down. I'm trying to work."

"Yes, sir," said Scott.

Mr. Spencer turned and disappeared at the top of the stairs.

Scott picked up a baseball and started throwing it back and forth in his hands. Evan wasn't sure what to do. He put the gloves and goggles down on the floor. The racecars were still zooming by on the TV screen, but without any sound, they seemed silly and fake.

"Your dad works a lot, huh?" said Evan.

"Even on a Saturday," said Scott, throwing the ball.

"My mom works a lot, too," said Evan, but in his head he thought, *But at least she doesn't yell at us for making noise.*

"Yeah, whatever," said Scott. "You wanna play

Crisis? It's cool." And with that, he chucked the baseball to the corner of the room. Only it was harder than a chuck, and his aim was off. Way off. The ball winged across the room and caught the corner of the TV screen. There was a loud crash, and then the TV went dead.

Both boys froze. Evan couldn't make a sound. He felt like he had a sock stuffed down his throat. There was a foot-long crack in the TV screen and a bunch of smaller cracks that looked like a spider web. The house was completely silent except for the noise of Mr. Spencer's footsteps running down the stairs. And then he was there, standing in the doorway, staring at the TV.

"Did you do that on purpose?" he shouted at Scott.

"No!" said Scott. "I didn't . . ."

"Because you are going to pay for that. Every penny of it. Your allowance, your birthday money— forget Christmas presents this year. Do you understand?" A vein popped out on Mr. Spencer's forehead, like something in an alien movie. Every time he said a word that started with *p*—*pay, penny, presents*—white flecks of spit flew out of his mouth. Evan thought he was going to explode or something.

"Dad, I didn't . . ."

"That television is brand-new. *Brand-new,* do you hear me?"

Evan took half a sideways step toward Scott. "We're sorry. We didn't mean to do it. It was an accident."

Mr. Spencer looked at Evan for the first time since coming downstairs. It was almost like he'd forgotten there was anyone else in the room. Slowly, he breathed in and out. His teeth were clenched; his jaw was as hard as a rock wall. "Did *you* throw the ball?"

"No, but, we were, you know, playing, and the ball just kind of—hit the TV by mistake. We didn't do it on purpose." Evan was scared, but he couldn't help thinking what a jerk Mr. Spencer was. Sure, his mom got mad—plenty of times—and sometimes she yelled, but not when it was an honest accident.

"We're sorry, Dad," said Scott in a low voice.

"Well, that doesn't fix the TV, does it?" said Mr. Spencer. Without another word, he walked out.

The room was quiet.

"Okay, then," said Evan, just to fill the awkward silence.

Scott looked down at the ground. "Yeah," he said. He looked like his dog had just died.

Evan picked up his baseball cap and jammed it on his head, backwards. "So, this was fun," he said, deadpan, but Scott didn't smile, or even lift his eyes off the floor. Evan could understand. It was lousy when your own parent yelled like that in front of another kid. It made you feel like your whole family was just dirt. Scott probably wanted him to leave.

"Well, I'd better get home."

"Okay," said Scott. "And thanks. You know. For stepping in like that."

"Sure. No problem."

" 'Cause, like, my dad loves that TV. I mean, he really loves it. So thanks."

"It's what friends do," said Evan, turning to leave.

That caught him by surprise. He hadn't meant to say *that*. It was a little hard to think of Scott as a friend after everything that had happened. But— where were they? He and Scott? Not friends. But not enemies. Somewhere between. Someplace that didn't have a name, or even any rules.

Evan scratched the back of his neck. "So, you know, I'm sorry," he said. "I'm sorry about the basketball game yesterday and the trial and everything. Look, you say you didn't take the money, and that means you didn't take the money. And I'm sorry I made such a big deal out of it and that I was such a jerk."

Scott nodded his head once. "Yeah, well, forget about the Morning Meeting thing. You know, you and Jessie apologizing. Because—well, just forget about it."

Okay. Evan felt better. He felt better than he had all week. It was like he'd been carrying a backpack full of rocks for days and days, but now he felt so light, he could practically fly. And man, was he *hun-*

*gry.* He could hear the chocolate chip cookies calling to him from all the way down the street.

Scott still looked pretty miserable, though, so Evan just said "See ya" and turned to leave.

He was at the top of the stairs when Scott called out, "Hang on." Evan turned and watched as Scott reached into his pocket and pulled out a key, then used it to unlock the file cabinet in the corner. Evan hoped he was going to offer him a Yodel for the road. A Yodel would taste pretty good right now.

But it wasn't a Yodel that Scott pulled out of the file cabinet. It was an envelope, and Evan recognized it right away.

It was Jessie's envelope. The one that had $208 in it.

Scott handed it to him. "I'm sorry I stole your money."

Evan took the fat envelope. He'd forgotten what a thick wad the $208 was. All that work. All that sweat. Mixing the lemonade and hauling it all over town and standing in the hot summer sun. And then having to tell Jessie that he'd lost the money. That had been the worst part of all.

"I guess you're pretty mad, huh?" said Scott.

Evan was surprised to hear himself say, "No." And surprised to know that he meant it. Maybe it was the crummy trial or the nasty basketball game or the fact that he hadn't eaten anything in nearly twenty-four hours. Whatever it was, Evan felt emptied out. There just wasn't any anger left inside him.

"Why'd you take it, though?" he asked, looking at the money.

Scott shrugged. "I don't know. 'Cause you had it, I guess."

"Oh," said Evan. That didn't make sense to him. It's not like Scott needed the money. After all, his parents bought him everything he wanted: the newest iPod, the best hockey skates, the biggest TV. It just didn't make sense to Evan.

But some things never do.

"I gotta go," Evan said, stuffing the envelope into the front of his shorts. The sun was low in the sky, and his mother didn't let him ride his bike after dark. Soon, he'd go over to Adam's house for the big meal that marked the end of the Day of Atonement. "See you," he said to Scott.

"Yeah, later." They both walked out into the front yard, then Evan climbed on his bike.

"Hey!" shouted Evan as he pedaled down the driveway. "The next time a ball goes over the fence, it's got *your* name on it. You owe me for that!"

Evan didn't stick around to hear Scott's reply. It would come up again—the ball in the swamp—the next time they were messing around on the basketball court.

# Solemn Pact of Silence

This contract is <u>legal</u> and <u>binding</u> for all parties who sign below.

The undersigned do solemnly swear to never reveal to the members of classroom 4-O, or to any adults who might ask questions, what really happened to the two hundred and eight dollars that went missing from Evan Treski's shorts pocket on September 5th.

This matter is considered closed, now and forever, and the details of it will be sealed for all time.

*Evan Treski*

*Jessie Treski*

*Scott Spencer*

# The Bell Bandit

by Jacqueline Davies

Houghton Mifflin Harcourt
Boston  New York

This one is for Ann Rider,
who always sees straight to the heart of
a book—and doesn't flinch.

# Contents

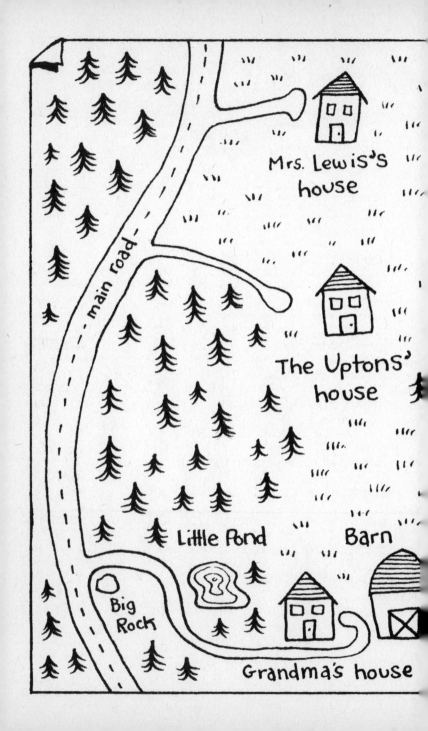

*excerpt from*

RING OUT, WILD BELLS
*by Alfred, Lord Tennyson*

Ring out, wild bells, to the wild sky,
  The flying cloud, the frosty light:
  The year is dying in the night;
Ring out, wild bells, and let him die.

Ring out the old, ring in the new,
  Ring, happy bells, across the snow:
  The year is going, let him go;
Ring out the false, ring in the true.

# Chapter 1
# Stuck in the Back

"How much longer?" Jessie asked from the back seat, tapping the window glass three times. Jessie always tapped the window three times when they passed under a bridge.

"Another hour," said Mrs. Treski. She glanced at the clock on the dashboard. "At least."

They had already been driving for three hours, climbing steadily higher and higher into the mountains, and Jessie could feel herself sinking into a sulk. Everything about this trip to Grandma's house was different.

First of all, Evan was sitting in the front seat.

Jessie could tell he was listening to his iPod. From behind, she could see his head bobbing slightly

1

to the beat of the music as he stared out the window.

Evan had never been allowed to sit up front before. But this time when he'd asked—for the ten thousandth time—Mrs. Treski had given him a long, thoughtful look and said yes. He was ten and tall for his age, so Mrs. Treski said he was old enough to move up front.

Jessie was nine—and stuck in the back.

"Hey," Jessie said, trying to get Evan to turn around and notice her. But he didn't. He couldn't hear her. It was like he wasn't even in the car with her.

Jessie stared out the window at the farmland as it whizzed by them. Usually, she loved this drive. She loved to count things along the way—cows, hawks, Mini Coopers, out-of-state license plates. She kept tally marks in her notebook, and at the end of the trip, she would count them all up to see who had won. It was almost always the cows.

She also tracked their progress by looking for important landmarks along the way—like the pest control building that had a forty-foot fiberglass cockroach creeping over the roof, or the two-story carved wooden totem pole that was really a cell phone tower, or the billboard for a diner that had a big metal teapot with real steam coming out of it.

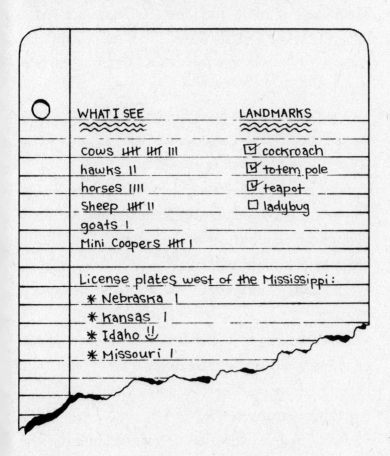

WHAT I SEE

cows HH HH III
hawks II
horses IIII
sheep HH II
goats I
Mini Coopers HH I

LANDMARKS

☑ cockroach
☑ totem pole
☑ teapot
☐ ladybug

License plates west of the Mississippi:
 ✻ Nebraska I
 ✻ Kansas I
 ✻ Idaho ☺
 ✻ Missouri I

Evan used to be on the lookout for these landmarks, too, and it was a race to see who could spot each one first. But this year, he didn't seem to care. Even when the giant water storage tank painted like a ladybug came into view and Jessie pointed it out to him, he just shrugged, as if he couldn't be bothered. He was no fun, and suddenly the trip felt long.

They passed under another bridge, and Jessie tapped the window three times. "Why did Grandma set her house on fire?" she asked.

Mrs. Treski's eyes shifted from the road to the rearview mirror, locking on Jessie's reflection for a second before returning to the highway. "She didn't mean to. It was an accident."

"I know," said Jessie. "But why did it happen *this* time?"

Mrs. Treski tipped her head to one side. "Accidents happen. Sometimes there's no reason. She left something on the stove, and it caught on fire. It could happen to anyone."

But it hadn't happened to her grandmother be-

4

fore. Jessie thought about all the times Grandma had cooked noodles for her or made hot chocolate for her or heated up soup for her. Not once had she set the house on fire.

It was because of the fire that they were driving up to Grandma's two days *after* Christmas instead of the day *before,* the way they always did. And it was because of the fire that they weren't even sure if they would be staying at Grandma's for New Year's Eve the way they did every year. And that was the really big thing that was different this time.

For as long as Jessie could remember, New Year's Eve meant staying at Grandma's house and the long, slow climb to the top of Lovell's Hill, where the trees parted and the sky opened and there stood the old iron bell hanging on its heavy wooden crossbeam.

Just before midnight they would gather, walking through the snow-covered woods, coming from all sides of the hill—neighbors and friends, family and sometimes even strangers—to sing the old songs and talk about the year gone by.

And then, just before midnight, the youngest

one in the crowd and the oldest one, too, would step forward and both take hold of the rope that hung from the clapper of the dark and heavy bell, and at precisely the right moment, they would ring in the New Year, as loudly and joyously and for as long as they wanted.

Jessie remembered the year when *she* had been the youngest one on the hill, and what it felt like when Mrs. Lewis, who was eighty-four that year, had closed her soft, papery hand over hers. They had swung the rope back and forth, over and over, until the noise of the bell filled the snow-covered valley below and the echoes of each peal bounced off of Black Bear Mountain and came racing back to them, like an old faithful dog that always comes home.

But this year, everything was upside down. They might not even spend New Year's Eve at Grandma's house. It all depended, Mrs. Treski said. On what? Jessie wondered. She tapped her right knee twice. Not spend New Year's Eve at Grandma's? Who would ring the bell?

Jessie jiggled her legs up and down. Her left foot was feeling prickly because she'd had it tucked up under her for the last half-hour. "How much longer to the Crossroads Store?" she asked.

"Oh, Jessie . . ." said her mother, looking in the rearview mirror again. "Do you need to stop?"

"What do you mean?" asked Jessie. It wasn't a question of whether she *needed* to—although now that she thought of it, a trip to the bathroom sounded like a good idea. "We always stop at the Crossroads Store," she said, with a hint of a whine in her voice.

"It's just that I thought this time we could drive straight through," said Mrs. Treski. "We're making such good time, and you know how the weather is in the mountains. You never know what might blow in."

"Mo-o-om," said Jessie. Everything was messed up on this trip. "Evan, you want to stop at the Crossroads, don't you?"

Evan just kept looking out the window, nodding his head in time to the music on his iPod.

"Evan!" Jessie didn't mean to hit him quite so hard on the shoulder.

"Quit it!" he said, turning around to glare at her.

"I'm asking you a question!" she shouted. Evan took out one of the ear buds and let it dangle from his ear like a dead worm on a hook. "Do you want to stop at the Crossroads?" Jessie couldn't help thinking the question sounded dumb. Of course he would want to stop.

But Evan just shrugged and put the ear bud back in his ear. "I don't care."

Jessie threw herself against the seat and folded her arms over her chest.

"Relax, Jessie," said Mrs. Treski. "We'll stop. I could use a break to stretch my legs, anyway. But we can't stay too long. I don't want to get to Grandma's after dark."

\* \* \*

The Crossroads Store was a ten-minute detour off the main highway. It was on the corner of two roads

8

that were so dinky, Mrs. Treski called it the inter-section of Nowhere and Oblivion. But the store itself was miraculous. It was a combination gas station, deli, bakery, gift shop, bookshop, hunting/fishing/clothing store, and post office. They sold kayaks, guns, taxidermied animals, hunting knives, Get Well cards, umbrellas, joke books, night crawlers, candy, and decorative wall calendars. Jessie could wander the store for hours, wishing she had the money to buy just about everything.

She had only five dollars in her pocket, though. That was all the money she'd allowed herself to bring on this trip. Back home in her lock box, she had al-most thirty dollars. Most of that was from the money she'd made during the lemonade war, or at least what was left over after she made that $104 contribution to the Animal Rescue League. ("You don't have to give as much as I did," Megan had said, but Jessie had insisted. "I said I was going to, and I'm going to," she said, even though it almost killed her to give all that money away—and to animals!)

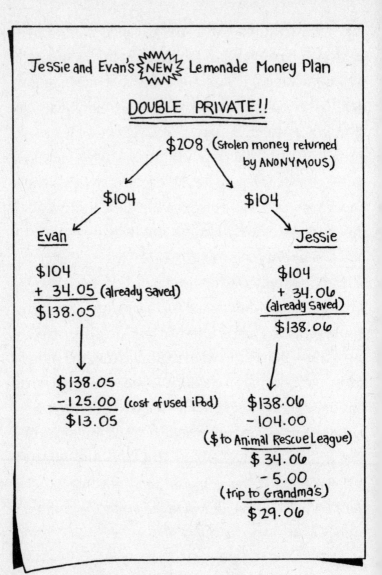

Jessie and Evan's $NEW$ Lemonade Money Plan

## DOUBLE PRIVATE!!

$208 (Stolen money returned by ANONYMOUS)

$104                    $104

Evan                    Jessie

$104                    $104
+ 34.05 (already saved)    + 34.06
$138.05                 (already saved)
                        $138.06

$138.05                 $138.06
-125.00 (cost of used iPod)   -104.00
$13.05                  ($ to Animal Rescue League)
                        $34.06
                        - 5.00
                        (trip to Grandma's)
                        $29.06

But no matter how enticing everything in the Crossroads Store looked to her (a squirrel nutcracker! fake mustaches!), Jessie wasn't about to spend thirty dollars. She liked to have money saved. Just in case.

After using the bathroom, she walked over to where Evan was standing, halfway between the deli and the bakery. He was looking at fancy gift bags of candy, all done up with curlicue ribbons.

"Look!" he said, holding up a bag. The label on the bag said "Moose Droppings." "Want some?" he asked, dangling the bag in front of her face.

"That is so gross!" Jessie said. But she loved it. The candy really did look exactly like moose droppings, only smaller. On closer inspection, she saw that it was actually chocolate-covered blueberries. "Are you going to get a bag? We could split one." But Evan had wandered off and wasn't listening to her anymore.

Jessie put the bag back on the shelf and walked over to the corner of the store devoted to jigsaw puzzles. There were a dozen puzzles to choose from, but Jessie's eyes went immediately to the one that was a picture of jellybeans. The brightly colored candies looked like rocks on a pebbly beach, and Jessie knew the puzzle would be hard to do. It had a thousand pieces!

"Jessie, are you ready?" asked her mother, shoving a few dollars back into her wallet after paying for the gas.

"Can we get this? Please?" asked Jessie, pulling the jellybean puzzle down from the shelf. "For Grandma?" Jessie and Grandma always worked on jigsaw puzzles when the family visited, and Jessie often brought a new puzzle for them to try. They had never done a thousand-piece puzzle, though.

Jessie's mom paused, the money still hanging out from her wallet. Jessie knew her mom had to be careful with money, and she tried hard not to ask for things she didn't need. "I have five dollars," said Jessie. "I could chip in."

Mrs. Treski took the puzzle and said, "It's a good idea, Jess. You and Grandma can work on it when she gets home from the hospital."

Jessie smiled, glad she could have the puzzle without spending her own money, and turned to the circular spinning postcard rack that was next to the jigsaw puzzles. There were eight columns of cards, and Jessie liked to make the rack squeak as she turned it slowly. She started at the top and began to work her way straight down one column, and then went back up to the top of the next column. She didn't want to miss a single card.

"Jess, can we go now?" asked her mother, looking through the various compartments of her wallet as if money would magically appear if she looked hard enough.

"No, I'm looking at the cards."

"You must own every card on that rack."

"Sometimes they have a new one," said Jessie.

"Five minutes, okay? Five minutes, I want to be pulling out of the parking lot." Mrs. Treski walked off to the checkout counter to pay for the puzzle.

Why was her mom so impatient? Usually she loved to stop at the Crossroads, but this time it was all about making good time and getting back on the road. Well, Jessie wasn't going to be rushed. She finished looking at the second column of postcards, and then started on the third.

"Ever been there?"

Jessie looked up. An old man with a stubbly beard was squinting through his glasses at a postcard that showed the Olympic Stadium in Lake Placid. Jessie noticed that the glasses sat crooked on his face. "The stadium where they had the Olympics? Ever been there?"

Jessie shook her head. "No."

The man tapped the card. "I was there in 1980 *and* 1932. Yes, I was. I saw Sonja Henie win the gold medal for figure skating. Do you believe that?" He nodded his head up and down as if he could make Jessie do the same.

Jessie looked closely at the man standing beside her. He started to scratch his face like he had a bad rash. "Were you in the Olympics?" she asked.

"No!" said the man. "But I had dreams." He was nodding his head more vigorously now—nodding and scratching—and his eyes were locked on the far end of the store.

"Hey, Jess, come on," said Evan, grabbing hold of one elbow and pulling her toward the door.

"I'm not done!" she said. But Evan didn't let go of her until they were outside. When Jessie looked back through the window, she saw that the man was still scratching his face and talking, even though no one was near.

"That guy was crazy," Evan said, matter-of-factly.

"How do you know?" asked Jessie, looking up at her big brother.

Evan shrugged and put his headphones back on. "You can just tell."

But Jessie couldn't tell. It hadn't occurred to her that there was anything wrong with the old man. Why did old people get like that? Did something break down inside their heads, the way a shoelace eventually snaps after being tied too many times? And how exactly did Evan know?

As soon as they got back on the highway, it started to snow. At first the flakes were large and wet, sticking for an instant to the windshield like giant white moths before dissolving into quarter-size drops of water. Then the snow became steadier

15

and more fierce, and the ground on either side of the highway turned white and shapeless. It was dusk when they pulled up to the end of Grandma's long, winding driveway and got their first look at the house.

"Oh my," said Mrs. Treski, turning off the ignition and letting the car lights die.

# Chapter 2
# The Man Of the Family

Normally, they would have walked into the house through the back door. But there was no back door. There was hardly even a back wall.

Evan couldn't believe it once they unlocked the front door and made their way through the dark into the kitchen. There was a hole in the back kitchen wall big enough to drive a car through. It looked like someone *had* driven a car straight through it, except that the edges of the hole were as black as coal and the smell of smoke was everywhere. Someone had taped heavy clear plastic to the wall, but one edge had come undone and was flapping in the wind.

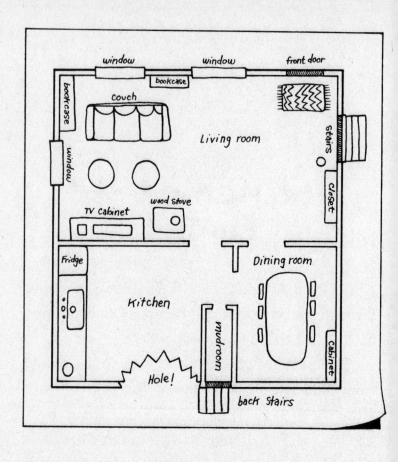

"Where's Grandma's stove?" asked Jessie.

"Well, *duh*," said Evan, a little more sharply than he'd meant to. "They had to get rid of it. It was probably melted down to nothing."

"I thought you said it was a little fire," said Jessie.

"I thought it was," said Mrs. Treski.

"And why's it so cold?"

"I guess the heat isn't working?" answered their mom. "I didn't realize . . ."

Evan had never seen his mom so surprised. Usually, she handled just about anything that came her way: bats in the basement, a squirrel trapped in the chimney flue, the time that Jessie got her head stuck between the railings on the stairs. No matter what, you could count on their mom to solve pretty much any problem. But now she just stared at the hole in the wall and didn't move.

Evan reached under the sink and found the heavy Maglite that Grandma always kept there. He flashed the beam across the walls, looking for something— *anything*—that looked the way it was supposed to.

"What's that?" asked Jessie. Evan shone the flashlight where Jessie was pointing.

"Wow," said Evan.

"That's a hole," said Mrs. Treski. There was a two-foot-wide hole that went straight through the kitchen ceiling, which meant there was a hole in the floor upstairs. "What room are we under?"

Evan thought about how the rooms upstairs were laid out, but it was hard to piece it together. Was it Grandma's bedroom? Or Mom's old room? Jessie came up with the answer first. She was good with maps.

"It's Evan's room."

*Oh, great,* thought Evan.

All three of them trooped upstairs, Evan leading the way with the flashlight. Sure enough, all the doors to the upstairs rooms were open except for the one that led to Grandma's office, which doubled as Evan's bedroom when he visited. That door was shut tight with a layer of thick plastic taped over it. When they pushed it open, they found the hole in the floor. Both windows were shattered, the glass lying in shards scattered across the room. Again, someone had taped plastic around the edges, but the wind had teased its way in. When it blew outside, handfuls of snow gusted into the room and landed on the floor.

"You can't sleep in here, Evan," said his mom. "I

don't even want the two of you coming into this room at all. I'll clean up the glass tomorrow."

"Where am I going to sleep?" Evan asked. Ever since he was out of a crib, this had been his room at Grandma's house. He couldn't imagine sleeping anywhere else.

"Well, for tonight, why don't you sleep in Grandma's room?"

"No way," said Evan. There was something just not right about sleeping in his grandmother's bed. It was hers. "I'll sleep on the couch in the living room."

"Okay. It's probably going to be the warmest room in the house." The living room had a wood-burning stove that heated the whole downstairs. "I'll get the fire going, while you two unpack the car. Is it a plan?"

That sounded like the mother Evan was used to. He headed back out into the dark yard to start hauling in the suitcases and bags of groceries.

"This is weird," said Jessie, grabbing the handle of the biggest suitcase in the car.

"You can't carry that," said Evan. His sister was small for her age and weighed less than fifty pounds, but for some reason she always thought she could lift heavy stuff. "Let me do it. You take that one." He threw his weight into pulling the suitcase out of the trunk. It landed on the ground with a loud *ca-thunk*. "What's weird?" he asked.

"Everything," said Jessie. "Nothing is the way it's supposed to be."

"Well, relax. Grandma will be here tomorrow, and Mom said she already hired some guy to fix the wall. Anyway, we're not staying long. Maybe just three days. And it's still Grandma's house. How weird can it be?" But he knew exactly what Jessie meant.

Evan dragged the suitcase into the house, then walked back out to the car to get the food. Three days of sleeping on the couch. Three days with no room of his own. Three days without his friends.

Evan couldn't wait to go home.

As he pulled the last grocery bag out of the back seat, Evan heard a car coming up the long driveway. Night had fallen. Evan felt a moment of panic, the sudden feeling that he should protect the house and his mother and sister from whatever was coming toward them. For a second, he thought about running inside and locking the door, but then he remembered the hole in the kitchen wall. There was no way to keep an intruder out. Headlights rounded the bend and flashed on the house. Evan decided to stand his ground.

A gray pickup truck rattled to a stop right behind the Treskis' car, and a man stepped out. He was tall and rail thin, with a scraggly, pointy beard. He was wearing a long-sleeve T-shirt under a down vest, jeans, and heavy work boots, and he had a pair of headphones dangling loosely around his neck.

"Hey," said the man. "Is your mom around?"

Evan stood there looking at the man, trying to figure him out. Was he dangerous? Who was he?

The man stopped walking and stood in front of Evan. Then he stuck his hand out. "I'm Pete. I'm the one doing the work on your grandma's house."

Evan relaxed and shook Pete's hand. Up close, he could see that the guy wasn't that old. He looked about the same age as Adam's brother who was in college.

"So, is your mom around, or did you drive here by yourself?"

Evan smiled. "Yeah, right," he said. "She's inside. Mom! Mom!" He ran into the house and found his mother in the living room, closing the little door of the wood stove. A fire burned brightly inside, but the house was still as cold as a skating rink.

Pete introduced himself to Mrs. Treski and then went down to the basement to turn the electricity on. When he came back up, he walked her through the damage. The sink in the kitchen didn't have running water, and the electricity on the first floor had been knocked out. "I rigged up a couple of by-passes, but you're going to have to get a plumber and an electrician to do the real repair work," said Pete. "It's going to take a few weeks, maybe a month, before the house is really whole again. Are you staying here tonight?"

Mrs. Treski nodded.

"It'll be cold," said Pete, "even with the stove." He turned to Evan. "You need to keep that fire going all night. Can you do that?"

Evan straightened up. He'd been following Pete and his mother through the whole house, fascinated by the things that Pete described—the inner workings of the house, like it was an animal that lived and breathed. "Yeah," he said. "I know how to take care of a fire. I've been to sleep-away camp."

"Good," said Pete. "That's your job, then." He turned back to Mrs. Treski. "Do you want me to bring over a couple of space heaters for upstairs? I live just a mile up the road." But Mrs. Treski said no thanks, they'd be fine with the stove.

"Probably for the best," he said, nodding. "You'd blow a fuse for sure."

Evan followed Pete out to his truck, even though the snow was coming down harder now. Before climbing in, Pete said, "Are you the man of the family?"

Evan shrugged. "I guess so." His mom didn't really go for that "man of the family" thing. And even though Evan's dad had been gone for more than two years, Evan still didn't think of himself that way. He tried to help his mom as much as he could, but he was only ten.

"Okay, then," said Pete. "You'll help me tomorrow. Right?"

"Sure," said Evan. And all of a sudden, he wasn't so desperate to leave Grandma's house and go back home.

# Chapter 3
# You Don't See That Every Day

The plan had been to go get Grandma in the morning. She was getting discharged from the hospital first thing, which meant she could finally come home. Mrs. Treski decided they would stay through New Year's Day to make sure Grandma was settled. Jessie couldn't wait for Grandma to walk in the door. Maybe then things would go back to normal.

But the plan had to change, thanks to the storm. Overnight the snow had turned the whole world into a scene from the book that Jessie was reading—*The Lion, the Witch and the Wardrobe*—all winter white and silent. The driveway had disappeared under the heavy, fresh snow, and the local news reported that road conditions were "challenging." On top of that, the battery in the car was dead (because Jessie had left one of the interior lights on overnight), and it was going to be a while before the guy from AAA could come out to the house. Apparently, a lot of people were having car trouble because of the weather.

Jessie spent part of the morning curled up in front of the wood stove reading her book and eating from the box of store-bought powdered doughnuts that Pete had brought with him. Pete and Evan were down in the basement now, checking out the furnace. There was a lot of banging, and every once in a while she heard them laughing. Jessie didn't get it. What was so funny about a broken furnace?

After that, Jessie climbed the stairs to see what her mother was doing. She found Mrs. Treski in the room with the hole in the floor, going through boxes of papers that had gotten wet after the fire. She was looking for Grandma's homeowner's insurance policy. The woven rug with swirls of maroon and deepest blue was pulled back and folded over on itself, revealing the bare wooden floor beneath it.

"Ruined," said Mrs. Treski, as she worked her way through the box. "I don't think any of this can be saved." But she kept plucking through the papers.

Jessie started to wander over to the built-in bookcase that ran along one wall of the room. Grandma had bookcases in every room in the house, each one stuffed to overflowing, but the books in her office were the ones that were most important to her.

"Jessie, stop," said Mrs. Treski. "I'm not sure I got all the glass off the floor."

"I'm wearing shoes. I'll be careful," said Jessie, walking delicately across the floor. "Are Grandma's books ruined, too?"

"Some, probably. I hope not her favorites."

"They're all her favorites," said Jessie, staring at the bookcase.

These books were like old friends to Jessie. She'd known them since she was old enough to crawl into her grandmother's lap and sit patiently while Grandma turned the pages. Books on birds, books on meditation, books on string instruments and baseball and antique quilts. Aesop's fables and Greek mythology. She looked quickly for her favorite and found it exactly where she had left it the last time she visited.

It was called *The Big Book of Bells,* and it was more than one hundred years old. Jessie loved this book for a lot of reasons: the red tooled leather cover with gold lettering on the spine, the thick pages that made a whispery sound when you turned them, the photographs of men in bowler hats and ladies in long skirts. But mostly Jessie loved this book because it had a photograph of Grandma's bell in it, the very same bell that hung on Lovell's Hill.

Jessie tipped the book off the shelf and into her hand, relieved to see that it wasn't wet or burned. She carried it downstairs, settled herself on the couch, and turned first to the photo of Grandma's bell, feeling proud that it was so famous and important that it appeared in a book. Then she turned to the diagram that showed all the different parts of a bell.

The parts were named for parts of the human body, and most of them went in the order you would expect: the crown, the shoulder, the waist, the hip. But then came the lip! That always made Jessie laugh, to think of having lips on your hips.

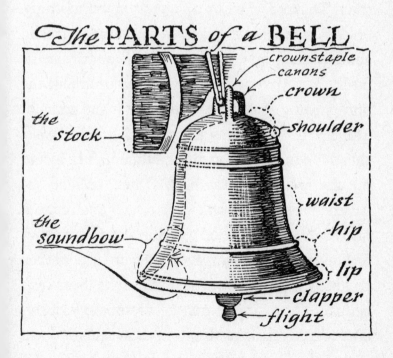

The PARTS of a BELL

crownstaple
canons
crown
shoulder
the stock
waist
hip
the soundbow
lip
clapper
flight

She was still poring over the book two hours later, reading about the largest bell in the world, which was in Russia, when the guy from AAA showed up and told Mrs. Treski that she needed an entirely new battery—which he didn't have on his truck. She would have to wait until later this afternoon when he could come back.

"No, no!" said Mrs. Treski. "You don't understand. I have to go pick up my mother this morning. She's getting discharged from the hospital." Then she explained how her mother had put the kettle on the stove but accidentally turned on the wrong burner and then forgotten all about it and gone for a long walk, and when she came back from her walk, she found her house on fire and tried to rush inside, but the fire department blocked her way, and she fell and broke her wrist.

The AAA guy listened very quietly and even nodded his head as if he was agreeing with her, but then he said what he'd already said. "I'm sorry, but I can't get back out this way until the afternoon. Probably after four." Mrs. Treski threw up her hands and said something under her breath, then she went back upstairs to continue sorting through Grandma's papers.

Jessie closed the book and went in the kitchen to try to convince Evan to go play in the snow with her. Evan was so wrapped up in helping Pete— they were tearing out the old wood from the wall—that she could hardly get him to even listen to her.

When Mrs. Treski finally drove off in the Subaru to get Grandma at the hospital, the afternoon sun was just beginning to draw long shadows on the blue-white snow. Jessie decided it was time to go visit Grandma's bell on the hill. She strapped a pair of snowshoes on her feet and headed outside.

The woods around the house were magical in any season, but especially in the wintertime. Two feet of fresh snow had fallen overnight. Jessie tried to imagine Mr. Tumnus, the faun in *The Lion, the Witch and the Wardrobe,* peeking out from behind a tree, his slender umbrella held in his hand. She wondered how fauns balanced on their two goat feet. It must be hard! She was pretty sure she would fall over, if she were half-human, half-goat.

She had reached the edge of the first woods and had come out into the clearing that was at the foot of a small hill. If she climbed over this hill and the next, she would come to Lovell's Hill with the bell at the top. But first she wanted to see if the tepee was still standing.

The summer before last, Jessie and Evan had built a tepee deep in the woods. First, they had found a dead tree trunk that stood about ten feet tall with all of its branches rotted away. Then they scoured the ground for deadwood branches that were at least eight feet long and mostly straight. Evan hauled the heavy branches back to the tree trunk. Sometimes he had to drag them a quarter of a mile over the bumpy floor of the woods. It was Jessie's job to snap off the spindly twigs that grew off the dead branches so that they were as straight and smooth as poles.

When they had a dozen straight branches, Evan and Jessie leaned them up against the trunk of the tree so that they made a circle all the way around. They covered the poles with fresh pine branches, using the stiff twine that Grandma kept in the barn to lash the branches to the poles. Over the opening, they hung a waterproof tarp that could be pulled aside like a door.

Before they had started building, Evan had made a diagram of the tepee. Jessie still had that drawing hanging on her bedroom wall back home.

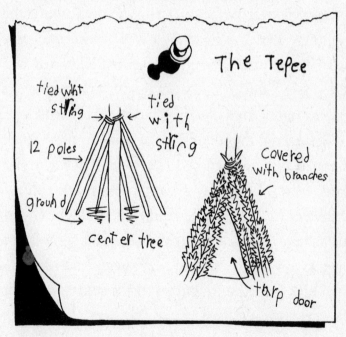

The Tepee

tied wiht string

tied with string

12 poles

ground

center tree

covered with branches

tarp door

It took them two whole weeks to finish the tepee, but when they were done, they brought Grandma to see it and told her she could use it anytime she wanted. Evan had said, "This tepee will last a hundred years," and Grandma had agreed. Since then, she told Jessie that she often checked in on the tepee when she was out walking in the woods, just to make sure it was still in good shape. It was a nice place to rest, she said.

Jessie skirted the foot of the hills until she found the Lightning Tree that marked the way. Years ago the tree had been struck by lightning, leaving it scarred and black. Jessie and Evan always used it as a marker; its one remaining stub of a branch pointed to the tepee.

Following the direction of the branch, Jessie plunged into the woods. There was still plenty of light, even though it was late afternoon, and after a couple of minutes, Jessie could see the tepee ahead, just where it was supposed to be. She snowshoed over to it, walked once all the way around to check for holes, and then climbed inside and sat on the dry dirt floor.

Jessie loved the tepee. It made her feel safe and warm and hidden away from the world. She lay on her back and stared up at the branches over her head. *This will never change,* she thought with satisfaction. She stayed inside for a few minutes, then crawled out of the tepee and snowshoed back to the foot of the first small hill.

But when she began to climb the hill, she saw that she wasn't alone. A boy was cross-country skiing toward her, his head down, goggles strapped to his face. It took Jessie a minute to realize that the boy didn't see her. He was headed straight for her, and he was picking up speed as he came down the hill.

"Hey!" she shouted. She lifted her big floppy snowshoes awkwardly and tried to back up into the woods. But the tail of one of the shoes stepped on the tail of the other one, and she ended up falling over backwards. "Hey!" she shouted again, as the boy *shooshed* straight toward her.

"Whoa!" he said, sliding to a snowplow stop. "You don't see that every day."

"What?" asked Jessie.

"My name's Maxwell. Who are you?" He made a funny move, shuffling his right foot forward and leaning his weight on it, and then stepping back onto his left. It almost looked like a dance move, except that he was on skis.

"I'm Jessie. You practically ran me over!"

"But I didn't!" he said, doing the dance move again. "That's 'cause I'm smart!" He made a funny noise that was like a steam engine puffing on a track.

"I wouldn't exactly call it smart," said Jessie, struggling to her feet. "But at least you didn't kill me."

She snowshoed her way past Maxwell and started to trudge up the hill that he'd just skied down.

"Where are you going?"

"That way," said Jessie, pointing up the hill.

"Can I come?"

"I don't care," said Jessie. She didn't say it angrily. It was just the honest truth.

Jessie noticed that Maxwell liked to talk. A lot.

On the way up the hill, she learned that Maxwell lived in the house closest to Grandma's and that his family had just moved in before the school year started. He spent a lot of time at Grandma's house. In fact, it had been Maxwell who discovered the house on fire after Grandma had left her stove on and then gone out for a walk. He'd run home to tell his mother, and she was the one who called the fire department.

"You don't see that every day!" said Maxwell, after describing what the fire had looked like.

Jessie looked at him. There was something funny about this kid.

They had crossed the first hill and the second, and now they were at the bottom of Lovell's Hill, the highest of the little hills on this part of Grandma's property. In five minutes Jessie would reach the top and be able to see the wooden crossbeam and the bell. The crossbeam was made out of two heavy oak beams that were joined in the shape of an upside-down L. When Jessie was younger, she would ask Evan to lift her up so that she could hang on the end of the top beam and swing her legs back and forth, pretending that she was a second bell, ringing. Now that she was older, the crossbeam was only a little taller than she was, so she didn't need anyone to lift her up.

Jessie trudged forward, Maxwell gliding alongside. She was almost there. She could just see the top of the crossbeam. The afternoon sun was starting to set, slicing its way down Black Bear Mountain. It was hard to look up at the crest of the hill, because the sun was setting directly behind it, causing the snow to glint fiercely. Jessie shielded her eyes and tried to see the top of the hill. Maxwell was *shooshing* by her side, swinging his poles back and forth with wild flailing motions, cutting new tracks in the untouched snow.

*Trudge, trudge, trudge.* Jessie looked up once more just as the sun dipped below the mountain, throwing the hillside into sudden shadow. There was the crest. There was the wooden crossbeam.

But the bell was gone.

# Chapter 4
# That Bad Feeling

Evan stared in amazement. The hole in the wall was gone. He and Pete had worked all day, first ripping out the damaged studs and replacing them with clean, dry wood, then trimming the old boards so that the ragged hole became a neat rectangle, then measuring and cutting and nailing in the new sheets of plywood. There was still the dry wall to hang and the outside shingles to replace, but the hole was gone. Evan had never felt such a sense of accomplishment in his life, not even when he and Jessie had won the Labor Day Poster Contest at the end of the summer.

Now he was sweeping up the sawdust that lay as thick as a carpet under his feet. Pete said no carpenter worth his salt leaves a mess behind at the end of the day. So Evan was sweeping up the sawdust and bent nails and small chips of wood, while Pete hauled the bigger scraps out to the truck. But every once in a while, Evan stopped and held the broom still in his hands so that he could admire the work they had done. He couldn't wait to show his mom when she got back from the hospital.

He was dumping the last pile of sawdust into the large gray plastic barrel when he heard loud clomping on the front porch, followed by the front door opening. Evan walked into the living room just as Jessie tried to step over the threshold wearing her snowshoes.

"Evan! The bell is gone!" She tripped over the doormat and fell face first into the living room, landing hard on her hands and knees. Behind her was an older boy Evan had never seen before. He had funny-looking cross-country shoe-boots on his feet, and he was carrying a pair of ski poles. Evan guessed he was at least twelve, maybe thirteen.

"I can't get these off," said Jessie. She had rolled onto her back in the living room and was holding her feet up in the air. The snowshoes were dripping clumps of snow onto her face and the floor. "Help me, Evan!"

"Oh, for Pete's sake," he said. He crossed over to where she was squirming and grabbed hold of one of the snowshoes. The boy had a funny smile on his face and was rocking back and forth, one foot out in front of the other. "Hey," said Evan, as a way of introducing himself.

"You don't see that every day," said the boy, looking at Jessie, who looked like a ladybug caught on her back.

"Yeah, actually, I do," said Evan. Jessie was always tripping over something or getting caught on something or dragging something along behind her. Evan unclipped one snowshoe and then the other and flipped them off Jessie's feet.

"The bell is gone, Evan! Gone!"

"What do you mean? Grandma's bell?"

"Yes! The New Year's Eve bell!"

"It can't be gone. You must have climbed the wrong hill."

43

"No, we didn't. The wooden post was there, just like always, but the bell is gone!"

Evan shook his head. "That thing weighs—I don't know—a hundred pounds. There's no way someone could just walk off with it. And besides, who would want to take it?"

"Who *wouldn't* want to take it?" Jessie asked, bouncing from one foot to the other. "It's an antique and it's famous—"

"It's not famous, Jessie," said Evan, shaking his head. "Just 'cause it's in that book doesn't make it famous."

"Well, it's worth two thousand five hundred dollars!"

"Is not!"

"I'll show you!" Jessie ran to the couch where she'd left *The Big Book of Bells* that morning and pulled out a letter that was tucked into the back cover of the book. She handed it to Evan, who read it slowly, not understanding all the words but getting the general idea. About five years ago, Grandma had had the bell appraised to find out how much it was worth, and Jessie was right: the letter said the bell was worth $2,500.

"Wow," said Evan.

Maxwell bobbed his head several times, rocking back and forth on his feet.

"We've got to find it," said Jessie, pulling on Evan's arm. "New Year's Eve is in three days! If we don't ring the bell on New Year's Eve..." Jessie couldn't get the words out, and Evan knew what she was feeling. It was hard to imagine not ringing the bell on New Year's Eve. They had always done that, for as long as he could remember.

Evan looked at the boy and then back at his sister. "Jessie...?" He half pointed at Maxwell, hoping his sister would get the hint, but as usual, she didn't. "Uh, my name's Evan," he said to the boy, sticking out his hand the way grownups did.

"How do you do," said the boy, shaking Evan's hand. "My name's Maxwell. I'm smart!" Then he rocked forward on his left foot and shook his right hand in the air. Evan looked at him closely.

"Maxwell lives in the yellow house. The one with

the big rock out front," said Jessie. "He knows Grandma really well."

"Yep," said Maxwell. "I come here all the time." Maxwell was rocking back and forth steadily now, snapping his right hand in the air with each forward motion. "We watch TV. And we do puzzles. And we feed the birds. And I'm smart! That's what Mrs. Joyce says. She says, 'Maxwell, you are smart!'"

There was a moment's silence, and then Evan asked, "What grade are you in?"

"Sixth grade," said Maxwell. "Hardy Middle School. Grade six."

"Mom's home!" shouted Jessie, running for the front door. Evan had heard it, too—the old Subaru making its way up the long driveway. He hurried back into the kitchen. He wanted to get the trash barrel outside before his mom walked in.

He was carrying it down the makeshift back steps he and Pete had rigged up, when Pete came around the house. "Your grandma's home, so I'm heading out for the day," said Pete. "We'll hang the dry wall tomorrow, then we'll start on the upstairs the next day. Sound good?"

"Yeah, sure," said Evan. He wanted to sound casual about it, so Pete wouldn't think this was the first construction job he'd ever done, but he couldn't keep the eagerness out of his voice.

"Okay, then. See you tomorrow." Pete plugged in his headphones and headed for his truck.

Evan walked back into the kitchen and took one more look around. It was still definitely a disaster area, but they'd accomplished a lot: the wall was repaired, and the back door was framed and hung, and you could walk up and down the back steps if you were careful. Plus, it was a whole lot cleaner than it had been an hour ago. When Evan heard voices (mostly Jessie's) in the living room, he hurried in to say hello.

His grandmother stood just inside the doorway, next to the coat rack and umbrella stand. Her winter parka was draped over her shoulders as if it were a cape, and Evan could see that her arm was in a cast, cradled in a sling around her neck. She fumbled one-handed with the coat until Evan's mother took it from her and hung it up on the rack.

Evan watched as Jessie tried to grab hold of

Grandma's hand, but Grandma pulled her hand in, hunching forward protectively, and covered the sling with her good arm, as if she were afraid someone might try to steal something away from her. She began to walk toward the middle of the room, taking small steps, which was not at all the way his grandmother usually walked. Then she stopped and looked at the stairs that led to the second floor and then back at the front door.

It was her face that surprised Evan the most. It looked pale, and she had bags under her eyes, which Evan had never noticed before. Most of all, she couldn't seem to settle her gaze on anything. Her eyes kept flitting around the room, like a bird that won't perch on any one thing.

Jessie was hopping around like a bird, too, chattering nonstop about the bell. Maxwell was walking behind them, carrying on his own conversation and making a strange puffing noise that sounded like he was trying to blow feathers out of his mouth. Evan's mother had an arm around his grandma's shoulder, guiding her slowly toward the couch, and when

Evan caught sight of his mother's face, he knew right away that something was very wrong.

"Hi, Grandma," said Evan cheerfully, from across the room. But Grandma didn't look at him.

"She's tired," said his mom. "Jessie, would you please stop asking so many questions. Grandma needs a couple of minutes to get used to being home."

"Why?" asked Jessie. "Why do you need to get used to being home, Grandma? That doesn't make any sense."

"Jessie, shut it," said Evan, feeling a little panicked. What he really wanted to do was run up to his mother and get a hug from her, but with Maxwell standing right there, there was no way he was going to do that.

"Come see the kitchen, Grandma," said Jessie. "See how good it looks."

"Jessie," warned her mother, "you need to slow down."

"A cup of tea," said Grandma. "That's what I need. A good strong cup of green tea."

She started to walk toward the kitchen. Evan hurried ahead of her, scooping up two last stray nails that were on the Formica counter. Then he stood beside the patched hole. His mother and grandmother walked into the kitchen, trailed by Jessie and Maxwell, who had finally stopped talking. Everyone looked at Evan and the repair work that he and Pete had done that day. It was his grandmother who spoke first.

"What is this? What has happened here?"

"Mom," said Mrs. Treski. "There was a fire. Do you remember the fire?"

"Where's my stove? How am I going to make my tea without a stove?"

"The stove was ruined, Grandma," said Jessie. "They had to take it out because it was no good anymore."

"What do you mean, Jessie?" asked Grandma. "Who did this? Where was I?" She looked at Mrs. Treski. "Susan, what has been going on here?"

"Mom—"

"You don't see that every day!" said Maxwell, rocking back and forth nervously. His right hand snapped in the air like he was cracking the whip on an imaginary horse.

"No, you certainly don't, Maxwell," said Evan's grandma. "You certainly don't."

"Grandma," said Evan. "It's going to be okay. Me and Pete are fixing the whole thing. We're going to work some more tomorrow. We'll get it just the way it used to be." Evan could feel that bad feeling rising up in him. The feeling he got just before taking a test. The feeling he sometimes got late at night when the house was too quiet and too dark and he wished his dad had never left.

For the first time that afternoon, Evan's grandmother looked right at him. She peered sharply at his face and then looked him over once, from top to bottom. She turned to Evan's mom.

"Who is that boy?" she asked angrily. "Did he do this to my kitchen?"

"Mom," said Mrs. Treski. "It's Evan. Your grandson."

Evan's grandmother shook her head. "I don't know him. Make him go away."

## Chapter 5
# A Thousand Pieces

The next morning, Jessie sat with her grandmother at the dining room table and ripped the cellophane wrapper off the box of the new jigsaw puzzle. She couldn't wait to get started. Grandma looked like herself this morning. She had slept twelve hours last night, and at breakfast she'd given Jessie and Evan a giant bear hug. They'd even exchanged their Christmas gifts. Grandma was wearing the scarf that Jessie had knit for her draped over her shoulders, and Jessie had a brand-new calligraphy pen and two jars of metallic ink waiting for her upstairs in her room. Evan's present from Grandma was a magic set, and he had given her a Christmas cactus covered in pink blossoms.

"That looks good enough to eat," said Grandma, staring at the picture of the puzzle that Jessie set up on one end of the table like a billboard. The brightly colored jellybeans reminded Jessie of Christmas lights all in a tangled pile. They even seemed to glisten and glow like lights on a tree. It was the most beautiful puzzle she had ever seen.

And the hardest. It took Jessie and Grandma nearly ten minutes just to spread out all the pieces on the table and turn each one right side up. Then they had to separate out all the straight-edge pieces that would form the outside frame. When they had finished, they stopped and studied the puzzle.

"They all look the same," said Jessie. It was true. Even though the pieces were different shapes, the picture on each one was basically the same. There was no way to pick one out from all the others. Jessie had never done a puzzle like this before. She didn't know where to begin.

"Four corners," said Grandma, tapping the table. "That's how we always start, right?"

So they searched through the puzzle pieces until

they found the four corner pieces and matched those up to the picture to figure out which corner went where. Then they began the slow process of building off the corners to create the outside frame of the puzzle.

"Grandma, tell me about the New Year's Eve bell," said Jessie. She'd been waiting all morning to ask her grandmother about the bell, but she was nervous. Mrs. Treski had warned both children: "Try not to say anything that might upset her," and she had told Jessie specifically, "Don't talk about how the bell is missing."

"Well, what do you want to know?" asked Grandma, fitting a puzzle piece onto her side of the frame.

"Where did it come from?"

"My great-grandfather put it there to call the neighbors in case of an emergency."

"Like what?" asked Jessie. "What kind of emergency?" She was hunting for a straight-edge piece with a purple jellybean on it.

"Oh, all kinds of things. If someone was sick or

if there was a lost child or a fire or a pack of wolves getting into the sheep."

"Back in 1884?" Over the years, Jessie had traced her fingers over that date on the bell a hundred times. She knew the inscription by heart:

**THE JONES TROY BELL**
**FOUNDRY COMPANY,**
**TROY, N.Y. 1884.**
**I SOUND THE ALARM**
**TO KEEP THE PEACE.**

The letters were as tall as her thumb.

"That's when the bell was cast." Jessie's grandma nodded. "That's when the bell was hung."

"How did they hang it?" asked Jessie. "It must weigh a thousand pounds!"

"Oh, no," said Grandma, scratching her earlobe, which is what she did when she concentrated. "It doesn't weigh that much. Maybe a hundred pounds. Two men could hang that bell easily. One time, years and years ago, the bell needed to be cleaned, so I lifted it off the hooks and dragged it back to the house on a sledge all by myself. Of course, it's a lot easier to take a bell down than it is to hang it up."

"You took the bell down?" asked Jessie. "When?"

"Oh, years ago. A long time ago. Just after your grandfather died. I was still young and strong back then. Not like now." Grandma turned a puzzle piece around in her hand, seeing if it would fit, but then put it back with the others on the table.

"Grandma?" Jessie asked in a near whisper. "Did you take the bell down—sometime this year?"

Grandma laughed. "What a thing! No, I couldn't take that bell down anymore. That old bell is still up there on Lovell's Hill. Always will be." She had stopped working on the puzzle and was using her good hand to rub her shoulder as if it ached.

"Maybe you wanted to sell it?" asked Jessie, thinking of the appraisal letter.

"No, Jessie. I would never sell the New Year's Eve bell."

"Maybe you . . . forgot."

"I didn't forget, Jessie," said Grandma, shaking her head.

"But you could have—"

"No!" Her grandmother dropped her hand to the table so that it made a sharp rapping sound. "Now stop, Jessie! The bell is on the hill. It's always been there, and it always will be there. So, enough."

"Okay, Grandma," said Jessie, but inside she wondered if maybe her grandmother's forgetfulness was a clue to the mystery of the missing bell.

They worked on the puzzle for another minute in silence, and then Jessie heard a strange thud on the front door. When she got up to investigate, she found Maxwell standing in front of the house with skis on his feet and ski poles in one hand. In his other hand, he had a snowball, and Jessie noticed the *splot* of white on the front door where he had already thrown one.

"You're home," said Maxwell.

"Uh-huh," said Jessie. They stared at each other for a minute, Maxwell rocking back and forth on his skis, Jessie with her arms crossed in front of her.

"It's not polite to ask someone to invite you in," said Maxwell.

"Why not?" asked Jessie.

"I don't know," said Maxwell. "It's just a rule my mother taught me."

"It doesn't make sense," said Jessie. "How's the person supposed to know you want to get invited in if you don't ask?" She wondered why they were talking about this. It was a strange topic for Maxwell to bring up out of the blue.

Maxwell nodded his head. "But it's a rule," he said.

"Maxwell!" Jessie's grandma had come to the open door. "Do you want to come inside?"

"Uh-huh!" he said, using his pole to unsnap his boots from his skis. Jessie followed her grandma back into the house with Maxwell right behind.

"It's a good thing you're here," said Grandma. "I need to go lie down for a few minutes, and Jessie needs a puzzle partner. Want to take over?" she asked, pointing to the dining room table.

Maxwell didn't even answer. He just walked over to the table and sat down in the chair that Grandma had left empty.

"Prepare to be amazed," Grandma said to Jessie, and then she headed up the stairs.

When Jessie sat in her seat, Maxwell had already fit together three pieces. But they weren't pieces of the outside frame of the puzzle. They were pieces that belonged in the vast, empty middle—the part of the puzzle Jessie hadn't even tried to solve yet.

And he kept finding more. He fit another piece onto the three he'd already joined. And then another. His eyes roamed quickly over the pieces, and he moved his hands over them, too, his fingers snapping and wiggling as he thought about which piece to pick up next. Sometimes he made a mistake—a near miss—but just as often he got the right piece on the first try. *Snap.* The piece fit in perfectly, and then Maxwell started to look for the next one.

"How do you do that?" asked Jessie. She was really good at jigsaw puzzles, the best in the family, the best of anyone she knew. But she couldn't start *in the middle* of a thousand-piece puzzle, especially one that was a picture of nothing but jellybeans.

"I'm smart," said Maxwell, continuing to add pieces. *Snap. Snap.*

"Well, I'm smart, too, but I can't do that," she said. She tried to concentrate on the frame she was building, but Maxwell's movements were so annoying, she couldn't keep her mind on what she was doing.

"Jellybeans," said Maxwell, snapping his fingers and looking at the pieces.

"Yeah, jellybeans," said Jessie, absent-mindedly. "Grandma calls me Jessie Bean."

"Why?" asked Maxwell.

"It's a nickname."

"I hate nicknames," Maxwell said loudly. "Nick-names are mean."

Jessie looked up, surprised. She'd always thought the same thing but had never heard anyone say it before. "Yeah, I hate nicknames, too! I wish everyone would just call people by their real names. Right?"

"Right," said Maxwell, snapping another piece in place. He pointed at the cluster of puzzle pieces he had fit together. "You don't see that every day."

"What?" asked Jessie, looking at the pieces.

"Oklahoma," said Maxwell. And sure enough, Jessie could see that the pieces made a shape that looked like Oklahoma.

Jessie watched as Maxwell added piece after piece to the puzzle. She was starting to get annoyed. At this rate, she wasn't going to get to do any of her own puzzle. "You know what?" she said. "I like to do puzzles all by myself, without any help." This wasn't true, but it was no fun doing a puzzle with someone who could finish the whole thing before you even got a corner done. It was like someone giving you the answer to a math problem before you even started. "Let's do something else. What do you want to do?"

"*Get Smart*!" said Maxwell.

"What?"

"The best TV show ever made. *Get Smart*. Six seasons, 1965 to 1970, one hundred and thirty-eight episodes produced in all." Maxwell walked over to the TV cabinet and opened the lower cupboard. Inside, Grandma had a few DVDs, mostly babyish movies that Jessie and Evan didn't watch anymore. But Maxwell pulled out a boxed set that Jessie had never seen before. *Get Smart* was the title, and there was a picture of a man in a suit and a tie looking very surprised.

"Season one, the pilot episode," said Maxwell. He popped the DVD in the player, and they both sat down on the couch to watch. The title of the first episode was "Mr. Big."

It was a funny show. Jessie laughed and laughed. There was this dopey secret agent who worked for a super-secret government agency called CONTROL. The agent's name was Maxwell Smart, but his code name was Agent 86.

"I get it," she said, turning to Maxwell. "That's why you say you're smart all the time. Maxwell Smart! It's a joke!"

Maxwell bobbed his head up and down. "Yep! My name is Maxwell, and I'm smart. That's what Mrs. Joyce always says! She says, 'You're smart, Maxwell.' It's a joke!"

Maxwell Smart was a no-nonsense secret agent.

He liked to take charge, and he was always confident he would catch the criminal in the end. Some people might think he was kind of bossy, but Jessie thought he was great.

There was another secret agent—a dark-haired woman named Agent 99—and a dog named K-13. Together, they got to use all kinds of great gadgets, like bino-specs and an inflato-coat and a shoe phone. Jessie especially loved the bino-specs.

"We should do that," she said at the end of the first episode. "We should be like spies and have a stakeout and figure out who stole the bell. We could solve the crime, just like Maxwell Smart and Agent 99."

"Okay," said Maxwell. "Let's do that."

"No, I mean for real," said Jessie. "Real secret agents, not just pretend."

"Okay," said Maxwell. "Let's do that."

"Really?" said Jessie. She was surprised that Maxwell agreed with her right away. She figured it would take a while to convince a sixth-grader to go

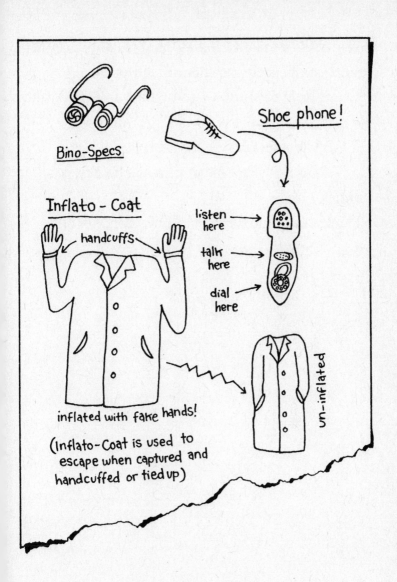

Bino-Specs

Shoe phone!

Inflato - Coat

handcuffs

listen → here

talk → here

dial → here

inflated with fake hands!

un-inflated

(Inflato-Coat is used to escape when captured and handcuffed or tied up)

along with her plan. After all, she was only a fourth-grader, and a pretty young one, at that.

"We have to think of something fast," she said. "New Year's Eve is the day after tomorrow."

"It's like a puzzle," said Maxwell.

"You're right. It's like a puzzle, and I'm good at puzzles."

"Me, too," said Maxwell. "I'm smart."

# Chapter 6
# Afternoon Shadows

Evan didn't want to stop. He and Pete were fixing the holes in the roof. Pete was outside, up on the extension ladder, ripping up shingles and tossing them through the hole to Evan. Evan was inside, crouching under the sloping ceiling so that he could catch the shingles as they fell and heave them into the garbage barrel. He also had to hand Pete whatever tools he needed.

So when Mrs. Treski appeared in the doorway of Grandma's office/construction site and asked Evan if he would please take Grandma for a walk, he made a face and said, "Can't Jessie do it?"

Evan, kneeling under the hole, looked up and caught sight of Pete's face looking right back at him. Pete didn't need to say a word. He just shook his head once, and Evan knew that was that.

"Yeah, okay, Mom," said Evan. He stood up and wiped the grit from the knees of his pants. "I'll be back in a few minutes," he hollered up to Pete.

"I'll be here," Pete called down. "Same as before. Take good care of your grandma, Big E."

Evan followed his mother, scowling. "Why can't Grandma take a walk by herself?" Grandma was a nut about walking. She took long walks by herself every day. Sometimes she'd walk five miles, circling her property, which covered a hundred acres at the foot of Black Bear Mountain.

"Evan, please," said his mother in the voice she used that meant there would be no more discussion.

Evan walked into the mudroom just off the kitchen. Grandma was looping her new purple scarf around her neck, the one that Jessie had knit for her for Christmas. Her injured arm was tucked inside her bulky winter coat, which was zipped closed over it.

"Hey, Grandma," said Evan.

"Something tells me you don't feel like going for a walk right now," said Grandma. Evan bent over his boots, tugging them onto his feet and hiding his face. Was it that obvious? The memory of what his grandmother had said to him two days ago in the kitchen flickered in his brain, but then he remembered his mother's explanation. *She's not herself, Evan.*

"No, I want to go," he said, knowing that it was okay to fudge the truth when you didn't want to hurt someone's feelings. "It's just that I was helping Pete, and he kind of needs me right now."

"Pete's a good boy," said Grandma.

"Boy!" said Evan. "He's a grown man."

"Not to me, he's not. Everyone looks young to me!" Grandma used her mouth to hold a mitten still while she wriggled her good hand into it. "Ready?"

"Ready," said Evan. Grandma opened the back door and was just about to step out, when Evan's mother called from upstairs. Evan tromped up to the second floor, feeling hot and puffy in his heavy ski coat and boots.

"Evan," said his mother, "try to make it a short walk, okay? Grandma thinks she's back to her old self, but I don't want her getting too tired. And try to hold on to her good arm, if she'll let you. Or at least keep close to her, so if she trips you can grab her before she falls. Okay?"

Evan didn't like the sound of any of this, but he nodded his head. He wasn't used to taking care of his grandma. She had always taken such good care of him and Jessie.

"And, Evan, one more thing," said his mother. "Don't let her go near the bell. Okay? I don't want her . . . Just keep her away from that hill, okay?"

Afternoon shadows came early to Grandma's woods because the sun set behind the mountain. Evan was surprised that the blue-gray light of late afternoon was already painting the snow. He turned to walk up the long, plowed driveway toward the main road—that would be a good half-mile walk—

but Grandma said she wanted to walk a different way, through the woods. She set out on the path that headed for the foot of Black Bear Mountain. There were footprints in the snow along this path and the steady slicing marks of skis, so Evan knew that Jessie and Maxwell had already come this way today.

Evan talked about the repair work that he and Pete were doing, especially the thrilling part about ripping out the old scorched studs in the wall and putting in new ones. It had been tricky, because the wall they were working on was a load-bearing wall, which meant it was holding up a lot of the weight of the second story. If they took out too many studs at once, the whole house could collapse. Evan thought it was like playing Jenga—the game where you build a tower of blocks, then try to pull out each block without causing the tower to fall.

Grandma didn't say much. It took some effort to walk on the packed-down snow, and there were branches and rocks you had to watch out for. Even Evan could feel his heart beating fast with the effort, and the cold intake of each breath of frozen air made his breathing seem heavier. He thought about Pete up on the roof all afternoon and wondered how he did it.

"Grandma, you want to go back now?" The light was definitely fading, and they'd already been walking for fifteen minutes. Evan wasn't even quite sure where they were, but Grandma knew her property like the back of her hand.

Grandma shook her head but didn't say anything. Her breathing was louder now, and she was grunting a little with the effort of climbing uphill. It was a pretty big hill, and the snow seemed deeper here. Evan looked around. There was something familiar about this place, but the light was so soft and lavender that he couldn't really trust his eyes.

They were just reaching the top now, Grandma ahead of him by a few feet. And as the crest of the hill came into view, Evan felt a sudden sense of coldness and dread.

Usually, they came up this hill from the other side, but it was still the same hill. Lovell's Hill. The one with the bell. There was the wooden crossbeam. And just like Jessie had said, the bell was gone.

"Grandma! Let's go back now," said Evan, afraid but not sure of what—which just made the fear feel all the worse. But Grandma wasn't stopping. She made a beeline for the bell, or at least where the bell should have been. Evan felt as though he had never seen a space so empty as the place where the bell was supposed to hang.

When she reached the wooden crossbeam, Grandma stopped. She looked around, and then looked back at the empty space. In the dim light, Evan couldn't see her face very well, but what he saw frightened him. She didn't look like his grandmother. She looked strange, with one arm missing inside her coat and the empty, flopping sleeve hanging like a dead fish. Her knitted cap was crooked on her head, and one strand of gray hair hung down and curled around her neck. Her eyes were searching for something, but the dying light made it harder and harder to see. Evan looked around to try to understand what she was looking for, but the thick blanket of snow seemed to transform every rock, every tree, every shape into something else. It was hard to make sense of any of it.

"Did you take the bell?" asked his grandmother sharply.

"No!" said Evan.

"Where is it? What have you done with it?"

"I don't know, Grandma. I didn't do anything with it."

"Give it back. Right now. It isn't yours to take."

"I didn't take it," said Evan, his panic growing. He had to figure out some way to get Grandma home. But when he took a step toward her, she backed up and nearly fell over. Evan froze in his tracks.

"Who are you?" she asked angrily.

"Grandma, it's me. It's Evan."

"Thief. You're a bell thief." Grandma looked at the crossbeam again and then at the sky. Evan tried desperately to think of how he was going to get Grandma home. She was tired. She was cold. He could see that now. He had to figure out how to take care of her. But he couldn't think. Should he leave her here and go get help? Should he try to force her to go home? How was he going to get her to safety without hurting her?

"Grandma, it's me. Evan. I'm your grandson. I need to get you home, okay?" Again Evan took a step toward her, and this time Grandma did fall over backwards, trying to move away from him. She landed sitting down in the soft snow, her bad arm still tucked inside her coat. Evan didn't think she was hurt, but the fall seemed to frighten her even more. She looked at Evan as if he had pushed her down, even though he was standing ten feet away from her.

"Stay away!" she said. "You won't get away with this." She looked around her again, and said, "Where's Susan?"

Evan didn't know what to do. He didn't know what to say. The truth made no sense as long as Grandma didn't know who he was.

He tried to think. He tried to imagine what it must feel like to be his grandmother right now.

Finally, he said, "Susan sent me, Mrs. Joyce. She asked me to bring you home. She's waiting for you at home." Evan waited to see how she would respond.

"Good," said Grandma. "I need to speak with her. There's been a problem. A very big problem." But she didn't seem to remember what the problem was.

"Can I help you up?" asked Evan. He didn't move toward her.

"Yes. Help me up. Then take me to Susan. I need to speak with her."

Evan slowly walked over to his grandmother and helped lift her to her feet. It was hard to get her up, and he could feel his muscles straining, but he was able to do it.

"What's your name?" asked Grandma, straightening her cap on her head.

Suddenly, Evan recalled a character in a story that he and Jessie had made up when they were younger. "Grumpminster Fink. At your service, madam." He crooked out his arm.

"That's a very strange name," she said, but she took hold of his elbow, and slowly they made their way down off the hill, out of the woods, away from the falling night, and into the warmth and brightness of the house.

# Chapter 7
# Chickens

Jessie looked up from her notebook as Evan walked into the living room. She and Maxwell had spent most of the day walking all over Grandma's property, looking for someone to spy on. Now they were watching *Get Smart* while Jessie wrote important notes that would help them with their spy mission. They'd finished watching the episode called "Diplomat's Daughter" and were about to watch the one where Maxwell Smart disguises himself as a giant chicken. At the top of the first page of her notebook, Jessie had written, "The Bell Bandit," which she thought sounded just like the title of a real episode from the show.

When Evan walked in, Jessie was surprised to

see that he had his snow boots on. "Not allowed!" she said, pointing her pencil at the dripping boots. "You're tracking in snow!"

"Mom!" shouted Evan. "Mom, can you come here?" Jessie looked at Evan's face. It didn't look the way it usually did. It almost looked like Evan was scared of something. But that didn't make any sense, because there was nothing to be afraid of here in the house. Jessie looked over at Maxwell. He hadn't even noticed that Evan had come in the room. He was busy watching the television.

"What is it?" shouted Mrs. Treski from the second floor.

Evan took the stairs two at a time. Ten seconds later, Mrs. Treski came hurrying down with Evan right behind her. Without saying a word, they disappeared into the kitchen. Jessie slowly got up from the couch and wandered after them, not sure she wanted to see what was going on.

In the kitchen, Jessie's mom was trying to take Grandma's coat off, but Grandma kept twisting away, saying it was time to feed the chickens.

Chickens! Just like on *Get Smart*. But Jessie knew that Grandma didn't keep chickens anymore. She used to, for years and years, and Jessie remembered the smelly coop and the soft fluff of feathers when she held a hen and the warm, smooth eggs that came in all different colors. That had been a long time ago, when Jessie was just a little kid. Why was Grandma saying she had to feed the chickens now?

"I'll feed the chickens, Mrs. Joyce," said Evan. Why was Evan calling Grandma *Mrs. Joyce*? "I'll take care of everything."

"You don't know how!" said Grandma angrily. "Susan, stop it. I have my chores to do." She swatted at Jessie's mom with her good hand and twisted away again.

"Yes, I do," said Evan. "The feed is in the barn, in the barrel to the left of the door. I fill the empty milk jug then shake it into the two feeders. And then I refill the pan with fresh water."

Grandma stopped struggling. "How do you know that?"

"I used to feed the chickens for you all the time," said Evan. Jessie thought his voice sounded funny, like it was being squeezed out of a toothpaste tube.

"Did you?" Her voice was quiet. She looked at Evan for a long time. "All right, then."

Evan walked out the back door and headed for the barn. Where was he going?

"Come on, Mom," said Mrs. Treski, helping Grandma out of her coat. Grandma was very quiet now. It looked as if she was concentrating really hard on a particularly difficult jigsaw puzzle.

Mrs. Treski led Grandma out of the kitchen. Jessie followed them into the living room and watched them go upstairs.

"You don't see that every day," Jessie murmured.

"You certainly don't," said Maxwell, right on cue, his eyes still glued to the TV set.

Seconds later Evan walked in through the front door.

"Why did you pretend to feed the chickens?" Jessie blurted out.

Evan pointed to the ceiling. "Is she upstairs?"

"Yeah, with Mom." Jessie looked at Evan's face. "There are no chickens, Evan!"

Evan shrugged. "Yeah, I know. I just thought it would be the easiest thing. I don't know."

"Is she pretending she doesn't know you again?"

"It's not pretending, Jessie!" Evan sounded angry. Why would he be angry? What had she done?

"That doesn't make sense," said Jessie. "You don't just forget someone in your family. That's not possible."

"Yeah, well, tell Grandma that. *You* can talk to her. She remembers *you*." And now Jessie was positive that Evan was angry.

"None of this makes sense," said Jessie. "I'm going to go get Mom."

"No!" said Evan. "Leave her alone. She's taking care of Grandma."

"So?" said Jessie. "She can still talk to me." She headed for the stairs.

"Don't!" And the way he said it made Jessie stop and turn around. Maxwell laughed loudly at something that was on the TV, and Evan looked at him.

Then in a quiet voice, Evan said, "Why does he have to be here?"

"Because we're watching TV," Jessie said. What was wrong with Maxwell? Why didn't Evan want him around?

"Whatever," said Evan, and he headed for the kitchen. But before he left the room, he turned and said, "You were right. The bell's gone. We saw it, Grandma and me. Just before she went loopy."

Jessie went back to the couch and sat down next to Maxwell. Maybe there was something about the bell being gone that made Grandma forget. Jessie had been talking about the missing bell the first time Grandma went loopy. Now Grandma had *seen* that the bell was gone. Jessie wondered if the bell was part of the problem. If the bell were back where it belonged, the way it had always been, would Grandma be better?

"Tomorrow is New Year's Eve," Jessie said to Maxwell. "We've got to find that bell before midnight tomorrow."

# Chapter 8
# Out of Whack

The next morning, Pete showed Evan how to use a plumb bob to determine a true vertical. They were replacing the windows on the second floor, and they needed to get the window casings set in straight. It turned out to be a lot trickier than he thought.

"You can't just set 'em according to the studs," said Pete, "because this is an old house and the studs are cockeyed. And you can't use the floor or the ceiling to mark against, because the floor slopes and the ceiling sags. Old houses. Everything is out of whack."

Evan nodded. Old houses *and* old people, he thought.

Pete showed him how the plumb bob worked. It was a heavy metal weight tied to a length of string, and when you let the weight hang free, the string made a straight line "that goes all the way to the center of the earth," according to Pete.

"Really?" asked Evan.

"Yep. No matter where you go, no matter what you're standing on, if you have a plumb bob, it points straight to the center of the earth." He handed the plumb bob to Evan to try out. "That's gravity for you."

Evan hung the plumb bob from his finger like a yoyo. "That is so cool."

"Well, like my dad always said, 'Gravity is our friend.'"

Now that Pete had gone to the hardware store to buy a new box of galvanized screws, Evan was wandering around the house with the plumb bob to see if he could find even one thing that was the way it was supposed to be. It was surprising. Evan would look at a door and think it was straight, but then when he held up the string, he could see that it was crooked. The front door was out of whack. The railings on the stairs were out of whack. All the windows in the living room were out of whack.

"This house is crazy!" he announced loudly, even though there was no one there to hear him. His mother had gone into town to talk with the insurance agent handling the fire claim, Jessie was off with Maxwell, and Grandma was taking a nap.

"You can say that again!" A voice came from the kitchen. Evan walked in to find his grandmother wrapping her new scarf around her neck. Her injured arm was still in its sling, but she managed to get the scarf on with just one good hand.

"Grandma, you're supposed to be napping." He put the plumb bob on the kitchen counter next to the toaster and noticed that his mom's cell phone was plugged into the outlet, charging. His mother's phone was old, and the battery ran out just about every day. She kept saying she was going to replace it, but she never did.

"Says who?" said Grandma.

"Mom said."

"I'm not four, Evan. I know when I'm tired, and I know when I'm not."

Evan was so relieved to hear that she knew who he was, he smiled. But then he saw that she was putting on her snow boots, and the smile disappeared from his face. "Where are you going?"

"For a walk," said Grandma. "It makes me crazy being all cooped up."

"No," said Evan firmly. "Mom doesn't want you going out—" He was about to say *alone,* but he stopped himself.

"Since when does your mother tell me what to do?" Grandma had gotten both boots on her feet and was now reaching for her dark green barn jacket. She slipped her good arm through one sleeve and buttoned the loose coat over her injured arm. Evan was surprised to see how quickly and easily she managed the buttons. His grandmother really was amazing.

"Please don't go, Grandma," said Evan. "It's getting late. It'll be dark soon."

"I'll be quick. I just need to stretch my legs and see the sky. The trees are calling to me. Can't stand being in the house all day."

She was going. Evan could see that there was nothing he could do to stop her. That panicked feeling came back. Something bad was going to happen. How could he stop it? What was he supposed to do?

"I'll come with you," he said.

"Fine, but be quick. There's not much daylight left. I'll wait for you out front." Grandma pulled her hat on her head, looped Jessie's scarf once more around her neck, and walked out the back door.

Evan slipped his coat on first and checked to make sure he had both gloves in his pockets. Then he started to hunt for his boots. One of them was in the boot bin, but the second one was missing. He emptied out the entire bin, looked under the bench, and even checked in the kitchen, but the boot was nowhere to be seen. After five minutes had gone by, he finally thought to look between the clothes dryer and the wall, and there was his boot, wedged in tight. He wrestled it out and got it on his foot, then hurried out the back door and around the house to the front yard.

But Grandma was gone.

# Chapter 9
# Stakeout

"We need a map," said Jessie. She and Maxwell were at his house planning their stakeout. "Tonight's New Year's Eve, for crying out loud!" Luckily, it was early afternoon. There was still time, if they worked fast.

Maxwell had lots of drawing materials in his room: paper, markers, colored pencils, rulers, protractors. He even had one of those big slanting desks that architects use to draw up their plans. It was perfect. Jessie climbed up on the tall stool and began to draw.

There were only four houses within a mile of Grandma's house: the Uptons', Mrs. Lewis's, Maxwell's house, and the old Jansen house, which no

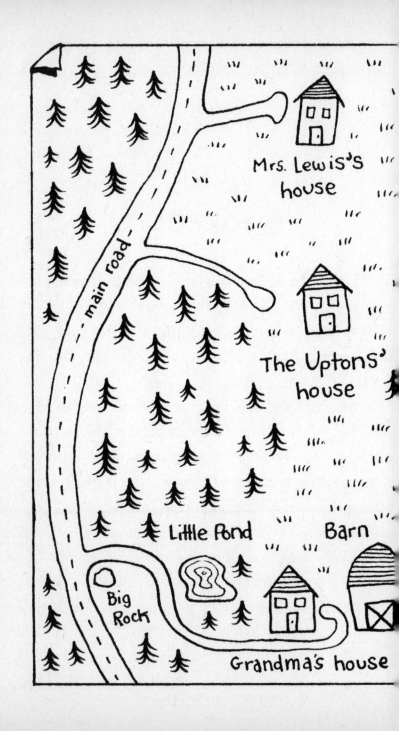

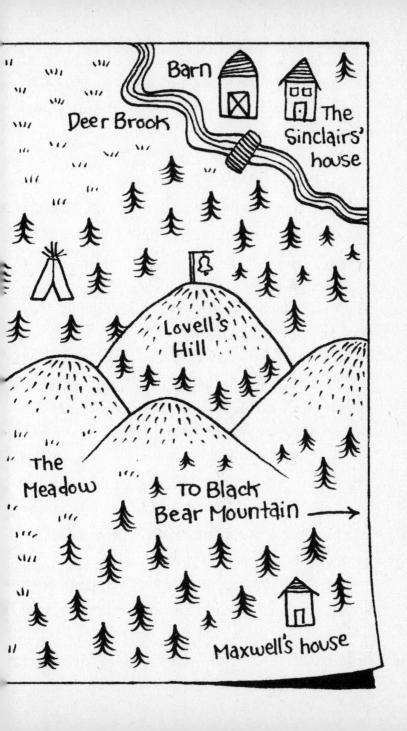

one had lived in for years. Last summer Jessie and Evan had looked in the windows, and the house was as empty as a seashell.

But people moved around. So Jessie asked, "Is anyone living in that old empty house?"

Maxwell made a face. "That's where the Sinclairs live," he said. "They moved in right after me. But I was here first!"

Jessie wrote "The Sinclairs' House" on her map. Then she called Maxwell over, and together they stared at the piece of paper.

Jessie was pretty sure that Mrs. Lewis, who lived alone, hadn't taken the bell. Mrs. Lewis was close to ninety years old. There was no way an old lady like that could lift a hundred-pound bell.

The Uptons were good friends of Grandma's. They're the ones who had driven her to the hospital when she fell. The Uptons checked in on Grandma at least once a week, and Jessie's mom talked to them on the phone from time to time.

"I don't think the Uptons took Grandma's bell," Jessie said. She pointed to the Sinclair house on the other side of the bridge. "What are they like? Do they have any kids?"

"Mean boys," said Maxwell. He started rocking back and forth, taking that odd half-step with his right foot before shifting his weight back to his left. "Two of 'em. Mean, mean boys."

"What makes them mean?" asked Jessie, thinking back to the girls in her last-year class who had played a rotten joke on her. Jessie felt her face go hot, just remembering what they'd done.

Maxwell shook his head. "Won't say it. Mean boys. Both of 'em. Mean."

Jessie frowned. She needed Maxwell's help. If she was going to be Agent 99, she needed an Agent 86.

"Well, how old are they?"

"Jeff's in fifth grade and Mike's in fourth." Maxwell's rocking was getting faster, and then he stopped rocking and started walking in circles, snapping the fingers on his right hand like he was cracking a whip and making that strange puffing noise.

"Huh. They're not so big," said Jessie. But in her mind she imagined boys that towered over her, boys even taller than Evan, and he was one of the tallest boys in his fourth-grade class.

"They don't have to be big. They're mean," Maxwell said.

"You keep saying that," Jessie pointed out. "Stop repeating yourself. And sit down, for Pete's sake. You're making a lot of noise." Sometimes Maxwell could be very distracting.

Maxwell sat down on the edge of the bed, but he kept snapping his fingers and moving his feet back and forth, quietly blowing air through his lips.

"Did you ever hear them talk about Grandma's bell?" Jessie asked.

"Uh-huh. On the bus. They said they were going to take it."

"Really?" said Jessie. "They really *said* that? Why didn't you tell me?"

"You never asked."

"A person doesn't need to ask a question like that. A person should just know that that's the kind of information you'd tell a secret agent." Honestly, sometimes she just didn't get Maxwell. He was a smart kid, but there were times when he acted like he had rocks in his head.

"When did you hear them talking about Grandma's bell?"

"Wednesday. December eighth. At 2:23 p.m."

Jessie stared at him. "How do you remember that?"

Maxwell shrugged.

Jessie wasn't sure if Maxwell was going to turn out to be a terrible spy or the best spy who ever lived. Either way, they had their suspects, and that meant it was spying time.

Jessie pointed to the map. "That's where we need to go for the stakeout," she said. "We need to watch those boys. See what they do and where they hide their stuff."

"Nope, nope, nope," said Maxwell, shaking his head. "I'm not going there. They're mean boys."

"They'll never even see us. We'll hide in the woods," said Jessie. "We'll need bino-specs, though. Do you have anything like that?"

"I won't go," said Maxwell. "I won't go."

"Fine," said Jessie. "I'll go alone."

"Okay."

Jessie shook her head. "A friend is not supposed to make another friend go on a stakeout alone. You don't know anything about being a friend." Jessie thought of all the times Evan had explained to her the rules for getting along with other kids. Now, here she was explaining those rules to Maxwell. It felt weird.

But it didn't matter much, because Maxwell didn't seem to care one bit that she was calling him a bad friend. It seemed to Jessie that all he cared about was staying away from the Sinclair house. She thought for a minute and decided to try a different approach.

"I thought you said you were smart."

"I am," he said. "Maxwell Smart."

"Well, if you're really Maxwell Smart, then tell me what you always say to the Chief." Jessie started talking in a deep voice that she hoped sounded like the Chief on *Get Smart.* "Maxwell, you'll be facing every kind of danger imaginable . . ." Jessie waited for Maxwell to reply. She knew that Maxwell had memorized every line of dialogue in all 138 episodes of the show.

Maxwell whispered his line so quietly, Jessie couldn't hear it. "Louder!" she shouted. "Maxwell, you'll be facing every kind of danger imaginable . . ."

". . . and loving it!" shouted Maxwell. He broke into a big grin.

"You see! It'll be fun. We'll be just like Agent 99 and Maxwell Smart, and we'll find the bell!"

"We're not going to find the bell," said Maxwell.

"Don't be a pessimist," said Jessie, using one of her favorite big words. She headed for the door with the map in her hand. "We need to find binoculars. And flashlights. And maybe some kind of a weapon."

*   *   *

An hour later they were crouched behind a clump of young pine trees that grew on the edge of the woods. In front of them lay the bridge that crossed Deer Brook, and beyond that was the Sinclairs' house, their barn, and more woods.

Jessie stared through the binoculars they had borrowed from Maxwell's mom, but there wasn't much to see. She wished the binoculars were attached to a pair of eyeglasses, like the bino-specs on *Get Smart,* but there hadn't been time for that.

"We need to get closer," she said.

"Nuh-uh," said Maxwell, backing up slowly and bouncing a little.

Without waiting for Maxwell to agree, Jessie started running toward the house in a crouched-over position, keeping as low to the ground as she could. It was hard going because the snow was still deep, but she was determined to see what was happening inside the house.

When Jessie got to the porch steps, she scampered up and then pressed herself against the outside wall of the house. This, she thought, was the way a real agent would behave. She was good at this! It gave her a thrill to think that she was about to spy on a real suspect of a real crime.

She waited a minute without moving to see if Maxwell was going to follow her, but when she looked through her binoculars at the clump of pines she had just left, she could see that he was still there, hunkered down in the snow.

*What a scaredy-cat!* Of course, her own heart was pounding like a drum, but at least she had made it

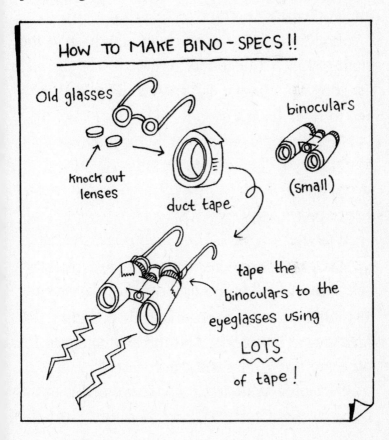

to the porch. What should she do now? Continue with the spy mission, or go back and get Maxwell? She thought about what the real Agent 99 would do, and she knew she didn't have a choice. Secret agents always stuck together. That was the whole point of having a partner.

Jessie tiptoed off the porch and ran back to the clump of pines. She found Maxwell just as she had left him, squatting in the snow and rocking back and forth on his heels.

"You have to come right now," she said.

"No!"

"Yes!"

"I won't."

"You will!"

He closed his eyes and shook his head furiously.

"Maxwell Smart, you listen to me. You've got a mission to do, and you're going to do it. We're spies. And they're the enemy. And this is what spies do. We creep up on the enemy, and we spy!"

She grabbed the sleeve of Maxwell's coat, and—

Jessie couldn't believe it—he came along. Just like that, he followed her across the yard and up the porch. In less than a minute, they were both pressed up against the wall with their heads just inches below the window.

But when they dared to lift their heads and peek in—there was nothing to see. They were just staring at a regular old dining room.

Silently, Jessie motioned with her hand for Maxwell to follow her. Crouched down, she crossed the porch to the window on the other side of the front door, and Maxwell came along right after her.

Again, they slowly raised their heads to look inside the window and saw . . . nothing. Just the living room, with no one in it.

Jessie sank down, pressing her back against the house. She looked at Maxwell, hoping he'd have a great idea, but he just looked like he wanted to go home. Spying was more difficult than Jessie had imagined.

Suddenly, there was a clattering and banging

noise inside the house. The front door flew open, and two boys in ski jackets and boots came charging out of the house and onto the porch.

# Chapter 10
# Shattering Glass

Evan started running down the driveway. Grandma would be easy to spot, he was sure. She was wearing a dark green coat that would stand out like a flag with all that white snow blanketing the ground. He wished he could follow her tracks, but Jessie and Maxwell and Pete and Evan had made so many footprints since yesterday, it was impossible to make sense out of the mishmash that covered the driveway.

And what if she hadn't stuck to the driveway? What if she was in the woods that spread out on both sides? Evan ran past Little Pond, looking left and right. The woods were shaded and filled with the shifting shadows of brown and green cast by tall pine trees. The sun was low in the sky, and the woods seemed to be sprouting strange shapes right before his eyes. If Grandma had stopped to sit down, if she was hurt and lying on the ground surrounded by the thickness and silence of those trees, he would never see her.

He started to run faster. He thought of calling out, but a voice inside told him not to. Maybe Grandma had forgotten who he was again. Maybe she would be afraid of him. If she heard his voice calling, she might hide, and then he would never find her.

The thought banged against the inside of his skull with every crashing step he took. It was cold, and it was getting dark. She was old and didn't re-member things right. People died up here in the mountains. Kids lost in a snowstorm. Grownups when their cars broke down. Hikers who left the trails and became disoriented. Evan had heard the stories. People died up here.

Evan kept running. The driveway was long and curved and stretched for over half a mile before reaching the road. He was breathing hard, and each breath felt like a rusty knife sawing through his lungs. His eyes stung from the cold, and two puddles of snot collected under his nostrils. But he kept running. Running toward the road. How far could she have gotten? As far as the road? She was wearing a dark green coat. No one would be able to see that coat if she was walking on the side of the road after dark. What if a car came around a curve too fast?

When Evan reached the Big Rock, he heard a car—the crunch and grind of its wheels as it turned from the main road onto the driveway. Mom! Evan would have screamed if his throat weren't so dry and raw from running in the cold. He waved his arms wildly, running toward the road.

But it wasn't his mother's car. It was Pete's truck, and Pete rolled down his window to find out why Evan was acting like a crazy person in the middle of the road. Breathing hard, trying to keep from crying, Evan explained.

Pete listened seriously. "Okay, first thing, let's call your mom."

"She doesn't have her cell phone with her—she

left it at home! And I don't know exactly where she is. Somewhere in town. Meeting with an insurance agent."

Pete nodded his head slowly, letting this information sink in.

"All right, then. Here's the plan. Someone needs to stay at the house. Can you do that? Can you be the person who answers the phone if anyone calls and who waits there in case your grandmother comes back on her own?"

Evan nodded his head.

"I'll call the police, and they'll put together a search. When's your mom expected back?"

Evan shook his head. "She said by dinnertime."

"I think I better drive into town and track her down," said Pete. "If she gets back before I do, have her call me on my cell, okay?"

"Okay." Evan was glad Pete was here, giving orders. Still, nothing Pete had said so far made Evan feel like Grandma was any closer to being found.

"I'll take you back to the house," said Pete.

"No, I'll walk," said Evan. He wanted Pete to go get his mother as soon as possible. And there was nothing waiting back at the house for him. Evan was sure of that.

Pete backed up the truck to the road and then spun the wheel and roared off. Evan started walking slowly toward the house. With every step he took, he became more convinced that Grandma was out in the woods, out in the falling darkness, out in the cold. And he couldn't help feeling that it was his fault. He should have convinced her not to go for a walk. He should have talked her into waiting with him in the mudroom. He should have found his boot more quickly. Heard her leaving. Figured out which way she'd gone. Not been the one she forgot. The one she didn't like.

When Evan got back to the house, he went first to the barn. No one was there. Then he stood in the front yard, the last place Grandma had been, and stared at the house. No lights were on. Grandma wasn't back. Pete had told him to wait inside. That was his job. And over the last few days, Pete had taught him the importance of each man doing his job and doing it well.

But what if Grandma had gone to the bell? What

if the bell had "called to her"? That's what Grandma said. Sometimes things called to her, and she had to follow their voices. A bird. A cluster of irises. The pond. The moon. All these things called to Grandma from time to time. And she always went when she was called.

Evan dove into the woods, finding the path that led through the trees to Lovell's Hill. The sun was dipping below Black Bear Mountain and everything had gone flat and gray, but Evan knew the path. He hurried until he made it to the top of the steep rise where the old oak crossbeam stood.

Evan looked around. Black Bear Mountain rose behind him like a giant tidal wave. The trees looked like soldiers guarding a gate. The snow under his feet seemed to deaden all sound, and the cold was beginning to creep up into his boots and snake its way up his legs.

Evan stared at the crossbeam, empty like an eye socket. Grandma wasn't here. The bell wasn't here. Nothing was the way it was supposed to be. Nothing was ever going to be the way it was supposed to be.

Evan had that feeling that he got sometimes—that out-of-nowhere feeling—of missing his dad. His dad was supposed to be here in an emergency. But his dad wasn't here and hadn't been for a long time. Sometimes he sent e-mails with pictures attached of all the places he traveled for work, and sometimes he sent gifts—a felt hat from Pakistan or a tiny bottle made out of blue glass from Afghanistan. But Evan hadn't seen his dad in almost a year.

And suddenly Evan knew who it was he needed to help him find Grandma. It wasn't his father. It wasn't his mother. He needed someone who would treat it like a math problem, who would keep a clear head. Someone who would be able to solve the puzzle. He needed Jessie.

Evan knew the way to Maxwell's house and figured he could be there in ten minutes if he ran the whole way. But as he turned to head down the hill, the air splintered with sound—first a scream and then the noise of shattering glass. The sound came from the direction of the little bridge that crossed Deer Brook. Evan started to run.

# Chapter 11
# Agent 99 Goes Solo

Jessie felt as if someone had waved a wand and turned her entire body to stone. Every muscle froze; the air locked in her lungs; even her eyes refused to blink. She pressed her back against the wall of the house and prayed to become invisible.

The two boys, though, never turned around. They raced off the porch without a single backward glance and ran toward the barn. Within ten seconds they were gone, and Jessie and Maxwell were left alone on the wide wooden porch.

"That was a close one," whispered Jessie, surprised her voice was working at all.

But Maxwell didn't say anything. His face had gone sort of grayish white, and his eyes kept staring where the boys had been.

Finally he whispered, "They would have killed us if they found us."

"They would not!" Jessie whispered back. "Maybe they would have yelled and told their mother, and maybe we would have gotten in trouble, but they would not have killed us."

"You don't know them!" said Maxwell, his voice rising dangerously.

"Shhh! You want to get us caught? Jeepers, Maxwell, act like a spy, would you?"

Maxwell stood up and started walking in circles. Jessie stared through her binoculars at the barn.

"They were carrying stuff," she said. "Did you notice?" Jessie had seen that both boys had something in their hands, but she'd been too scared to see what.

"A shoebox and a hammer," said Maxwell, still walking. "Jeff had the shoebox. Mike had the hammer."

"Wow. You *are* a good spy," said Jessie. She wished

she'd noticed those things, but it had all happened so fast.

Jessie looked at the barn again. Maxwell started to walk slower and slower, and then he stopped and just stood in one spot, rocking back and forth.

"We need to go see what they're doing in that barn," said Jessie.

Maxwell started shaking his head.

"Yes, we do," she said. "I bet that's where they hide things. I bet they've got a secret compartment in that barn, and that's where they are right now, and if we find that secret compartment, we'll find the bell."

"No," said Maxwell. "No, we won't. We will not find the bell in that barn."

"Well, we're going to find something, that's for sure," said Jessie. "Come on." She scooted off the porch in her low-to-the-ground crouch and hurried across the open front yard to the barn. One quick glance over her shoulder told her that Maxwell was staying behind. She'd have to do this bit of spying alone. *Agent 99 goes solo.*

The large sliding door to the barn was open just

a foot, but Jessie didn't want to spy from there. If the boys came barreling out the door, she'd get caught for sure, and she could still remember what it felt like to be on the porch, pressed up against the wall of the house, with nowhere to hide. She could hear music coming from inside the barn, a pop song that she recognized.

Nope, this time she was going to be smart. She and Evan had circled this barn a dozen times over the years. She knew there were windows on the sides and back of the barn. She walked to the left until she came to the first of two small windows. The boys had turned on all the overhead lights—rows and rows of them, which lit up the barn like a stage. This was lucky for her, because it made it much easier to see inside the barn, and she knew that with the fading daylight she would be almost invisible if the boys looked up.

She peeked her head around to look in the barn, but all she could see was the usual stuff: a tractor, old tools hanging on the wall, a workbench with piles of magazines all over it, baled hay. It looked like her grandma's barn. Jessie couldn't see the boys anywhere. But she could hear hammering.

She crouched down again and scuttled over to the second window, but she still couldn't see the boys. The hammering stopped, and then it started up again.

Jessie continued to walk around the outside of the barn. She was starting to think she might need to sneak inside the barn itself, when she popped her head up at the single small window on the back of the barn and came practically face-to-face with the older of the two boys. It was as if she was standing just three feet away from him and he was looking right at her.

Jessie was so surprised, she immediately ducked her head back down and waited to hear a shout from the boy. But the hammering continued, and Jessie realized that the bright light inside and the growing darkness outside had turned the window into a one-way mirror. She could peek in without being seen.

Slowly, she inched her head up.

Jeff and Mike were in one of the stalls that ran along the back of the barn. The ceiling here was low, the floor covered in rough wood. Jessie looked around and realized the compartment was used for storing firewood. The split firewood was stacked in racks that jutted out of one of the side walls of the small room. The racks were made of long two-by-fours nailed into the floor and the ceiling. The room looked dirty and creepy to Jessie, but it was a perfect place to hide something.

Both boys were standing in front of the middle rack. Jessie could see that they had pounded a couple of nails into the two-by-fours along with some thin splints of wood that formed an *X*. Two strings dangled from the nails. The boys were pounding something else onto the two-by-fours, but Jessie couldn't see what it was. The younger one—Mike— held the nail steady, while the older one—Jeff— hammered it in. She reached into her backpack and took out her notebook to make a quick diagram. This might be important information she was gathering, and she wanted to get it right.

As she watched, Jessie figured out what the boys were nailing to the board: two large spools of thread, each one set on a nail so that it could turn easily. She added the spools to her diagram.

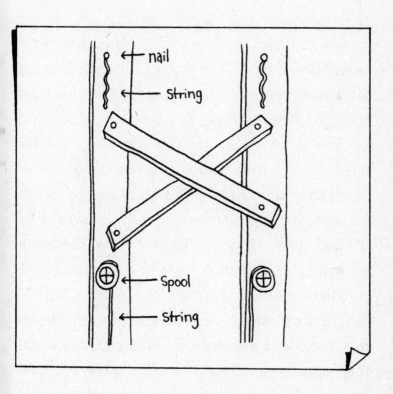

nail
String
Spool
String

"What are they doing?" a voice whispered nearby.

Jessie nearly dropped her pencil, she was so startled. In the dim light, she could just see Maxwell peeking around the corner of the barn. He'd snuck up close to her without her even hearing him! He really did have all the skills of a good spy.

She motioned for him to come over, and Maxwell glided noiselessly over the snow. She pointed to her diagram and then pointed at the window and shrugged her shoulders to show that she didn't know what was going on inside. Maxwell poked his head up and looked through the window.

"What's in the box?" Maxwell whispered to Jessie. Jessie had forgotten all about the shoebox that Jeff had been carrying before. It sat on the floor a few feet away from the boys with a rock resting on its lid. Jessie shook her head.

The boys tested the spools by spinning them on their nails. The spools spun wildly, making a whirring, clacking noise that made Jeff and Mike laugh. Jessie was intrigued. The boys didn't seem mean at all! They were building something new, and Jessie liked to do that, too—whether it was making a complicated track for racing marbles or a lemonade stand with hand-painted signs and a canopy.

Next to her, Maxwell started to make his puffing sound. Jessie looked over at him and shook her head sharply. If they blew this stakeout, they weren't going to get a second chance to find the bell before tonight. Maxwell put a hand over his own mouth and started to rock back and forth. His eyes were glued to the window like he was watching a horror movie.

Jessie turned back in time to see Mike pick up the shoebox and reach a hand under the lid. Jeff crowded close to Mike, and for a minute, Jessie couldn't see what they were doing.

Then Mike held up his hands, and Jessie could see that he was holding a frog—a live frog! Its back legs kicked a couple of times, dangling below Mike's hands. Mike held the frog up while Jeff tied one of the strings attached to the nail to one of the frog's front legs. Then he tied the other string to the other front leg. Jessie couldn't figure out what they were planning to do. Maxwell started to make a noise Jessie had never heard from him. It was like a moan, but it came out in short bursts. The hand over his mouth muffled the sound, but Jessie was still worried the boys would hear it. There was nothing she could do, though. She couldn't take her eyes off the scene inside the barn.

Now the frog was dangling by its front legs, its back pressed against the wooden splints the boys had hammered into place, its pale green belly facing out. It tried to kick itself free, but its powerful hind legs had nothing to push against.

The boys set to work on the frog's jumping legs. Jeff grabbed the left leg and started to wrap the thread from one of the spools around it. Mike did the same with the right leg and the other spool. Jessie started to see a picture in her head, a picture of how the spools would turn, how the strings would get tighter, how the legs of the frog would stretch and stretch and stretch until . . .

Out of the corner of her eye, Jessie saw Maxwell press his other hand over his mouth. The sounds from his mouth were coming out faster and louder. Jessie felt like she was deep underwater—everywhere heaviness pressed on her. Her legs felt heavy. Her arms felt heavy. Her mouth felt sealed shut, as if a big hand had clamped down on it. She couldn't move. She couldn't think.

Jeff began to turn the spool on the left as Mike turned the one on the right. The frog began to kick furiously, but soon the kicks became little quivers as the strings pulled in all directions. And then the quivering stopped. The frog couldn't move. All four legs were stretched as far as they could go. Only the soft green belly of the frog moved, vibrating in and out, as if its heart would beat right out of its chest. And the frog's mouth opened and closed, in what looked to Jessie like a silent scream.

Suddenly, there *was* a scream, and Jessie had the strange thought that it came from the frog! It was a cry like Jessie had never heard before. She turned and saw Maxwell screaming wildly as he kicked at the snow, looking for something buried underneath. When he found what he wanted—a rock the size of his fist—he picked it up and hurled it through the window. The glass smashed to pieces, and Jessie jumped back. Maxwell continued to scream as if he were being skinned alive.

And then he bolted, running back over the bridge, leaving Jessie in the dark with the two Sinclair boys staring right at her through the hole in the shattered glass.

## Chapter 12
# A Fair Fight

Evan ran toward the bridge, stumbling in the deepening darkness. On the other side, he could see someone running toward him, but the light was so dim, he couldn't tell who it was. The person was running as if a wild animal were chasing it, arms clawing madly at the air, legs galloping down the hill toward the bridge. Evan had to stop abruptly at the bridge to prevent a collision.

That's when he saw it was Maxwell. But Maxwell was supposed to be with Jessie. Where was Jessie? Who had screamed? What broke the glass?

"Maxwell, what happened?" Evan shouted, but Maxwell wasn't stopping. He barreled over the bridge, running past Evan as if Evan didn't even exist.

"Stop! Stop!" Evan yelled, but it seemed like Maxwell never heard him. He ran up the hill and into the woods, and then he was out of sight.

Evan turned and raced over the bridge and up the hill where Maxwell had come from. There was a house up here, the old Jansen house. He saw that the lights were on, so he headed for the porch but then stopped. He heard voices. Coming from behind the barn. And one of them was Jessie's.

When Evan rounded the back corner of the barn, he practically ran over his little sister. She was standing with her legs apart, buried halfway up to her knees in the deep snow, with both arms crooked at the elbow. In each hand, she held a rock the size of a baseball.

In front of her were two boys. It took Evan just a split second to size them up. The bigger one looked to be just about Evan's size; the other one wasn't much smaller. When Jessie saw Evan, she took three quick steps backwards but kept the rocks held tightly in her fists. She'd been holding her own against the boys—that was Jessie!—but Evan could tell she was scared.

126

"Hey!" Evan shouted, and took a step toward the boys.

"Is this your brother?" shouted the older boy at Jessie. "He's not so big! We could beat him up with our hands tied behind our backs." The younger boy laughed and said, "Yeah!"

"Come on, then," said Evan. He made a move toward the older boy, pushing his chest out and balling up his fists, but just then a rock landed on the ground right between them.

"Stop it!" said Jessie. "Fighting is for morons!"

"Yeah, like that moron who broke our window!"

"He's not a moron. You're the morons! It's disgusting what you were doing!"

"What is going on?" shouted Evan.

"They were torturing a frog in there, Evan!" Jessie said, and Evan could tell she was on the very edge of crying. "Maxwell and me were spying on them—"

"Yeah, you were spying on us. On our property—"

"So what! You should go to jail for what you did!"

"You're the one who's going to jail! Trespassing. Spying. Breaking windows!"

"Shut up!" Evan yelled, and everyone did. "Jessie, did you break the window?"

"No. Maxwell broke the window. Because they had a frog tied up and were trying to pull its legs off. While it was still *alive*."

Evan looked at the two boys, and suddenly they didn't seem to have anything to say. The older one looked at the ground. The younger one looked at the older one, and then he looked down at the ground, too.

Evan shook his head. "That is *sick*. That is really, really sick." Evan was a tough kid who liked guts and gore as much as anyone. But the thought of hurting a real animal made his stomach turn.

"It's our property. We can do whatever we want on it. And you're still trespassing." The older boy made a move toward Evan, and the younger one backed him up from behind.

Evan stepped forward to show he wasn't afraid. But two of them at once. That was going to be hard, and Evan didn't have a lot of experience with fighting. He tightened his fists at his sides, wishing he had one of his friends from home. Paul or Jack or even Scott Spencer. It would be a fair fight if it were two against two.

*Wham.* Another rock came sailing at them, and this time it hit the older boy in the shoulder.

"Jeez, what are you doing?" he shouted. "You can't throw rocks."

"Who says?" said Jessie. "Show me the rule book." Her voice sounded funny, and Evan could tell she was shaking. But there she was, standing up to those boys. Just like she'd stood up to Scott Spencer when she put him on trial for stealing the lemonade money. She might be the smallest fourth-grader in the world because she'd skipped a grade, but Jessie had bossed around the whole class. When it came to justice, she was fearless. Maybe this was going to be a fair fight after all.

"Hold her down," said the older boy to the younger boy, and as soon as the smaller one took a step toward Jessie, Evan let loose. He shoved the younger boy so hard, the kid fell to the ground, then he turned on the older boy with both his hands up, ready to swing. The older boy quickly backed away.

"Hey, calm down. It's no big deal," he said. "Jeez, you two are really a pain in the neck. Just take your stupid sister and get out of here."

Evan kept his fists up in front of him, standing his ground. Out of the corner of his eye, he could see that the younger brother was crying but had gotten up on his feet. Bullies! It was like his mother said—stand up to them and they always back down.

"Come on, Jess," said Evan, lowering his hands halfway.

"No," said Jessie.

Evan could see that she was holding two more rocks, one in each hand. *No? What was she thinking?*

"Jess, we're going."

"Not until we get that frog out of there."

The older boy took a step forward. "You are *not* going inside our barn. There is no way I'm letting you in there."

Evan could tell the boy meant it. You didn't mess

with farm families and their property. Evan had spent enough time in these woods to know that. Jessie was pushing their luck, and she was going to get them both in a lot of trouble.

But Jessie didn't care. "I'm going to break every window in your barn until your mother comes out here to see what all the noise is, and then *you* can tell her what you're doing in there."

*Oh man,* thought Evan, feeling his insides crumple up. *Now we're going to get murdered.*

"If you throw even one more rock—" The boy took a step toward Jessie. Evan took a step toward the boy. The younger kid circled around behind Evan. *Here it comes,* thought Evan.

But a voice called out. "Jeff! Mike! Where are you?" It was a woman's voice, and it came from the direction of the house.

"Good!" said Jessie. "Now you have to go inside, or she's going to come looking for you. And then what? Huh?"

To Evan's surprise, the older boy hesitated. The younger boy stopped, too—frozen.

131

"Right now, you two!" The voice rolled across the yard like a bowling ball. "If I have to call you a second time, you'll be sorry I did!"

The younger boy took off.

The older boy looked at Evan and Jessie and said, "You better be gone in five minutes. I'm going to come back out here, and you better be gone." He started walking toward the house, but once he passed the barn, Evan saw that he broke into a run and didn't stop until he was on the porch. He disappeared inside the house, swallowed up by the front door.

Before Evan could say anything, Jessie started to run inside the barn. "We have to get that frog out of there!"

But when they got inside the barn and found their way to the wood storage room, the frog looked more dead than alive. It was hanging by its front legs, its back legs making weak kicking movements that seemed like the feeble waving of a surrender flag. Jessie didn't want to touch the frog, so Evan held the frog's body in his hands while Jessie plucked at the strings tied to each leg. When they got the last one off, Evan put the frog down on the dirt floor of the barn.

It was as if the frog had forgotten how to move. It wiggled its back legs, but couldn't seem to get a solid footing on the cold ground. First one leg and then the other shot out from its body, kicking at the air, but unable to move forward. Evan and Jessie watched, waiting.

"It's going to die," said Jessie, and Evan thought she was probably right. The frog had forgotten how to jump, or maybe its legs had been broken or permanently damaged in some way. Evan felt a sudden wave of sadness for all the things in the world that were damaged and broken.

Evan looked down at the frog and said, "We can't just leave it here to die. We need to take it home." But what he was thinking was, *And put it out of its misery.* He reached down to pick up the small animal, and when his hand was just an inch away, the frog leaped through the air and disappeared under the woodpile.

"Hey!" said Jessie. "He's okay! Did you see him jump? Wow!"

Jessie smiled at Evan, and he wanted to smile back, but he couldn't. The dark thought was still banging inside his head. "C'mon," he said. "We gotta go. And we don't have a lot of time."

## Chapter 13
# The Missing Bell

They went back to the top of Lovell's Hill, where the empty crossbeam stood, because they needed a place to start their search and Jessie couldn't think of anywhere else. Night had fallen, and a thick cover of clouds hung low in the sky. Luckily, Jessie had brought a flashlight on the stakeout. The thin yellow beam illuminated the ground just enough for them to make their way.

At the top of the hill, Jessie flashed the light ahead of her. There was the heavy wooden crossbeam with its empty space where the bell should have hung.

The missing bell. What a lousy spy she'd turned out to be! She hadn't learned a thing on the stakeout. She still didn't have any proof that the Sinclair boys had stolen the bell in the first place. And Maxwell had ended up half out of his mind, running off—to where? Where was Maxwell now? Was he missing, too?

"Maybe Grandma was here," said Jessie, skipping the flashlight beam over the ground. There were hundreds of footprints in the snow. Both Jessie and Maxwell had crossed this hill several times over the last few days, and Evan had come straight over the hill when he heard Maxwell's scream and the broken glass. There were footprints everywhere. The ground was a tangled-up dance of feet.

"Think, Jessie," said Evan. "It's like a puzzle. You're good at puzzles. Where would she go?"

Jessie looked up toward Black Bear Mountain, but there was no way she could see it in the darkness. The woods behind her were a thick brushstroke of blackness, too. Blackness in front of her. Blackness behind her. Where could Grandma be in all that dark?

Something cold and wet landed on Jessie's cheek. Then another and another. It was beginning to snow.

"Oh, Grandma," said Jessie, quietly.

"C'mon, Jess," said Evan. "You can think this out. I know you can."

In her mind, Jessie made a list. "She wouldn't walk on the road. She hates walking on the road. So forget that. She didn't go to a neighbor, because they would have brought her back. She's not in the barn?"

"I checked."

"Don't you think she's on the farm somewhere?"

Evan nodded his head. "Yeah, but where?" It was a big farm. A hundred acres.

"Let's go back to where she started. The house. And then we'll take the backward loop." That was Grandma's favorite walk, the one that took you all the way to the foot of Black Bear Mountain and then looped back through the woods, up the hill to the New Year's Eve bell. Jessie had done that walk a hundred times with Grandma.

When they got to the dark house, Evan ran inside to grab an extra flashlight and leave a note for their mother. Then they both strapped on snowshoes—the snow was coming down faster now—and headed down the path.

Mom
Jessie and I are looking for grandma. Don't worry. We'll stay close to the house. We have snowshoes and we'll stick together Evan

It was hard going. Evan led the way, and Jessie trudged behind. As they walked, they swung the beams of their flashlights from the path, to the woods on the left, back to the path, and then over to the woods on the right. Jessie called out "Grandma!" from time to time. Once she heard something scrabbling close to her feet, but she told herself it was just a squirrel or maybe a rabbit. Nothing to be afraid of. Still, she picked up her pace so that she was right behind Evan—so close that the tip of her snowshoe caught the tail of his and caused him to stumble. She thought he was going to turn around and yell at her, but he didn't. He just kept going.

When they reached the foot of Black Bear Mountain, Jessie was hot and sweaty under her ski hat, her bangs plastered to her forehead. Her mittened fingers were damp, too, but her cheeks were stinging from the cold.

Jessie wiped her hand across her face. "We haven't found her yet," she said, pausing to rest at the bend in the path that turned away from the mountain and into the woods. She wanted Evan to say something back, something that would give them hope. But Evan didn't say anything. He just shone his light in a circle all around them. The feeble yellow beam danced across trees and rocks and drifts of snow— snow everywhere, covering everything and falling thicker and faster now.

They kept on walking. Now they were cutting

through the woods that covered the far side of Lovell's Hill. There wasn't even a real path here. The only way to navigate was to look for the marked trees, but the markings were invisible in the pitch-black. Even when they focused the beams of their flashlights directly on the trunks of the trees, the falling snow made it impossible to see.

"Grandma!" Jessie called out, but more softly now. The woods were so silent that every sound seemed amplified. Evan kept stopping. Jessie could tell he was trying to get his bearings. It was easy to veer off course in the woods, even in the daytime. At night, with no moon to guide by, it would take all their concentration to find their way to the top of the hill.

*Where are you, Grandma?*

When they reached the top of the hill, they stood on either side of the heavy wooden crossbeam and stared at the darkness all around them.

"Evan?" said Jessie. "I don't know where she is." Jessie felt a heaviness sink into her body, and she knew she was not going to be able to solve this puzzle. She had failed.

Evan's voice came out weak and bedraggled. "You'll figure it out, Jessie. I know you will."

Jessie looked at her big brother and saw that he was crying. There were wet patches on his cheeks, and his long eyelashes glistened in the dim glow of the flashlight.

"Why are you crying?" asked Jessie.

"Because I'm cold! And I'm scared! And—." Evan waved his arms at the nothingness all around them. "It's dark. It's dark, Jessie. And she's all alone out there somewhere. And I bet she's feeling like I am. Cold and scared and afraid of the dark."

Jessie thought about this. This was new information, and she tried to add it to the puzzle.

"Well, if she's cold . . . then she's going to want to go someplace warm," said Jessie. "And if she's scared, then I guess . . ." Jessie thought about the places she went when she was feeling frightened or overwhelmed: the nurse's office at school, her bedroom, the pages of a favorite book. "She probably wants to hide away somewhere."

What kind of place was like that on the farm? A place that was warm. A place that was hidden away.

A place that made you feel safe. Jessie tried to imagine such a place. She closed her eyes so she could concentrate. She tricked her brain into feeling cozy and safe and protected.

Then she opened her eyes and looked at Evan. "I know where she is."

# Chapter 14
# Waiting for a Bus

They couldn't find the tepee. If you'd asked Evan yesterday, he would have said, *I can find that tepee blindfolded.* But here they were, as good as blindfolded because of the darkness, and Evan had no idea where to look. He and Jessie wandered through the woods, flashing their lights in every direction, but either they'd gone too far or not far enough, because the tepee wasn't there.

What if they couldn't find it in the dark? Evan knew his grandmother wouldn't survive a night out in the cold like this. Even if the police managed to get together a search party soon—and Evan hadn't seen a single flashlight or heard any voices in the woods yet—it might be too late by the time they found her. His grandmother was old, and she had a broken wrist. She got confused. She needed help. He started walking faster, but he had no idea if he was getting closer to the tepee or farther away.

"Stop," said Jessie. "We need a system. We can't just keep walking around hoping we're going to find it."

So they followed their tracks back to the bell and stared at the edge of the woods they had just come out of.

"Where's the Lightning Tree?" asked Evan. They swept their flashlight beams back and forth, but they couldn't see through the thick falling snow. So they split up, each starting at one edge of the woods and working their way to the middle, checking each tree that they came to.

Finally, Evan said, "I found it!" And he had. Up close, the tree was unmistakable, burned black and naked without any branches except the single stubby one. The branch pointed their way into the woods, and they plunged deeper and deeper in. Evan kept telling himself, *We're getting closer, we're getting closer,* but it seemed to him that they were taking way too long to find Grandma.

"There it is," said Jessie, pointing with her flashlight through the trees.

And there it was. Just where it had always been. The tepee they'd built the summer before last. The tepee that was strong enough to survive a hundred winters. Evan broke into an awkward run, his snowshoes flopping and slapping the ground. When he reached the opening, he stopped, suddenly afraid to see what was inside.

Jessie caught up behind him, looked at him, then reached out to pull back the tarp.

"No!" said Evan, grabbing her hand and pulling it back. He didn't know what they would find inside, but if it was bad, he didn't want Jessie seeing it first.

He took a step forward so that his body blocked Jessie's view, then he slowly pulled back the top edge of the tarp, just enough for him to poke his flashlight inside and peer into the circle of light.

There was Grandma.

Sitting on the ground, cross-legged.

Her eyes blinked like an owl's, caught in an un-expected light. How long had she been sitting like that?

"Hi," said Evan, afraid to call her *Grandma* in case that spooked her. It felt to him as though she were standing on the edge of a cliff and any sudden move-ment could topple her over. He noticed that her hat was crooked and Jessie's scarf dangled from one shoulder.

"Is the bus here?" asked Grandma. "I've been waiting for hours."

"Grandma!" shouted Jessie from behind Evan. Suddenly he felt Jessie shoving his body out of the way, sliding past him and into the tepee. He wanted to grab her and keep her back, but he was holding the flashlight and the tarp, and she slipped by before he could stop her.

"Why are you here, Grandma?" Jessie was prac-tically shouting, or at least it seemed that way to Evan. "Why didn't you come home?"

Grandma looked bewildered. "I'm waiting for the bus. It's been hours. What's the delay?"

"What are you talking about Grandma? There's no bus!"

"No bus! What do you mean? Of course, there's a bus. I take this bus three times a week."

"Grandma," said Jessie, sounding like she was about to cry. "Stop it. Stop pretending. It isn't funny!"

Grandma gave Jessie a disapproving stare. "Who are you? Why are you yelling at me? Where's the bus?"

"Evan!" yelled Jessie, and now she was crying. Evan could see the first few tears pooling up in her eyes, and he knew if she really got going, there would be no stopping her. She hardly ever cried, but when she did, it was a thunderstorm.

"Jess, it's okay," said Evan, pulling on her arm. She tried to shake her arm free, but he got a good firm hold of her. "C'mon. Come out here."

She let him pull her out of the tepee, where they stood side by side in the falling snow. "She's tired," he said. "And she's old. This is how it is now. We have to get used to it."

"No! No, no, no!" said Jessie, shaking her head.

"I won't get used to it. I'll never get used to it! She doesn't even know me!"

"Yeah, she does," said Evan. "Somewhere in her brain she knows exactly who you are. She just can't reach it right now. It's like my bedroom at Grandma's house. It's still there. We just can't get to it for a while. It's off-limits. But she'll remember you again. When she's not so cold and tired."

"I hate this," whispered Jessie.

He bent his head closer to hers. "I know. But look, we've got to get her home. Can you go in there and talk to her? Get her to come out?"

Jessie shook her head. "I can't. I can't."

"Okay," said Evan. "It's okay. You don't have to. I'll go in. Just try to keep quiet, okay? Because I think, you know, we're scaring her."

Jessie clamped her mouth shut and nodded her head yes. Evan stood for a minute outside the tepee, thinking. Then he undid the buckles on his snowshoes and stepped out of them, pulled back the tarp, and ducked inside.

Two summers ago, when they first built the tepee, Evan could stand inside at the tallest spot. But now his head butted up against the sloping branches that leaned against the center tree pole. He started to lean over, then realized it would be easier just to kneel on the ground. This brought him eye to eye with Grandma, and one look at her face told him she was very scared.

"Ma'am?" he said. "Are you waiting for the bus?"

"Yes!" she said. "I've been waiting for hours!" She looked so relieved then—almost happy—that Evan wished more than anything he could make a bus appear, right here in the middle of the woods.

"It isn't coming," he said. "There's been a problem. A flat tire. The bus can't make it here today."

"Well, send another!" said Grandma. "That's ridiculous. There's a bus every hour on this route. I've been taking this bus for years. I know the schedule."

"All the buses are broken," said Evan. "I'm sorry."

"That's inexcusable!" said Grandma. "I'm going to write a letter." The hand on her good arm started to pluck at her coat.

"Yes, you should," said Evan. "But right now, we have to get you home."

"Wait a minute. Who are you?" she asked suddenly.

"I work for the bus company. They told me to tell you that the bus isn't coming and that I should take you home."

"I've been waiting for hours!"

"I know," said Evan. "It's awful. You should write a letter."

"I'm going to!"

All the time they were talking, Evan slowly moved closer to Grandma. When he rested a hand on her arm, she didn't back away, and when he helped her to her feet, she leaned on his shoulder and went along.

"There's another passenger outside," said Evan. "She's been waiting for hours, too. Do you mind if she walks with us?"

"Inexcusable. You can't expect people to wait for hours. People depend on the bus. And what happened to the bench? Who took the bench?"

Evan ushered Grandma outside the tepee and nodded to Jessie, who had taken several steps back. "You know, kids probably," said Evan. "Kids do some really stupid things these days."

He put her arm over his shoulder and his hand on her back, then shone his flashlight on the snow ahead of them. Jessie walked right behind, but Grandma never once turned around to look at her.

Evan kept talking. Grandma seemed to think she was young again, in the days when she rode the bus three times a week to her classes at the community college. Every once in a while, she would stop walking and ask Evan, "Who are you again?" and Evan would remind her that he was with the bus company and it was his job to escort her home. Once she said, "I can't go home! I have to get to class!" But Evan told her that all the classes were canceled because of the snow. Grandma said she thought that was ridiculous, but she kept on walking.

When they reached the house, Evan could see his mother's car and Pete's truck parked out front. He suddenly felt so tired, he wanted to stop right where he was and lie down in the snow. Grandma, however, seemed to perk up when she saw the house in front of her.

"Thank you," she said, taking her arm off his shoulder and patting the front of his ski coat. "It was nice of you to walk me home. But you can go now." And she turned to go into the house.

Evan watched her walk up the stairs, knock the snow off her boots, and push open the front door. He could tell she knew exactly where she was. She was home.

"Evan?" said Jessie. "Is she okay?"

"Sure," said Evan. "Look at her. She's fine." He paused for a second. "She's just different than she was."

"Really different."

Evan shrugged. "Not all that different. Still Grandma." He took a few steps toward the house, then turned around. Jessie wasn't following. "C'mon. Let's go inside."

"No," said Jessie. "I need to go see Maxwell."

The picture came into Evan's mind of Maxwell

running like a wild animal, screaming as he went. It seemed to Evan as if there were an endless number of people to worry about. "You have to come inside first. Mom has to *see* you, to make sure you're okay."

Jessie nodded. Evan waved his arm toward the house. "C'mon. I'll walk you over to Maxwell's later."

# Chapter 15
# What's wrong
# with Maxwell?

Evan kept his promise to her. But it took a while.
First there was the commotion of Mrs. Treski hug-
ging them both about a hundred times. Then Pete
phoned the police to call off the search party. Then
Evan told everyone how they'd found Grandma because *Jessie* had figured it out, because *Jessie* was so
smart. She liked that part.

Then there was dinner, which was just canned
soup and cold sandwiches because no one had the
energy to cook a real meal but everyone was starv-
ing. And then Mrs. Treski said she wanted to get
Grandma to bed early, never mind that it was New

Year's Eve. Which is when Jessie said she wanted to go see Maxwell, and Evan said he'd walk her over. The snow had stopped falling and a bright moon had broken through the clouds, so Mrs. Treski said yes. But be back soon.

When Maxwell's house came into view, Evan stopped on the path. "I'll wait back at the house, okay? Just call when you want to come home." Evan had never been inside Maxwell's house, so maybe he felt funny about going in.

Or maybe Evan just didn't want to talk to Maxwell's mom about what had happened that afternoon. Jessie could understand that.

She had hoped to avoid Mrs. Cooper altogether—somehow slip inside unnoticed. Maybe she wasn't even home? But instead, Maxwell's mom answered the door and asked Jessie to sit in the living room while she finished loading the dishwasher. Jessie sat down on the couch and looked at the photographs on top of the piano. There were dozens of them, and they were all of Maxwell.

Mrs. Cooper walked out of the kitchen, drying

her hands on a dishtowel. She sat on the couch next to Jessie. Usually, Jessie felt comfortable around grownups—sometimes more comfortable than with kids. But not this time.

Mrs. Cooper stared at her, with a look as hard as granite. "So. What happened this afternoon?"

Jessie took a minute to think. Should she tell the whole story? Or would Maxwell get in trouble? Had they broken any rules? What if she just left out the part about spying?

In the end, she figured the whole story was going to come out anyway. She might as well give it up now.

So she told Mrs. Cooper everything, from the very beginning. About the missing bell. And what Maxwell overheard on the bus. And the stakeout and how wrong it had gone. She described the frog and then the rock through the window and how Maxwell ran away screaming. Mrs. Cooper listened without saying a word.

When she was done talking, Jessie waited for Mrs. Cooper's response, but all she said was

"I wish those boys had never moved to the neighborhood."

"Me, too," said Jessie, thinking about the missing bell. She was sure the boys had it hidden somewhere. "But why is Maxwell afraid of them? He's bigger than they are."

"They tease him. Play mean jokes on him. About a month ago, they tricked Maxwell into climbing inside a cardboard moving box. They said it was a game. But instead of a game, they taped him up inside the box and left him like that—for hours. Maxwell doesn't like tight spaces."

"That's horrible," said Jessie. She couldn't imagine being trapped like that. It made her legs and arms feel twitchy just to think about it.

Mrs. Cooper looked across the room, then shook her head slowly. "They're just *mean* boys."

They sure were. But why? Were they born that way? Were some people born one way and some people another?

"You can go see Maxwell now, if you want," said Mrs. Cooper, standing up and snapping the dishtowel over her shoulder. "He's in his room playing a video game."

Jessie jumped off the couch and headed for the stairs that led down to the basement, which was where Maxwell's bedroom was. She was on the third step when she stopped and turned around. "Mrs. Cooper?" said Jessie. "What's wrong with Maxwell?"

Mrs. Cooper paused in the doorway to the kitchen and looked at her. "He's just different, that's all. He sees things differently than we do. He feels the world in a different way, too. Things bother him that wouldn't you or me, like loud noises or changes in his routine or new people. To us, they're no big deal, but to Maxwell, they're a very big deal. And even though Maxwell's incredibly smart, there are some things he has trouble understanding. Like feelings. He has a really tough time understanding feelings."

"Oh," said Jessie.

*Like me,* she thought.

She found Maxwell leaning against the giant gorilla pillow that sat at the head of his bed. The arms of the gorilla wrapped around Maxwell, as if the big furry ape were trying to reach the game controller Maxwell held in his hands.

Maxwell didn't even look up when Jessie walked in.

"Hey," she said.

Maxwell nodded his head, his eyes never leaving the screen.

Jessie stared at the TV. The game was one of those questing games, where dwarves and dragons and giants and other magical characters fight each other and collect treasure. Pretty soon she was sitting on the edge of the bed, as caught up in the game as Maxwell was.

"Can I try?" asked Jessie.

"No, I'm right in the middle of a quest. Later."

"When, later?"

"When I die."

"When are you going to die?"

Maxwell shrugged. "Probably not for a while. I'm really good at this game."

Jessie watched the treasure points pile up on the

counter in the upper-right corner of the screen. Maxwell's character, a twinkly-eyed dwarf with a mohawk, seemed invincible. He killed a dragon, two evil elf twins, and a giant with a weapon that could shoot lightning bolts.

"I wish we'd had one of those when Jeff and Mike tried to hurt that frog," said Jessie.

Maxwell nodded his head. "I would have killed them both."

"You're not supposed to want to kill people in real life," she said, but she knew what he meant. She really didn't like those boys. And even though Evan and Jessie and Maxwell had managed to save the frog, she knew that the Sinclair boys would do something just as awful again someday. Who would be around then to stand up to them?

Besides that, Jessie was sure they had the bell—hidden in the barn or stashed under the porch or maybe buried out in the woods. "Do you think they've got it?" she asked Maxwell. "The bell, I mean?"

"Nope," said Maxwell, punching furiously on

the controller buttons. It was amazing how fast he was. Jessie watched as his dwarf decapitated a black-robed warlock.

"Why not?"

"Because I know where it is."

Jessie continued looking at the screen, not understanding what Maxwell had just said. Was he talking about something in the game? Maybe he didn't get what she was talking about.

"You know where *what* is?"

"The bell," said Maxwell. "Dang!" He pointed at the screen. "I lost a life, but I can buy it back." Ten thousand points fell off the counter, and Maxwell's dead dwarf jumped to his feet and started fighting again.

"You know where the bell is?" Jessie's voice was weirdly quiet. She felt like she'd walked into a mental hospital, and you were not supposed to yell in hospitals.

"Yep."

"Where is it?" Her voice grew a little louder.

"In my closet."

"In your *closet?*" Jessie jumped off the bed and pushed open the sliding door to the closet. On the floor was a laundry basket, an old box filled with LEGO pieces, and Grandma's bell.

"Why did you steal Grandma's bell?" Now Jessie was yelling.

"I didn't steal it. I protected it. Mrs. Joyce was in the hospital for a whole week. I didn't want Jeff and Mike to take it like they said they would. So I took it down and hid it in my closet."

"But . . . but . . . why didn't you tell me that?"

"Because you didn't ask."

"But . . . you knew I was looking for it! When someone's looking for something and you know where it is, you tell them!"

Maxwell kept playing his game. "You said it was a puzzle. You said you like to solve puzzles by yourself. I thought you wanted to figure it out on your own."

"But you can't just take something from someone without telling them. That's *stealing.*"

"Is not. I told Mrs. Joyce. I told her when I visited

her in the hospital. I guess she forgot."

*Well, duh!* thought Jessie.

She stared at the bell. It looked just like it always had. Except it was sitting on the floor of Maxwell's closet! She really did feel like the whole world had gone crazy and left her behind—the only sane person on the planet. She couldn't think of what to say. "You're really . . . you're . . ."

"Smart," said Maxwell. "I'm Maxwell, and I'm smart."

Jessie looked at Maxwell, who was still furiously playing the video game, killing gnomes and druids left and right. It was just like his mother had said: Maxwell was different.

She grabbed hold of the top of the bell and tried to pull on it, to see how heavy it really was. The bell tilted, but there was no way she could lift it.

"Well, if you're so smart," said Jessie, "then tell me how we're going to get this bell out of your basement and hanging up on the hill by tonight."

# Chapter 16
# Ring Out, Wild Bells

Pete would have been proud. That's what Evan thought as he neared the top of Lovell's Hill. There was the bell, hanging on the crossbeam, the way it had for as long as Evan could remember. Something about seeing it there gave him such a sense of gratitude and happiness that he reached out his arm and put it around Jessie's shoulder, giving her a quick squeeze as they climbed the last few steps to the top.

"It's still here," said Jessie. As if anyone could have gotten it down again! Evan, Maxwell, and Jessie had spent two hours hauling the bell back up the hill on a toboggan with only the moon lighting their way. Then they'd hoisted it onto the hooks and lashed it to the crossbeam with a rope that Jessie tied in a million knots. When they were done hanging the bell, Evan had noticed a few spots on the post that were splintered. Tomorrow, he would come up here with a sanding block and work on the wood until it was smooth, just the way Pete had taught him.

Evan nodded. "Still here." It was good to know that the bell would remain, right where it belonged.

The snow that had fallen earlier carpeted the hillside, and the moon shone brightly in the clear, cold air. The effect was like a stadium lit up for a night game. Evan could see all kinds of details: the letters inscribed on the bell, the grain in the wood of the crossbeam, and the faces of the people gathered. Some of them he recognized, like Mrs. Upton and the Bradleys, who had been friends of Grandma's for years. But lots of the people were new to Evan.

Grandma would have known them all, but Grandma was home resting with Mom. Evan was sorry about that. It didn't feel like New Year's Eve without Grandma.

Of course, Maxwell was there with his mom and dad, all three on cross-country skis. When he spotted Evan and Jessie, Maxwell *whooshed* over to them. He held up his wrist with its digital watch.

"Twelve minutes and thirty-eight seconds. Exactly," he said. "I set my watch to the official NIST clock. It's accurate to within six-tenths of a second." Then he *whooshed* back over to his parents, who were talking to a young couple Evan didn't recognize. The man was holding a small child in his arms and had his back to Evan. The woman was someone Evan had never seen before.

"I guess we know who the youngest is this year," said Evan to Jessie, pointing at the couple.

Jessie looked over at them and said, "I didn't know Pete had a kid!"

"That's not—" but then Evan looked closer and

saw that it *was* Pete. "I didn't know, either!" Evan walked over, feeling a little shy. "Hey," he said to Pete. "Man of the family, huh?"

Pete broke into a smile and put out his fist for Evan to bump. "You know it. This is my posse. Kayley, say hi to Big Man Evan." But the little girl in Pete's arms just buried her face against her dad's shoulder, too shy and sleepy to greet a stranger. "And this is my wife, Melissa."

Evan said hello and shook hands politely, the way he'd been taught. Melissa told him how relieved she was to hear that Grandma was okay. "You and your sister are heroes," she said.

Evan looked at Pete, and Pete raised his eyebrows in response. He'd already given Evan a talking-to in private about not sticking to the plan they'd agreed on. *Traipsing off in the woods and dragging your little sister with you!* But Evan could tell by the way Pete smiled now that he was just as glad as Melissa that Grandma had been found, safe and sound.

"All's well that ends well," said Melissa, tucking the leg of Kayley's snow pants into her boot. "Too bad she couldn't be here, though. It won't be the same without her."

They stood in the moonlight, talking about the events of the day and the trip home planned for tomorrow. Evan and Jessie and Mrs. Treski were driving back in the morning, and Grandma would be coming with them. Maybe for good. Pete would keep working on the house. He thought he'd have it all wrapped up by the end of January.

There was a pause in the conversation, and then Melissa asked, "So who's the oldest?" They all looked around, and a murmur began to sweep through the crowd. *Who's the oldest this year?* One man said, "I'm fifty-three," and a woman called out, "Fifty-eight, here." "Where's Mrs. Lewis?" asked someone, and a voice in the crowd said, "She's staying home. Said to say hello to everyone."

"Not so many of the older folks this year," said Pete. "On account of the snow, I guess."

Evan shook his head. If Grandma were here, she'd have them all beat by a couple of decades.

"Four minutes!" yelled Maxwell. "Precisely!"

Everyone on the hill began to crowd in closer, forming a warm circle around the New Year's Eve bell. "Another year!" shouted someone, and Mrs. Cooper said, "And not a day wiser!" which made people laugh. Evan watched as Pete moved into the very center of the circle, holding Kayley close to him and whispering in her ear. The woman who had announced her age as fifty-eight also moved into the center of the circle and said something to Pete that made him throw back his head and laugh.

"C'mon, Jess," said Evan. His sister was hanging on the outside of the circle, staring at the path that led back to the house. "What are you waiting for?"

"Three minutes!" shouted Maxwell.

Suddenly Jessie broke away from the circle and started running toward the woods. "It's Grandma. She's here. She made it!"

Everyone in the circle turned to look. It really was Grandma! Evan couldn't believe it. And his mother was right behind her.

Jessie had already grabbed hold of Grandma's good arm and was pulling her toward the circle.

A cheer rose up from the crowd as everyone on the hill burst into muffled mittened applause. The sound bounced off Black Bear Mountain and ricocheted back to the top of Lovell's Hill.

"Two minutes, thirty seconds!" shouted Maxwell.

"I'm guessing I'm the oldest?" said Grandma, breathing hard as she broke through the circle.

"Yes, ma'am," said Pete. "And Kayley here's the youngest."

"Well, then we're good to go!" said Grandma. "Except—" She looked around her, searching the crowd. "Except this year, I want—" She spotted Maxwell and waved him over. "Maxwell. And Jessie, you, too. And . . . and . . ."

"Grandma, we can't all ring the bell," said Jessie. "It's not the tradition!"

"I don't care!" said Grandma. "This year I want something different. I want . . ." She continued to look at each face in the crowd. Evan shuffled his feet uncomfortably. Grandma's eyes finally came to rest on his face. "You!" she said. "Come here. I want you here, too."

171

Evan walked forward, miserably. It was awful to be forgotten by Grandma at all, but even worse to have it happen in front of so many people. It made him feel like he had done something bad, something he was being punished for.

Grandma grabbed his shoulder with her good hand and pulled him in close to her. She bent her face down so that her forehead touched his. In the bright moonlight, he could see the spidery wrinkles around her mouth, the fine lines that trickled from her eyes. Her face looked frightened. He was frightened, too. What would she do? What would she say?

"I do know you," she whispered. "I do. I just can't . . . I can't quite put it all together. But I *know* you."

Evan nodded his head. "It's okay, Grandma. It's okay."

"Ten, nine, eight . . ." shouted Maxwell, his face lit up green by the glow of his digital watch.

They had to crowd together: Pete, holding Kayley, Evan, Jessie, Maxwell, and Grandma, each one grabbing a few inches of the rope that hung from the bell's heavy clapper.

Everyone on the hill joined in the countdown. ". . . five, four, three, two, one!"

Evan swung his hand back and forth wildly. The five of them pulled in different directions, and the first few peals of the bell were weak and halting. But then they found a rhythm, and they swung the rope back and forth in perfect unison, until the noise of the bell filled the snow-covered valley below and the echoes of each peal bounced off of Black Bear Mountain and came racing back to them.

Evan listened to the bell and thought that it sounded different this year. Maybe because he was ringing it? Maybe because it had been taken down and then hung again? It sounded lower, a little bit sadder. Then he listened again and thought, no, it sounded the same as always.

Different and the same.

In Pete's arms, Kayley pumped her legs wildly

and then threw her head back and crowed at the night sky.

"You don't see that every day!" shouted Maxwell, and Grandma laughed just like she used to, loud and rumbly.

Evan smiled at Jessie, and she smiled back at him. "Happy New Year, Jess!" he shouted, above the wild clamor of the bell.

"I SOUND THE ALARM
TO KEEP THE PEACE."

New Year's

Jessie Treski

# Read all the books in the
# Lemonade War
## series!